RED QUEEN

RED QUEEN

RED THORNS CREW BOOK 3

REBEL HART

1

MAX

"**I**'m sorry it came to this, son."

My eyes fell to the gun in his hand. The gun that didn't shake. His pinky wasn't flying around. It wasn't moving, or twitching, or crooked. He held that gun with all the confidence his voice held, and I knew he'd do it.

I knew he'd gun me down.

What my father didn't know was this: I loved her. The life I feared losing tonight wasn't my own. It was hers. And if I didn't do something, Dani would die right along with me. I was done tonight, either way. I had accepted that. I accepted it the second I crashed through that gate. I accepted it the second my father pulled his gun on me. I even accepted it when he apologized, lying straight through his fucking teeth.

What I refused to accept was her death.

Too much time has passed. You need to get her out.

The voice in my head tortured me with the truth. It screamed out exactly what I should do. And yet, there I stood. Facing off with my father. With Satan himself. It felt like my heart was being ripped out through my anus. It felt like a thousand tornadoes had descended upon my skull, wreaking as much havoc as possible. The physical pain was unbearable. A bullet would've been a great relief.

She's going to die because I didn't fight hard enough.

Dad sighed. "Whether or not you believe me, I do love you."

I snickered. "Your gun has a funny way of showing it."

He shrugged. "Suit yourself."

I watched his finger flex and I stepped to the side. I moved as quickly as I could, waiting for the sound of the gun to hit my ears.

CRACK!

The deafening sound made me squeeze my eyes shut. I waited for the pain. I waited to see where the bullet had landed before I determined whether or not I could get to Dani. Whether or not I had just enough time to scramble to the pool and get her out before I bled out on the back lawn. I paused in my tracks, drawing in deep breaths. Anything to keep myself steady. Anything to keep myself stable.

Two and a half minutes without oxygen.

The pain didn't come, even though I heard grunting. I opened my eyes and looked down, ready to see blood spilling from my body. Ready for the pain that I knew would slap me across the face once I pulled out of shock.

There was no blood.

What the fuck?

I searched around my body. I slid my jacket off and ripped my shirt off. I pushed through the pain, trying to figure out where the hell the bullet had landed. Then I heard a piercing voice behind me.

"Max! Catch!"

I whipped around at the sound of Rupert's voice. I saw him stumbling along the lawn with a gun held tightly in his hand. Something shiny soared through the air. I locked my eyes onto it as I heard scuffling along the concrete. The gurgling sound kicked up again as I caught the flying object. And as the sharp edge sliced at my finger, I whipped back around.

Only to see my father fall backwards into the pool.

"Get her out!" Rupert roared.

I gripped the knife in my hand and watched my father fall into the water. I saw the pool tinting with blood as it spilled from the wound in his gut. Was this real? Had Rupert killed my father?

Dani.

"Dani!"

The bellowing exclamation left my lips as I ran for the pool. I dove into the waters, piercing through the growing red as my father's body floated on the surface. I opened my eyes as I dove deeper, kicking my way towards the chair. I saw Dani lying there, bound to that fucking metal frame. The pain swirling around my body teased my lungs, forcing me to try and gasp. To try and drink a cup or two of the chlorinated water around me. I refused to give in, though. I refused to go out like that.

Panic gripped my heart when I saw how pale Dani's face looked.

Cut her free. Do it. She's dying.

The voice in my head spurred me forward. It gave me the strength to saw through the leather bonds on her ankles and wrists. I cut her free, watching as her body drifted in the middle of the water. Her black hair swirled around her face and her skin grew paler in front of my eyes.

Up! Now!

My lungs burned. My joints ached. My eyes watered as I wrapped my arm around her lifeless body. I looked upward at the rooftop of red. I kicked off the floor of the pool and soared up toward the top. I longed for fresh air. I longed for a hot shower. I longed for a good night's sleep with Dani cradled next to me.

Soon.

I gasped for air as my head breached the top. I smelled the iron of my father's blood as his body drifted away from me. I shoved the knife into my pocket, hoping and praying it didn't stab me in the fucking thigh. Because that's what I needed. Another damn wound to attend to.

"Take my hand!" Rupert yelled.

I watched him stumble to the edge of the pool as his hand thrust out toward me. I didn't need help, though. Dani did. I kicked to the edge and rested my hand against the concrete. I heaved Dani's body up and Rupert helped me get her out of the pool. I didn't like the way her head bobbed around, water trickling down her cheeks from her mouth. Her eyes were closed, her ankles and wrists swollen and blue.

I didn't like any of this.

"Do you know CPR? She's not breathing."

I hoisted myself out of the pool before I crawled over to her.

"Move," I growled.

Rupert shuffled out of the way as I threaded my fingers together.

"Come on, gorgeous. You've got this."

I pressed my palm against her chest and murmured the song out loud. It was a song John that had taught me would keep perfect time during something like this. Recalling the steps, I stopped pumping and pointed to Rupert.

"Breathe into her mouth," I said.

He paused. "What?"

I reached for the back of his neck. "Tilt her head back to open up her airway and breathe into her goddamn mouth, Rupert."

I shoved his head down to her face and he did as I asked. I kept a close eye on him, watching the way he breathed. And when I saw her throat expand, I patted his back.

"Let me do this, then you go again. Okay?"

He nodded. "Got it."

Stayin' alive. Stayin' alive. Ah. Ah. Ah. Ah.

"Now," I said.

Rupert bent forward and breathed before I started my pumps again.

Stayin' alive. Stayin' alive. Ah. Ah. Ah. Ah.

"Now."

He did as I commanded before I started the pattern over again.

Stayin' alive. Stayin' alive. Ah. Ah. Ah. Ah.

"Now!"

He sighed. "Max, we need--"

I glared at him. "Now, Rupert."

He nodded. "Okay."

Stayin' alive. Stayin' alive. Ah. Ah. Ah. Ah.

"Now."

"Max, I really think--"

"Shut up and do it!"

Stayin' alive. Stayin' alive. Ah. Ah. Ah. Ah.

"Now."

He put his hand on my shoulder. "She's gone, Max."

I gripped his wrist. "You'll be the next one in that pool if you don't fucking do as I ask. Now, breathe!"

Stayin' alive. Stayin' alive. Ah. Ah. Ah. Ah.

With every pump of my hands, I saw my life slipping away. I felt my future falling to the wayside. Everything I'd ever held dear was right in front of me, and I couldn't save her. I couldn't get her to breathe. Panic gripped my voice. Rupert and I fell into a rhythm that seemed to grow less and less useful as time ticked by.

Three minutes without air.

Four minutes without air.

"Max, we need to--"

I growled. "Breathe."

"Max, you have to stop."

"Damn it, Dani. Breathe!"

Rupert wrapped his arm around my neck. "Max, get back."

"Dani, breathe! Breathe, please!"

"Come here. Max. You have to--"

I struggled to get away from his grasp. I raked my nails down his forearm and heard him hiss. But he didn't relinquish me. I watched Dani slip further away from me, growing smaller as Rupert pulled me back.

"We have to call the guys," he whispered.

I shook my head. "No."

"We have to make sure she--"

"No!" I shrieked. Never in my life had I ever heard that sound come out of my face. A desperate, wanton plea for him to shut the absolute fuck up. I ripped away from his grasp and rushed back to Dani's side. I slid her hair off to the side, gazing into her doll-like face.

Then I dipped my lips to her ear.

"I know you can hear me. I know you're a fighter. And I'm begging you, on my knees--with everything I am--I need you to wake up."

I threaded my fingers back together and pressed my palms back into the same place. I heard Rupert coming back for me as I started pressing harder. Faster. As quickly as my body could work. I fought with Rupert. I kept knocking his hands away from me. And as I bent down to breathe life into her body once more, I felt him fist my shirt.

"Max, don't make me do this."

I drew in a deep breath. "Wake the fuck up!"

I slammed my open palms against her chest in frustration. I wanted to cry out to the earth and curse its existence. Why? Why in the world did things have to go like this tonight? Why was I born to such a fucking maniac? Why did I have to lead this kind of a life? Why did Dani have to pay this price for--

"Max!"

I growled. "What?"

"Look."

The first thing I felt was water splashing against my face. And the second thing that happened were my ears twitching. I heard coughing and sputtering. I felt the body beneath me writhing in pain. Broken moans combined with guttural coughs sounded against my eardrums as my eyes looked up to Dani's face.

A face with its eyes open.

"Dani?" I asked breathlessly.

She continued coughing up lungfuls of water as her hands reached out for me.

"Dani! Holy shit!"

Taking her hands within mine, I moved her onto her side and pressed my forehead into the crook of her neck. I rubbed her stomach, breathing in deeply the smell of her awakening body. I wasn't ashamed to admit that I cried. That my eyes welled with tears of happiness and dripped silently against her skin. It seemed like an eternity. Like forever had passed before I heard the sound of her voice again.

"Max?" she rasped.

I nuzzled against her. "I'm here. I'm right here. It's okay. You're okay. Holy fuck, you're alive."

She coughed. "Your--dad--"

I smoothed her hair away. "I know. I know he was behind this. I know--"

"No. Look."

I watched her trembling finger point at the pool. And when I looked over at the red water, I saw his body slowly sinking beneath the surface. I blinked a few times, watching him go under. Watching as the water accepted its second supposed victim of the night.

"Rupert?" I asked.

"Yeah?"

"Stay with Dani."

"Max, no," she whispered.

I looked down at her. "I can't just leave his body like that. I can't."

I stood up and dove back into the pool. I pierced through the thick blood and kicked my legs toward my father, watching small cascades of red swirl and inter-twine beneath the surface. Like a delicate ballet of good and evil as I swam closer to his lifeless body.

My father was the biggest piece of shit to ever walk this planet, but no one deserved to be found in a literal pool of their own blood.

Gotcha.

I wrapped my arms around his body and kicked back up to the surface. Time moved in a haze as I pulled him out of the water and settled him onto the concrete. I stood over his body, clenching my fists as I gazed down into the lifeless face of the man that had made my life a living nightmare.

Rupert's voice pierced the dead of night.

"Max! Move your ass!"

The sound of sirens caught my ear and I turned on my heel. I dipped down, scooping Dani into my arms as she continued to cough up the last little bit of water. She was wheezing. Her hands clung to me, even though her grip was weak. And as I cradled her against my naked torso, I saw Rupert scooping up my clothes.

"I've got my truck. It's in front. We need to get in it and get out of here."

I nodded. "Lead the way, Rupert."

The three of us raced across the grounds as sirens screamed closer. I felt Dani curling deeper into me. My legs bellowed out the need for rest as my knees began buckling. I paused, leaning against the brick side of the house and took one last look at my father's body beside the red pool.

Is he dead?

"Come on!"

Rupert's broken voice pierced through my thoughts and I pushed off the house, piling us into the backseat of his truck as he started backing down the driveway. The sirens grew closer and I heard tires squealing in the distance. I cradled Dani between my legs as Rupert took off, leaving the hellscape of my father's mansion behind. Dani started whimpering. My beautiful, sweet, innocent Bambi whimpered and shuddered in my grasp. I wrapped her up tightly in my arms and pressed my lips to her ear.

"You're okay. You're safe. I've got you, and we're headed out of here. Okay?"

And when I felt her nod, I could have broken down in tears all over again.

2

DANI

His arms were the only thing I knew. Their warmth. Their comfort. Their strength. It was the only thing I registered as I curled deeper into his body. A body I thought I'd never feel again. Tears streaked my cheeks, mingling with the droplets of water I still coughed up. I nuzzled against Max's bare torso and wondered why in the world he'd had to shed his clothes in the first place. We were both soaked. Was he the one that came in after me?

Of course he was.

I felt the seats beneath me soaking through and through. Water dripped from the edges of my clothes onto the floorboard. I heard Rupert and Max murmuring back and forth. I didn't catch what they were talking about, but I also didn't care.

I was alive.

And I wasn't sure how Max had pulled that off.

"I'm sorry," I whispered.

Max pressed a kiss to the top of my head. "What was that?"

I coughed, feeling a little more water lunge up the back of my throat. I turned my head off to the side and coughed it onto the back of Rupert's seat before I felt my cheeks flush.

"I'm sorry for ruining--your--your truck, Rupe."

He snickered. "Don't be silly. I'm just glad you're still alive, Bambi. You scared the hell out of me."

Max pulled me back against him. "Me, too."

I started coughing again as Max gripped my chin softly. He pulled my head toward his, and I watched as his eyes danced over my face. His hand fell from my chin and slid slowly down my body, but not in a sensual or a sexual way. His fingers were on a mission. I saw him nodding his head every time his fingertips pressed down into a part of me.

My ribs.

My thighs.

My kneecaps.

My chest.

"Are you sure you're all right, gorgeous? My father didn't hurt you at all, did he?"

I snickered, which caused me to start coughing again. How the hell did I even answer that question? 'Yeah, I'm okay, I just almost drowned. No biggie.' I managed to shake my head before I started coughing again.

"That cough sounds bad, Max. She needs a doctor."

"We need to get back to my place first. I'll call a doctor once we get there."

"Sure a doctor doesn't need to meet us there?"

I gasped for air. "Not. Hurt."

Max spread out in the back of Rupert's truck and held me against his chest. I found his heartbeat with my ear and settled into the comforting rhythm. Physically, I felt fine. I mean, my lungs felt like they'd been run through a wood chipper. My throat was still burning. I felt short of breath, like I couldn't catch it. And my head felt swimmy, for lack of a better word. Honestly? It reminded me of the time in high school when I'd had another swimmer cross into my lane by accident during a swim meet. Once she'd realized what had happened, she'd kicked out, anxious to get back into her lane before someone clocked her on it.

But not before her foot kicked out and caught me right in the chest.

The memory of inhaling that gulp of water felt a lot like this. I'd come up mid-stroke and started coughing so badly I threw up in the pool. The lifeguards dove in and pulled me up onto the side of the pool where sanctioned paramedics were already waiting for me. I had required medical care then. I remembered them wrapping me in blankets and my mother trying to bat people off as they tried cutting me out of my wet bathing suit.

I didn't remember much else, though.

Rupert piped up. "Here. She needs a blanket."

Max's voice filled my ear. "Thanks. We need to get her out of these wet clothes and get her warm."

"Call your doctor. Have him meet you at the house. Seriously. That cough sounds nasty."

I felt something warm against my skin. "Come here. Let's try to get you warmed up."

I groaned. "Huh?"

"You're shivering. Badly. We need to get you warm."

I felt my muscles tense. "I--I am?"

Rupert sighed. "Not good. She's disoriented."

Max growled. "Just give her a second, damn it."

The warm blanket wrapping around me felt like knives against my skin. I fought Max's movements, but I wasn't strong enough to bat them off. Tears rushed my eyes once more, trickling aimlessly down my cheeks. And every time I drew in a shuddered breath, I started coughing again.

Before throwing up more water onto the truck's floorboard.

"She needs a damn doctor."

"And I'll get her one."

"She needs one now, Max."

"Then fucking pull over and call 911! But if you want to make it out of this without handcuffs, keep driving until we get back to the damn house!"

I whimpered as I curled tighter into him. It felt as if my body was rebelling against his efforts. Why did the blanket hurt? Why did my feet feel as if they were on fire? Why couldn't I close my hands tight enough to hang on?

Why am I so helpless?

I was worried that I needed a hospital. But we were

in no position to go to the hospital. And I finally understood the predicament Max had been in the day he was jumped. The hospital wasn't an option. I mean, someone had just shot Max's father, for crying out loud!

"Who--who shot—?"

I managed to stammer the words out between my clattering teeth.

"I did," Rupert said.

I looked up into Max's face. "You--dove in?"

He grinned down at me. "Did you really expect me to do anything else?"

Yeah. No hospital for us. Rupert had just killed Max's father, and the police sure as hell didn't need to be catching up with us. Not after tonight. Because I honestly wasn't sure anyone would believe what had happened tonight. I placed my cheek against his shoulder and felt him wrap the rest of the blanket around my legs. It felt like my head was in a vise grip that someone kept tightening.

I closed my eyes and forced myself to focus on Max.

"Thank you for coming for me," I whispered.

He cupped my cheek. "Of course I came for you. I always will."

I felt his body shaking and heard the tears in his eyes. I felt his hand trembling against my cheek as his thumb stroked me softly, smoothing away my own tears while his dripped steadily onto my forehead. I looked to the side, watching as Max's thumb came into my view every once in a while.

And if his thumb was that bloodied, I was worried about the rest of him.

"What happened to you?" I asked.

I gazed back up into his face as my vision finally focused. When I saw the bruises and the swelling and the cuts, open and bleeding, I gasped. Which spurred on another coughing session. Which caused me to lunge off to the side and vomit, once again, onto the floorboard of the truck.

I saw the gash in Max's thigh now, how tattered his jeans were. How bruised his body was. His ribs were black, his knuckles split and red from fighting. His face was almost unrecognizable with all the bruises and scabs and the swelling that had taken over his eyes.

My breath caught in my throat. "Oh, my God."

Rupert craned his neck back. "We're still fifteen minutes out from the house. Sure you don't want to change your mind?"

I shook my head. "No hospitals. We can't--I can't--"

The coughing started up again, only this time I couldn't control it. It felt like something was lodged in my lungs. Something my body wanted to get out but couldn't. I pressed my hand into my chest. When the heel of my hand touched my sternum, I thought I was going to blow through the roof. My coughing became yelling. My body started shaking. And when Max pulled me back against his body, he turned me.

Max stumbled over his words. "I don't--I just--we--"

Rupert sighed. "Come on, Max. Listen to that cough."

My eyes widened as my hand fell against his chest. He jumped at my touch as my fingertips found the tattoo over his heart. The one that matched the tattoo I had on my thigh, to be exact. The skin beneath it was bruised and puckered. There was something that looked like a blood blister forming beneath it, threatening to break and destroy the entire masterpiece. Tears flooded my face. I felt my body trembling uncontrollably.

All of this had happened to Max because I hadn't listened to Rupert.

You should've stayed in your dorm room.

My lip quivered. "I'm so sorry."

Max's grip tightened on me. "Rupert, how far away are we from the hospital?"

"Less than fifteen minutes, I can tell you that."

I sniffled. "I'm so fucking sorry. Please forgive me. I--I only wanted t--oh, fuck."

The guilt was too much. It filled my stomach and pushed any of the contents I still had left in it over the top. Max turned me onto my side as I started to choke. I tried coughing, but I couldn't get it up. It felt lodged. It felt stuck. And no matter how hard I tried breathing, or coughing, or gagging, or gasping, nothing came loose.

Had I just listened, none of this would have happened. Had I listened to Rupert, Max would be fine. I'd be fine. But I had to go and play the hero. I had to go and get myself caught. I had to go and find

Max, which got us nothing but beaten to hell and almost killed. I was an idiot. Max had fallen in love with an idiot.

He deserves better.

I heard the boys fighting, but their voices seemed far away. My vision tunneled and my lungs started to burn again. I couldn't take it. The pain was too much. Part of my body begged for death, and the other part of me scrambled for life. I didn't deserve it, though. Not after getting Max into this situation. Not after putting Rupert in danger like I had.

I should've stayed dead. Maybe everyone would be better off.

"Turn around. Now."

Max's growling voice caught my ear and I shook my head. No. The last thing we needed was a hospital. I didn't need my boys in a bigger mess because of me. If I needed to die to keep them safe, I would.

Anything to keep Max safe.

I wheezed. "No. We have to get out of town. The police--"

I felt something burst in my throat before puke flooded my lungs. I heard Max growling again before the tires of the truck squealed. My body flew off to the side. Max held me as tightly as he could while my lungs tried to bury me underneath once more. I felt him rubbing my back and telling me to relax. As if that would magically solve all my problems. But the more Max stroked my back, the more I felt my muscles relaxing anyway.

And soon, my lungs felt relief.

"Oh--fuck--I--ugh."

Max sighed. "There it is. Get it up. Don't worry about anything else."

Rupert cleared his throat. "She throwing up finally?"

I nodded, but I couldn't speak. It felt like the pain was endless. And even though my stomach felt empty, my lungs still felt full. How was that possible? What in the world was my body doing? The coughing fit started again before I could catch my breath and I felt my brain squeezing in on itself. I felt my stomach protruding as if it were filled with too much water.

No.

Not my stomach.

Is that my bladder?

There was too much chaos in my mind. There were too many sounds happening all at once. I tried locking on to Max's voice. Or Rupert's. Anything that might ground me back into reality. But I couldn't. Every time I latched onto something, my mind gravitated back to the pain. My eyes reminded me of just how beat up Max really was. I hurt so badly my body almost forgot about it, as weird as that sounded. I had moments of lucidity followed by moments that didn't make sense. I saw flashes of light before darkness fell over my eyes. They'd focus, then unfocus. As if attempting to save me from the world still swirling around me.

And all of it culminated as a stark, disgusting reminder of who was really responsible for this.

Me.

I was responsible for all of this.

3

—————

MAX

The second she started coughing, I grew concerned. It was still wet. Still ferocious. Still making her heave. After all this time out of the water, with everything she had already brought up, she shouldn't still be struggling to breathe. She shouldn't have had to work so hard at it.

Rupert shook his head. "We have to turn around. This is serious, Max."

I brushed her hair back. "I'll call the doctor and have him meet us at the--"

"She needs a fucking team, Max! Look at her!"

My eyes fell to Dani's pale face. Her body shook uncontrollably. Goosebumps fled along her skin. No matter how tightly I held her, I couldn't warm her up. She kept growing colder and colder in my arms. Despite my muscles trying so hard to reverse the damage that had already been done.

"Max!"

I grunted. "I'm thinking."

"Well, think a bit faster before she dies in my backseat."

My eyes shot up to Rupert and I saw him glaring at me in the rearview mirror. He was right, though. Something was off. Dani had been submerged for much too long, and there was no telling the damage that might have been done. This was more than just lungfuls of water. This was more than just being underneath the surface for a bit too long.

Dani had effectively died. I wasn't sure how long she'd been out. But my thoughts were quickly pierced by the sound of the love of my life gagging again.

"Gorgeous?"

She turned to the side and her stomach started jumping again. But nothing came up.

"Dani! What's wrong? What can I do?"

Rupert growled. "You can take her to the hospital."

"Will you fucking shut up for one goddamn second!?"

Dani threw her head over to the side, away from my chest. It was all I could do to catch her before she fell to the floorboards of the truck. She gasped for air. I felt her stomach contracting. It was like her body was trying to get something up but couldn't. My heart raced out of control. I looked outside and felt more frustrated than ever.

More upset than ever.

More lost than ever.

"Turn around. Now," I said.

I heard Dani wheeze. "No. We have to get out of

town. The police--"

Rupert whipped the truck around. "Fucking finally. We're less than five minutes out. I can have us there in a jiff. Hang on."

I growled. "Hurry it up. She can't get whatever this is up."

"Fucking hell."

I heard the tires beneath his truck practically screaming for mercy. We kicked up burnt rubber in our wake as he sped down the road. I held on to Dani as tightly as I could. I placed my forehead against the back of her head, feeling her body rebel against itself. I rubbed her back, digging my fingers into her muscles. I tried desperately to get her to relax. To get her to stop freaking out long enough to let her body take control.

"It's okay, gorgeous. Relax. Just relax. I know it's hard, but you have to relax for me. Okay?"

"Oh--fuck--I--ugh."

I sighed with relief once I heard something splash against my feet. "There it is. Get it up. Don't worry about anything else. You're okay."

Rupert cleared his throat. "She throwing up finally?"

I nodded my head as I brushed Dani's hair away from her face. And when she was done emptying the contents of her body onto my boots, I rolled her back against me. I wiped away a crusted trail leaking down her chin. I gazed into her tired eyes, and the terror behind them gripped me. I felt helpless. For the first time in my life, I didn't know what the fuck I could do to make this better. It killed me inside, not being able to help. Not being able to relieve her of this pain and take it upon my shoulders.

I looked deep into her eyes. "You keep fighting, okay? You keep hanging on, and I promise you we'll get out of this."

She nodded as tears rushed her eyes. She tried to say something, but I pressed my finger against her lips.

"Save your energy. You're going to need it for the doctors at the hospital."

She shook her head side to side, but I gripped her chin.

"Yes. You need more than my doctor can provide. Understood?"

Tears lined her eyes and it broke my heart. And the entire time, I kept thinking about what kind of bullshit my father's death would leave behind. I knew it couldn't spell anything good for myself. Or for John. I mean, who knew the kind of debts my father still had out there. Who knew the kind of people he had been trying to cut his deals with. For all I knew, they'd come after us now. Looking for someone to fulfill the deals my father had created.

If he's even dead.

I looked back up at the rearview mirror and saw Rupert shooting us nervous glances. He was a fucking rock. Nothing made the man waver. So to see him worried meant that my worry was founded. Dani kept coughing, struggling to breathe. It was as if she was still drowning, even though she wasn't anywhere near water.

"Can you go any faster, Rupert?"

I felt his engine rev. "I'll push this truck to the limit, if that's what it takes."

"How far out?"

"One stoplight. Which I'm going to blaze through if it turns red."

I nodded. "Do it. If you get caught, I'll pay the ticket."

I tried my damndest to stay in control of my own panic. Because the last thing Dani needed to see every time she looked up at me was a frazzled, worried asshole. But every second that passed by--every cough I heard gurgle up her throat--sent my soul into a frenzied state. I felt more overwhelmed than I ever had in my entire life. I was in control of nothing. All I could do was sit there, hold her, and keep telling her shit would be all right.

When I had no idea.

"It's okay. Everything's going to be fine, all right, gorgeous?"

I looked down at her and found her eyes rolling back.

"Rupert!"

His tires skidded. "Pulling up to the emergency entrance now!"

I braced myself as the truck slung me into the back wall. I held Dani tightly against me as my shoulder slammed into the side. I swallowed down the roar of pain that threatened to burst from my throat. I looked outside and saw people watching us as burnt rubber swirled around the vehicle. Rupert leapt out of his truck and ripped the back door open. And before he could get a word in edgewise, I slid off the seat with Dani in my arms.

"You park. I'm finding a fucking doctor."

He patted my back. "I'll come find you guys."

I wasted no time charging through the doors of that emergency room.

"I need a doctor! Now!"

Everyone turned their heads to face me before a nurse jumped up from behind a desk.

"I need a doctor, a mobile bed, and some fucking answers!"

Staff converged onto me and someone took Dani from my arms. I balled up my fists, ready for a fight as I felt nurses' hands all over my torso. Someone shone a light into my eyes as Dani was placed on a moving bed and rushed off through a set of metal double doors as nurses poked and prodded at my body.

"He's got broken ribs."

"His nose looks crushed, too."

"We need to get the swelling down in that eye. He'll lose his sight if we don't."

I shook them off. "Dani! I'm coming!"

Someone grabbed my arm. "You need medical treatment, too."

I whipped around on the nurse before a man in a white coat came trotting up with a wheelchair. I looked at the pathetic device before glaring at the people standing in front of me.

I thumbed over my shoulder. "I'm not the one that needs help. She is."

The doctor nodded his head. "You need attention,

too. She's being taken care of. Let us take you back and--"

I shook my head. "The only thing you need to do right now is tell me where the fuck you've taken my girl."

"Sir, if you don't calm down, I'm going to have to sedate you."

I turned toward the voice and saw her holding a needle in her hand. I ripped it from her grasp and tossed it back to the doctor, who fumbled around with it. After catching it in his hands, needle point down, his eyes slowly came back up to mine.

"Tell me where she is. Now."

He sighed. "What happened to you two tonight? I need to know everything I can in order to help her."

"She was submerged underwater for over two minutes. I don't know how long she was unconscious before I pulled her from the pool."

"Chlorine, or salt water?"

I sighed. "Chlorine."

The doctor shook his head. "Did she suffer any trauma before that? A head injury? A punch to the gut or the chest? Anything that could've knocked her out or knocked her breathless before she went under?"

"She told me nothing like that happened."

"How did the drowning occur?"

I blinked. "She got herself hooked onto a chair that tipped backwards and she couldn't get herself free."

"And you're the one that found her?"

"Yes."

His eyes ran down my body. "Nurse, get him a bed

next to her room."

I growled. "I told you, I don't need--"

He pointed his finger at me. "I don't know who you are or who you think you're bossing around, but the second you stepped through those emergency doors, she and you became my priority. Make no mistake. I will have you bussed to a different hospital if you're going to stand in my way and refuse treatment when you so clearly need it. Got it?"

I choked down the want to make this man swallow his own fucking teeth.

"Yeah. Got it."

Rupert ran up behind me, panting. "Where is she? Where's Bambi?"

The doctor furrowed his brow. "Bambi?"

I sighed. "Nickname for the girl you just took back."

The doctor nodded. "You got her real name?"

My face fell flat. "Dani Young."

Rupert interjected. "Hi. Yes. Where is she? I'd like to see her."

I licked my lips. "We both would."

The doctor held his head high. "Do you consent to being treated? And acting accordingly in the presence of staff?"

I looked around at the nurses surrounding me. They were ready, willing, and capable of doing whatever it took to make sure I was all right. I needed to not be so angry. Why the fuck was I so angry?

"Put me beside her, and yes," I said.

The doctor nodded curtly. "Good. Follow me."

He and his team of nurses led us through the metal double doors. The second we turned down an isolated hallway, I heard that cough. Dani's barking, wet, incessant cough.

"Has she been coughing like that ever since you pulled her out?"

Worry grew in my gut. "Yes. It took several rounds of CPR to bring her back. And ever since, she's been barking like that and coughing shit up."

"Anything other than water?"

"Contents from her stomach. It's triggering her gag reflex."

The doctor pointed. "You'll be in this room. I want you hooked up to an IV and--"

I shook my head. "I want to see Dani first."

He spun around on me. "You do as I ask, or you're gone. Get in there and let my team of nurses get you started on some fluids and a round of pain medication. You're going to need it for when we start patching you up."

Rupert placed his hand on my shoulder. "Just do as they're asking. Okay?"

I shrugged his touch off. "Fine. Whatever."

A nurse led me into the room right next to Dani's before sitting me on the edge of the bed. She set the I.V. and got me started on pain medication. But I was focused on the coughing coming from the room beside me. I not only felt helpless; I also felt hopeless. And the more she coughed, the more I wondered if she'd actually pull out of this.

I wondered if any of us would be okay after this.

4

DANI

I couldn't remember much. After sedation, the only thing I recalled was waking up and asking for Max. I kept reaching out for his hand, searching the room for him. Trying to get him to call out to me. But the only response I ever got was from the doctor.

"He's being checked out. We'll get him in here soon."

"No, Miss Young. It's just me. Is there anyone else you want us to call?"

"I need you to hold still. Nurse, can you hold her down? I have to get her to stop moving."

"Miss Young! Stop talking and hold still."

I wanted this nightmare to be over. I wanted all of this to go away. I wanted to feel Max wrapped around me again so I could listen to his heartbeat. So I could remind myself that he was still alive.

It was the only thing that kept me grounded sometimes.

"Can you remember what happened?"

"Were your wrists and ankles tied together?"

"Nurse, I need another ice pack down here."

Everything felt like a whirlwind. It felt like my life was nothing but flashes and images of things taking place around me. But after what seemed like hours of tests and machines and things being shoved down my throat, I was upright. I was awake and coherent.

And I still needed Max.

"Miss Young, how are you feeling?"

I sighed. "Can I see him now? Max? Where is he?"

He patted my leg. "He's being checked out himself. The man was pretty beat up. He's got some injuries of his own that needed to be taken care of."

"Is he going to be all right? What happened? What was wrong?"

He licked his lips. "Miss Young, what happened tonight?"

I blinked. "What?"

"You have both suffered a great deal of trauma. Did you get into an argument?"

"What? No!"

"Has he hurt you in any way?"

"Get him in here now. Max!"

The doctor nodded. "Close the door, please."

I shook my head. "Don't you close that door. Where's Max? I want to see my boyfriend."

"Right after you answer some questions I have regarding yours and his injuries."

"You can ask him if you have questions."

"Well, I'm asking you. And I need you to answer. Okay?"

I sucked air between my teeth. "All right. Fine. What do you want to know?"

"What were you bound with?"

I blinked. "Come again?"

He sighed. "Your wrists and ankles have some serious abrasions on them. Almost like they were tied. Your boyfriend told us you got snagged onto a chair that tipped into a pool. Your injuries say differently."

"Look, it's been a long night, Doctor. Am I going to be okay?"

"Answer my questions."

"Try answering mine, and maybe I'll trust you."

He looked over at his nurse while I waited for my answer.

"You're going to be fine, Miss Young. While the abrasions are concerning, no lasting damage will come of them. We also vacuumed out your lungs. You were under for so long that the water started seeping into the small caverns of your lungs that usually expand with air. The coughing was to try and get the water up, but all the coughing did was push the water further into those pockets."

I paused. "Is that why I felt I had something lodged in my lungs?"

He nodded. "Correct. That's also why we had to sedate you. That process is incredibly painful when performed without sedation. Judging by the abrasions around your extremities, I figured you'd been through enough tonight."

"I appreciate that. Thank you."

"It also took us a while to raise your body temperature. But you're holding stable at 98.2 degrees. Which we'll take, for now. Even though it's still a tick below normal."

"If it helps, I'm always cold."

He sighed. "Forgive me if I don't take your word for things."

I snickered. "Fair enough."

"Did this man hurt you?"

I shook my head. "If anything, he's the one that saved me. He and Rupert--wait, is Rupert still here?"

"The redhead with the beanie?"

"That's the one."

He nodded. "He's still here. He's next door with Max. They're waiting until I'm done talking with you."

"Well, are we done talking?"

His eyes ran down my body before he drew in a deep breath.

"I'm not leaving any of you alone until you're fully discharged. I don't like the injuries that man came in here with, either. And until I know the two of you are going to be safe with one another after leaving, you'll be under my care. Understood?"

I paused. "Is that something you can do?"

He nodded. "I can keep you both here for up to three days, if I say the word. Don't give me a reason to do that."

"You really don't believe me. That man out there would never hurt me. He loves me. And I love him."

"And again, don't blame me if I don't take your word for it."

I leaned back against my pillows. "Okay, then. Can I at least see him?"

He narrowed his eyes. "I'll allow it. But mostly because he's pestering my nurses and I'm fearing for his own safety at this point."

I giggled. "Sounds like the man I love."

He grinned. "I'll get him in here. But you stay in this bed. Got it?"

I nodded. "Got it."

The second Max's face came around the corner, my heart surged with delight. I held my arms out for him and he strode to me, wrapping me up tight in his grasp. Someone had given him a shirt. I had to admit I was a bit disappointed. His muscles were always something to enjoy and admire every chance I got. Nonetheless, I placed my ear against his chest to hear his heart beat. I felt him cradle my head against him. And as he sat on the edge of my bed, I drew in a deep, relaxing breath.

"I'm so glad you're okay," I whispered.

He kissed the top of my head. "Are you all right? Did they get all the water out of your lungs?"

"They say they did. No more coughing for me."

"Thank fuck."

I nuzzled against him. "Max, I'm so--"

"I'm so sorry for the position I put you in tonight."

I paused. "The position *you* put me in?"

He crooked his finger beneath my chin and pulled my gaze up to his.

"The entire time we were in the truck, I kept thinking you were going to die because of me. Because of my selfishness and the life I lead. I couldn't stand the thought of it, Dani. Of something happening to you because of me."

I furrowed my brow. "I'm not sure it's you who got me into this situation tonight."

"It is. It's this life I've chosen for myself. A life that isn't suited for even the most dangerous of criminals. I'm sorry, gorgeous. I'm sorry for getting you caught up in all this."

I stared up at him with worry filling my gut. I didn't like where this conversation was going. The emotion behind his eyes froze me in my spot. But when his eyes grew glassy, my heart clenched in my chest.

"Max, this isn't your fault."

I tried to sound strong, but my raspy voice didn't do much in that department for me. If anything, it made the worry behind his eyes grow more fierce. Almost to the point where the glassiness of his stare scared me.

"Max?"

He blinked. "Yes?"

I cupped his cheek, lowering my voice. "This is your father's doing. Not yours. Plus, I never should've left my dorm. I never should've come looking for you. Rupert was right. All I did was make things--"

He shook his head. "Enough."

I swallowed down the rest of my words as he heaved a heavy sigh.

"What's done is done, gorgeous. You're safe, and that's all that matters to me. Okay?"

My forehead fell against his shoulder. "When can I get out of here? I don't want to be here any longer."

The doctor piped up from the doorway. "You'll have to stay overnight, I'm afraid."

My head whipped up. "What?"

"Overnight. You both will have to stay for some monitoring."

"But I thought you said--"

"This is protocol. You were without oxygen, Miss Young, for at least a minute. Maybe more. And if any signs of brain damage are going to manifest, the greatest chance of them doing so is within the first twenty-four hours. You'll have to stay for monitoring. Him, too. But if everything looks good with you both after that, you'll be free to go."

Max didn't take his eyes off me. "I want to stay with her. In this room."

The doctor walked into the room. "I'm not so sure that's a good idea. The whole point of being monitored like this is so you can rest easy."

I nodded. "Unfortunately, I think I agree with him. I'm tired."

Max shrugged. "Then I'll sleep in the corner. But I'm not leaving this room. Understood?"

As Max looked over at the doctor, my mind started to worry. What if that doctor had called the police on us? Would the authorities come looking for him? Wouldn't they have questions? Especially once they found his father dead at his own damn estate?

The law is going to ruin us.

"Whatever sleeping arrangements are going to be the best for you two, I'll do my best to make it happen. But, whatever happens, I expect you to obey. Got it?"

The doctor's voice ripped me from my trance as Max nodded.

"Got it, Doc."

I swallowed hard. "I don't know if--"

Max cupped my cheeks. "Things will work out."

He stared directly into my soul. As if he knew what I was thinking.

"They always do with me, okay? Trust me on that. I've got a lot of people who can help us through this."

The doctor grew curious. "Help you with what, exactly?"

I glared at him. "Can you give us some privacy?"

Max chuckled. "Please, Doc?"

The curious man sighed. "Ten minutes. Then someone will be around to take your vitals."

He left us in the room again. Alone. And my panic started to overflow.

"Max, what if he calls the police?" I asked.

His forehead fell against mine. "Do you trust me?"

"What if they come snooping around? What if they find your father's body and--"

"For all we know, my father might not actually be dead."

I froze. "Wait, do you think--?"

His thumbs stroked my cheeks. "I mean, there's no such thing as murder charges if nobody dies. Right?"

He chuckled like he'd just made a fantastic joke. But I didn't find it funny.

"I'm serious, Max."

He cleared his throat. "I am, too. And what I'm telling you I expect you to listen to. Right now, the only thing you need to be worried about is getting rest. Once we're out of this hospital, we'll figure out our next steps."

"Together?"

"Of course. How else would we do it?"

I paused. "I don't know. The way you were talking before, it almost sounded like…"

I couldn't even bring myself to finish the statement.

"Dani, you know how selfish I am."

I snickered. "Yeah. Yeah, I do."

"So why the hell would a selfish man like myself let go of the only thing good in his life right now? I mean, what kind of bullshit is that?"

I giggled. "I suppose you have a point."

He grinned. "Good. Now, lie down. I'm going to lie down with you for a while."

"I don't want to fall asleep yet, though."

"You need your rest. I'll be here while you fall asleep. Okay?"

I was too tired to put up a fight. So I simply did as he asked. I lay down in bed, scooting over so he had enough room to get in there with me. It was a squeeze, though. My Max was a brute of a human being. But once I felt that strong arm of his slink around my waist, all was right with the world. I closed my eyes and drew in a deep breath. And when I didn't start coughing, I wiggled around until I faced him.

"Sleep, gorgeous."

I scooted closer to him. "There. Perfect."

I drew in his scent and focused on his steady breathing, ignoring the lingering scent of chlorine and trying to rest as my mind raced.

5

MAX

THUMP!

The banging of the door closing caught my ear and my eyes popped open. I couldn't move, though. Something had me pinned to the bed. My eyes stared up at the popcorn ceiling of the hospital room as footsteps sounded around me. And even though my entire body wanted to move and shield Dani from the threat, my muscles simply lay there and ached.

"Ugh. Fuck."

The footsteps grew closer as whispering started. I didn't recognize the voices, but one of them was definitely female. Were the nurses in the room? They were usually quieter than that. And when I felt something shift against my chest, I groaned.

"Dani?"

She yawned. "Max. Morning."

"And a good morning to you, too."

The male voice was curt. Edgy. It had sharp razors

around the edge of his words, and I heard Dani gasp. She pushed herself away from my body and my muscles screamed out for mercy. I didn't let out a sound, though. Because as she came into focus, I saw recognition fly across her face.

"Mom? Dad? What are you doing here?"

My blood ran cold. My heart stopped in my chest. I groaned as I turned my head, facing the two fuzzy people standing at the end of the bed. I squinted to get my eyes to adjust. I felt Dani shuffling beside me, trying to prop herself up. I moved and tried to help her as I pulled her against me, fighting through my own pain as my eyes struggled to focus.

"Whenever you're ready," the man said.

I cleared my throat and brought my hands to my eyes. I dug the heels of my palms in before I let out a yelp. Holy shit, that hurt. Why the hell did that hurt so much?

Dani lowered her voice. "Your eyes look better, but they're still bruised. Be careful."

I nodded. "Thanks."

Her mother spoke. "Dani, please tell me you're all right. My gosh, what in the world happened to you?"

Dani sighed. "Hold on, Mom. Just--Max?"

I nodded. "I'm getting up. Give me a second. My legs don't want to start."

She giggled. "We need coffee."

I grinned. "Lots of it. I'm going to go find a way to track some down."

Her father spoke up. "Yeah, I think you should leave."

My head whipped up and my eyes finally cleared. Everything came into focus as I stared into the face of a staunch, serious Korean man. Wow, Dani looked a great deal like her father. The same kind of skin tone. The same kind of hair. The same kind of slanted eyes and lower lip pout. On Dani, it was adorable. But, on her father?

It made him look like he wanted to rip my head off.

Her father wore ratty blue jeans and a pair of sneakers. He had a gray blazer over what I could only assume was a Cheeto-stained white shirt. The man looked like hell. Bags beneath his eyes. His lips down-turned into a serious frown. The whites of his eyes were more red than anything else. And when I looked over at her mother, she didn't look much different. With her plump features and big brown eyes, I saw where Dani got those massive doe eyes from.

She was the perfect combination of her parents.

Dani put her hand on my arm. "You can stay if you want. You don't have to leave."

Her father spoke again. "We need to talk, Danika. Alone."

I nodded. "Do you want coffee? Because I have to leave in order to get it."

Her mother's voice was soft. "Please let us have some time with our daughter."

While I understood their requests, I wasn't moving until Dani asked me. She was my main priority right now. And whatever she wanted, I'd grant.

Dani sighed. "Coffee would be nice, thank you."

I paused. "Are you sure?"

Her father rounded to her side of the bed. "Of course she's sure. Now get the hell out of my daughter's bed."

Her mother gasped. "Peter!"

"Rena, a strange man is in bed with our daughter. And look at him! He looks worse off than she does! How do we know you didn't do this to our daughter?"

I managed to slip off the edge of the bed. "I would never lay a finger on your daughter like that. You have my word."

The man snickered. "Well, forgive me if I don't believe a word that comes out of your torn-up face."

Her mother put a hand on his shoulder. "Pipe down. You're going to have the nurses in here kicking us out in a second."

Dani caught her father's attention as my feet finally planted themselves onto the floor. I spotted a chair in the corner and walked over to it. I lifted it and walked it over to her mother, setting it beside her, offering her my hand. She took it so I could help her settle against the cushion.

"Would you like any coffee, ma'am?" I asked.

She smiled up at me. "Rena, please. And that would be nice."

Her father harrumphed. "You can drop the coffees off and head out. We've got it from here."

Dani cleared her throat. "Max doesn't leave."

Her mother's eyes studied me. "So you're Max."

I nodded. "Yes, ma'am."

She smiled. "Good to know."

I looked back over at her father, who was practically shooting daggers out of his eye sockets at me. My eyes fell to Dani one last time and the sweetest smile ever crossed her face. I wanted to walk back over and give her a good morning kiss. One of my favorite kinds of kisses from her. But with her father two seconds away from ripping my skull open, I decided against it.

"Sir, would you like--?"

"Out," he said curtly.

Dani sighed. "Dad, please stop it. I can't do this with you right now."

Her voice sounded so defeated, and the last thing I wanted to do was leave the woman I loved with more people that would stress her out. So, as I retreated back to the door, I made a mental note to tell the nursing staff my worries about them being here.

I mean, just because they were her parents didn't mean that they were who Dani needed right now.

"Mom, how did you find me?"

I paused near the doorway, wanting to hear more of the conversation.

Her mother snickered. "Hannah called us last night, sweetheart. She was frightened, and she said you ran off into some trouble."

Her father murmured. "Yeah. And trouble's got a beat-up face."

Dani hissed, "Dad, stop it."

Her father yelled across the room. "If you're going to stand there and listen, mind telling me what on earth happened to Danika?"

Her mother shushed him. "Pipe down. If you get us kicked out, I'm disowning you and finding a way to stay here. I told you to calm down on the ride here. I expect you to keep your cool now."

I slowly turned around and faced the two of them as Dani looked at me with wide eyes begging to be saved.

Her mother's eyes slid down my body. I saw her clocking the bruises and the stitches and the bandages I had wrapped around my various extremities. I saw the tension in her father's face. I felt it in the air as Dani tried to pull away from him. I looked at her, seeking some sort of direction. Because I sure as hell wasn't telling these people the truth. But she didn't look like she knew what to say, either. And I wasn't sure if I should actually stay and talk, or simply leave.

"Well? I'm waiting," he said.

I nodded. "I think maybe introductions are in order first. I'm Max."

He snickered. "Peter. I'm Dani's father. Now, what the hell happened to my daughter?"

I walked back across the room, trying to buy myself some time. I patted Rena on the shoulder softly before extending a hand to her father. I wanted to shake the man's hand. I mean, they were the parents of the woman I had fallen for. I had to try and make some sort of decent impression.

All he did was look at my hand, though.

As if I was offering him a rotten apple.

Peter turned his body to face mine and I watched Dani's eyes widen. I heard her mother suck in a short breath of air behind me. The man was short. He barely came up to my shoulder. But the angry glare in his eyes boasted of the ferocious worry he had flaring deep within his gut.

"Could you please afford me and my wife some privacy with our daughter? You can lengthen your coffee run, if necessary."

I put my hand down and nodded. I should have expected the cold brush-off. Even though I was attempting to make an effort to try and defuse the situation. Had I been in Peter's shoes with my own daughter lying in some hospital bed with some beat-up stranger lying next to her, that asshole would've been dead before his feet touched the floor.

Dani cleared her throat. "I don't want him to leave, Dad."

He whipped back around. "You, your mother, and I need to talk. Alone. Whether or not you want that to happen doesn't matter. What matters is the fact that we're going to talk."

Dani snickered. "So I don't get a say in this at all. Even though Max is the one that saved me and he's the one that's been looking after me all night, you're just going to kick him out. Just like that?"

Rena paused. "He saved you? From what?"

Peter glared at me hotly again. "If he'd leave, we could figure that out. Or do I need to remove him myself?"

Dani grinned. "I'd love to see you try, Dad."

Pride filled my chest, even though I wanted to tell Dani to stop antagonizing her parents. Something in the pit of my gut told me they'd never seen her like this before. Then the change that had occurred with her slapped me across my face. She was a completely different person with me. A person I wasn't sure was necessarily good. I felt my mind fighting with me. I felt my heart waging war. I felt my gut trying to get in on the action and pierce through the haze of pain and fear and dissent.

"Would any of you like coffee before I head out?" I asked.

Dani nodded. "Yes, please."

Peter held up his hand to her. "Black. Large. Thanks."

I looked down at Rena. "What about you, ma'am?"

She placed her hand against my arm. "Rena, again. Just use my name. And I'd love some coffee. However you take yours is fine."

Dani piped up. "He usually takes his morning coffee black, but sometimes I'll sneak some cream in it if it smells bitter."

Her father growled. "Morning coffee?"

I nodded. "I'll be back in a bit."

I shot a look to Dani before I headed back for the door. Things were getting too heated and too tense, and I felt my protective instinct rearing its head in unsavory ways. They were family, and they needed time to themselves. That much I understood.

Plus, I need a serious dose of caffeine.

I slipped into the hallway and closed the door behind me, only to find nurses standing around the desk staring at me. I sighed as I turned, heading straight for the elevator. But one of the nurses called out to me.

"If they cause problems, we'll kick them out," she said.

I lifted my hand in thanks and kept on walking.

It didn't take me long to make the coffee run. The cafeteria didn't have a line, and the coffee was freshly brewed. I picked up larges for all of us and stacked some extras in a small bag to go. I picked up some danishes that looked nice, as well as a couple of cinnamon rolls. Then I grabbed a big thing of fruit salad, just for something healthy thrown in. I wasn't sure what her parents had had on the road, if anything. I wasn't sure how long they'd driven or what had happened in order to get them here.

But I figured the least I could do was feed them.

I rode the elevator back up to Dani's floor and balanced everything in my arms. However, the door to her room still wasn't opened.

"No one's come out yet," another nurse said.

I nodded. "Thanks."

I set everything down and leaned against the wall. I wished with all my might that I was anyone else but myself right now. I wanted to be one of the doctors, or one of the nurses. One of Dani's friends, or a concerned volunteer member of the hospital. Anyone that could get into that room and stay there by Dani's side.

You know, without putting a disgusting taste in her parents' mouths.

I kept an ear out for yelling. Or shouting. Or

anything that might rile Dani up. I closed my eyes, drawing in deep breaths to try and swallow down the worry that kept creeping up the back of my throat. I wasn't sure what worried me more: the fear of yelling starting up or the fact that I couldn't hear a damn thing.

And as the coffees grew cold at my feet, I counted down the seconds until I was back in Dani's presence.

6

DANI

"Dad, why are you being so rude? That man saved me. Why in the world can't you just--"

Dad glared at me. "Who is that man?"

I sighed. "If you'd listen to me instead of demanding answers on the spot, you'd know."

Mom cut in. "That's Max, Peter."

Dad scoffed. "Who the hell is that?"

I sucked air through my teeth. "That's the man I've been seeing. He's the reason why I declined Kline's coffee date."

I resented the sharp, condescending tone of my father's voice, and I hated the anger that rose behind his eyes. I was already frustrated with this entire scenario. All I wanted was for Max to come back into this room. My father didn't own me. I wasn't my parents' property. I was of legal age to ask for any kind of care I wanted, which meant I could kick them out and bring Max in if I wanted.

Maybe my father needs me to remind him of that.

"What in the world are you doing with a man like that? Have we taught you nothing?" Dad asked.

I snickered. "Please don't forget that at any point in time, I can have you removed and bring him back in. Don't make me do that."

His eyes narrowed. "Who are you and what have you done with my daughter?"

I shrugged. "Maybe your daughter is sick and tired of the helicopter parenting tactics you employ."

Mom placed her hand on my shin. "Sweetheart, we're only here because we're worried. Try to be patient with us. I mean, look at you. You're in the hospital. We have a right, as your parents, to be worried."

Dad practically spat on me. "What in the world has gotten into you? First, Hannah calls us up rattling on about how you've gotten yourself into trouble. How's she's worried about you. You're falling behind on papers and assignments in your classes. Then you're dodging our--"

I held up my hand. "Wait, wait, wait, wait. How do you know *anything* about my school assignments?"

Dad held his head high. "Of course I know. I've got connections within some of the departments."

I blinked. "That's illegal. My grades are none of your concern unless I have them released to you."

Mom patted my leg. "All of that paperwork you signed your freshman year enabled us to view that information, honey."

I felt my eyes widening. "Are you fucking kid--!?"

Dad leaned over me. "What did you just say?"

I closed my eyes. I needed to gain control of this situation. I was tired of all this bullshit. Of people feeling they could control me. Use me. Direct me in whatever fashion they deemed suitable for my life. This was my life. And they had no reason to do all of the shit they were doing.

I wanted more time with Max. I wanted him instead of them. I needed space from all of this. I needed...

I don't know what I need.

But I knew it wasn't this.

I always feel stronger with him around. "I wish Max was still here."

Dad scoffed. "Has he brainwashed you?"

Mom gasped. "Peter! Are you kidding me right now?"

"Answer me, Dani. What has that man done to you? Did he do this to you? Did he put you in this hospital bed?"

I drew in a deep breath. "No, Dad. He didn't. He saved me. And my answer won't change just because you want it to. Max is the man I've been seeing, and I'm sorry I wasn't honest with you sooner. I was waiting for the right time to tell--"

Dad snickered. "Does now look like the right time, Danika?"

I blinked up at him as I leaned back against my pillows. I loved Max. There was no reason to hold that back from anyone. That was my truth. That was my reality. And I had no issues telling anyone who came into contact with me.

But, my father really needed to back off.

"No, Dad. Ideally, I would have told you the next time I made the drive home. Probably over Thanksgiving break. And, ideally, you'd give him a chance before you wrote him off entirely."

My father's face reddened. "Danika, you put yourself in an incredible amount of danger by being with this man. Why on earth would you think being with someone like him is a good idea? He almost got you killed!"

I sighed. "Is that what Hannah told you? Because that's not the truth."

Mom clicked her tongue. "Then just tell us the truth, sweetie."

I threw my hands in the air. "I am, Mom! I am telling you the truth! This isn't Max's fault. And even if I wanted to tell you the entire situation, you wouldn't understand. It's complicated, but the only thing you guys need to know--"

Dad gripped the railing of my bed. "You will tell us every detail of what happened last night before I call the police and have them drag it out of you."

"Peter!"

I sat up straight. "You do what you feel you have to. You have that right. But I'm not your little teenage girl any longer. You can't boss me around, nor can you protect me from everything. If anything, I've found my inner strength with Max. And I wouldn't trade it for the world."

"He's dangerous, Danika. Reckless. A damn criminal! You think I didn't talk to Hannah about him? About this crew he runs around with and the bike he rides and the stuff he gets into? You don't think I did my due diligence by looking up who in the world this man was, Danika? I mean, it's only a matter of time before something like this--or worse--happens again! Had it not been for Hannah in the first place--"

"Nothing," I interjected. "If it hadn't been for Hannah, then nothing. Because her calling you didn't save my life. Max did that. The only thing Hannah calling you did was worry you guys, drag you out of bed, shove you ten hours away from home, only to yell at me while I lie here in a hospital bed. So, who's the bad one now, Dad?"

My father drew in a sharp breath to retort, but Mom shoved him off to the side. She wiggled her way up to me and lowered herself, kissing me on the forehead. Dad harrumphed off into a corner. I practically saw the steam coming out of his ears. And as Mom took my hand, she brushed my hair away from my face.

"Peter, you need to stop it. For goodness sake, can't you see our daughter's in distress? Dani. Princess. I'm so sorry this happened. What can we do to help?"

Finally. "You both can start by shaking Max's hand."

Dad scoffed. "I'm doing no such thing. That man is a monster. Plain and simple. And you deserve better than the likes of some scumbag standing in the hallway."

I shrugged. "Then the two of you can leave."

Mom hissed. "Peter, at least try to be sympathetic. This is our daughter you're speaking to."

Dad came back over to the bed and sat on the edge of it. But my mouth was sealed. No matter what he did, or said, or asked, I wasn't answering a damn thing until he did as I asked him to do.

He placed his hand on my ankle. "What happened?"

I shrugged. "If you want a play by play, talk to the attending doctor."

"I'd rather hear it from you."

"Tough."

His jaw clenched. "Rena?"

Mom patted my shoulder. "Gentle, Peter. Try again."

He sighed. "You said Max saved you. What did he save you from?"

I blinked. "Shake his hand first."

"Just tell me what happened to you. I want to know what happened to my daughter."

"And if you want to hear it from me, you'll shake Max's hand with the respect he deserves. I'd be dead without him. And you'd be visiting the morgue instead of a hospital room."

He shot up from the bed. "You take that back."

"I won't, because it's a fact. And if you really want the dirty truth, I was already dead when Max found me. It was his life-saving CPR that saved my life."

Mom gasped. "Oh, honey."

Dad raked his hand through his hair. "You tell me

what in the world happened right now, or so help me God I will--"

I pointed to the door. "There's the way out. You can leave the way you came, or you can go find Max and try this again. But if you don't start lowering your voice and keeping a hold on your anger, I'll have this hospital remove you completely."

His face fell. "Where in the world is my sweet little girl?"

"I'm right here, Dad. You just don't like the fact that I'm not blindly following you any longer. And I shouldn't. Because this is my life, and my education, and my future. And the only person that should have an opinion about that is me."

I held my ground as I stared off with my father. I slipped my hands beneath the warm blanket and tucked them between my thighs. I didn't want my father to see how scared I was of him. Of his anger when he got like this. I wanted to portray the strong front I always had whenever Max was at my side. Because it was about time people saw this side of me.

Then Dad caved. "If I shake his hand, you'll talk to me?"

I nodded. "We both will."

I watched his eyes fall to the door as Mom squeezed my shoulder.

"Nice going, princess," she whispered.

I watched my father head for the door. "Thanks, Mom."

And I held my breath as my father started his journey toward the door.

Please don't blow up in my face. Please don't blow up in my face. Please don't blow up in my face.

7

———

MAX

I leaned my head against the painted cement wall and sighed. With the coffee and food growing cold at my feet, I crammed my hands into my pockets. Mostly to hide my bloodied knuckles. Every time a nurse or a patient passed by, they gave me 'the look.' You know, the one with the crooked eyebrow and the wandering eyes. The one with the soft pause as they gave me a once over.

"You sure you don't need any pain medication?"

"You really should go lie down. You haven't yet been discharged."

"If the doctor sees you like this--"

I licked my lips. "You let me handle the doctor, Nurse. Thanks."

They scoffed and snickered and whispered as they walked by. But it didn't rile me up. I knew I looked like a wreck. One of those class-A, super-duper train wrecks. I felt the swelling in my eyes finally going down, but I also felt the bruising creeping underneath my skin and my neck stiffening. My arms were hard to move. And my back—damn it, my fucking back hurt like hell.

It hurt to breathe. It hurt to blink. It hurt to stand, or sit, or generally exist. But nothing would get me back in that room. Nothing would get me in a bed without Dani at my side. So I dealt with the uneasy looks and the constant barrage of questions and the nurses trying to talk me into pain medication.

I was fine with the Tylenol I kept swallowing down.

Every once in a while, I thought I heard voices behind the door. But with the door closed, this damn cement wall in my way, and Dani on the other side of the room, it was hard to hear anything. I started pacing outside the door. The coffee stopped steaming from the little hole in the lid and the fruit looked to be sitting in a pool of its own juices. Hardly appetizing at this point.

It's the thought that counts.

For the first time in a very long time, I felt nervous. Truly, genuinely nervous. I mean, these were the parents of the woman I loved. If I couldn't make a good impression, what did that mean for Dani and me? Usually I didn't give a shit about this stuff. I didn't care about the girl's life, or her family, or what she did for a living, or what she'd do the next morning. We met, we fucked, she left. That's how it worked in my life.

But Dani stuck.

And I had to do my best to make sure her parents were on my side.

Now, how to sway her father…

The door ripped open and I turned around. With my hands still shoved in my pockets, I watched as the edge of the door caught the bag of danishes, and I heard the paper crunch. It didn't matter, though. Not to me.

Because staring back at me from beyond the doorway was Dani's father.

He stared at me for a long time. His eyes danced around my face before traveling down my body. I was familiar with the look. He was trying to size me up. Figure out how badly I was hurt. And I let him. I took no offense to it. I mean, his daughter was lying in a fucking hospital bed. I would've already killed the man at her side had the tables been turned and I'd been in Peter's position.

Then he did something that shocked me.

He extended his hand.

"It's been a trying morning, Max."

I looked down at his hand before I slipped mine out of my pocket.

"I apologize for how I acted in there. It wasn't kind, given the tense situation for all of us," he said.

I shook his hand. "I understand. I wish we were meeting under better circumstances."

He dropped my hand quickly and didn't respond to my sentiment. Which told me he wasn't out here of his own volition. He peeked over his shoulder and I resisted the urge to do it too. I wanted him to know that I was fully paying attention to him if he had anything else to say. His head came back around and his eyes met mine. After heaving a heavy sigh, he thumbed over his shoulder.

"You should come back in. Danika's been asking for you."

I nodded. "I've got coffee and things to munch on, if anyone's hungry."

Peter snickered. "I'm sure Danika will appreciate that."

I reached down and gathered everything into my arms before following Peter back into the room. I let the door close softly behind me, using my foot to stop its jarring movements so it wouldn't slam. Dani turned her head to me and the warm smile that crossed her face made me smile in return. I walked over and placed everything on the edge of her bed, giving her the first pick of the fruit and the danishes I had to offer.

"This looks great. Thank you, Max," she said.

I smiled. "If there's something here you want but don't see, let me know. I'll go track it down."

Her mother giggled. "That effort extend to all of us?"

I turned my gaze to her. "Of course. Though I think I got a decent-enough spread for what they had down there."

Peter sighed. "I'll be right back. I need to go let work know I won't be reachable for the next twenty-four hours."

I peered over my shoulder. "I'll save you a danish. Do you have a preference for flavor?"

He shrugged. "Surprise me."

I nodded slowly as he marched back out the door, closing it a bit too hard behind him. And when I turned to face the two women in the room, Rena gave me a tight-lipped smile.

"My husband handles stress poorly. Always has. I'm very sorry if he offended you."

I grinned. "It'll take more than that to offend me. I promise."

"Well, thank you for the coffee. And the food. The fruit looks fresh. Is it?"

I nodded. "Watched them cut it just before they put it out."

"Oh, fabulous. I love a good fruit salad."

Dani snickered. "Well, you can have it. I'd rather have a couple of those apple danishes."

Rena rolled her eyes. "My daughter, always chowing down on carbs. You'll lose that metabolism one of these days. Then you'll be just like me."

Dani shrugged. "Well, I hope Max here likes big women. Because I don't ever plan on giving up my danishes."

Her words brought silence between the three of us. That was such a heavy-handed statement, I didn't know where to start picking it apart. Did Dani really see us together that long? Did she dream about our future the way I did? I saw worry cross behind her mother's eyes and I wanted to say something to reassure her. But I figured keeping my mouth shut was probably for the best.

So I drew in a deep breath. "Rena, Peter is fine. I promise. I get where you guys are coming from. When my own brother was in the hospital…"

She giggled nervously. "Are you sure you don't need any medical attention yourself? Your face looks pretty…"

I chuckled. "You should see my ribs."

Dani murmured, "Max."

I nodded. "I'm just kidding. Kind of. I promise I'm all right. I don't need any sort of attention. Just rest, some Tylenol, and plenty of fluids."

Dani interjected quickly. "So, Mom. How in the world did you and Dad figure out where I was?"

Rena laughed. "You know how your father is. The second he drained Hannah of all the information she had, he started calling every police station and hospital in the area. Searching for your name. Wondering if you had been admitted. He did it for the majority of the ten-hour drive over. And, once this hospital confirmed you had been admitted, it was ninety the rest of the way here."

Dani sighed. "Yep. Sounds like Dad."

Her mother patted Dani's knee. "You know he's just worried. And he's got a right to be. We still don't have any answers. We haven't seen a doctor. All the nurses are telling us is that you were submerged underwater for too long. Which doesn't make any sense, given the fact that you're a great swimmer."

"Look, Mom, I really didn't mean to scare you guys. Things just sort of… got out of hand last night. It was no one's fault."

"Well, don't take offense if I don't believe you. Max?"

I nodded. "Yes?"

"Would you like to fill me in a bit on what happened last night? You know, since my daughter won't?"

I looked down at Dani and saw the panic behind her eyes. I felt that same panic wafting around in my gut, too. This wouldn't go over well. And it was hard to keep that feeling off my face. I knew I bore a great deal of the weight of what happened last night. If anyone was to blame, it was me and my actions. Had it not been for me being so damn selfish, I never would've pulled Dani into this lifestyle in the first place. Had I been thinking with my head and not my dick, I would've known that she was a girl fit for more than this. More than a few one-night stands with some jerk-off who didn't deserve her.

And if I hadn't dragged her into any of this, she never would've been on my father's radar.

Rena sighed. "I'm waiting, Max. Please don't make me wait much longer. It's making me concerned that the police should be involved at this point."

My mind spun with all sorts of things. I felt myself raging out of control again. I should've known that coming to the hospital would've set off this chain reaction. But I didn't realize her parents would get involved. I felt completely unprepared for something like this. Hell, I'd been completely unprepared for the whirlwind that was Danika Young. She had swept me off my feet in ways I'd never experienced before.

How in the world was I supposed to explain any of this to her fucking parents?

So many things ran through my mind. Like how Dani needed to be on campus right now. It was a Monday, and I knew she had morning classes she was missing right now. She had her ritual swimming in the afternoon, too. Which she would also miss. Instead of swimming those lengths and stretching those muscles and carrying on with her normal life, she was here. In the hospital.

Because she'd nearly drowned in my father's backyard.

Rena huffed. "Well?"

Dani sighed. "Mom, you have to understand that he's been through an ordeal, too."

"Yeah, I can see it from the bruises on his face. That doesn't mean we don't require answers. We're your parents, Dani. And while I get that you're trying to spread your wings and be a bit more independent, you're in the hospital. That warrants at least a bit of an explanation as to why a wonderful swimmer like you almost drowned."

"Technically, I did drown. It was Max who saved me."

My voice grew stern. "Dani."

She looked up at me. "Sorry. I just--it's true. And I think you guys are missing that point."

Rena shook her head. "We're not missing that

point. But you have to understand that even though you feel independent right now, you just admitted to drowning, Danika. You drowned. And yes, in time I will thank Max for saving you. But now isn't that time. Now is the time for answers."

Dani looked up at me and I had no clue on how to guide us. Where to take us. What to say from here. I expected to be dealing with the police. Not her parents. I'd have to have a talk with that fucking roommate of hers once we got ourselves out of this mess. I drew in a deep breath, preparing to tell the entire truth. Well, most of it. The story quickly threaded itself together in my head as I stood there, trying to buy myself a bit more time.

Before the door to the room swung open.

Thank fuck.

"Sorry that took so long," Peter said. "My boss wanted to know what was going on and it required a bit of an explanation. Though he's still got some questions. Just like I do."

Dani sighed. "I know, Dad."

Rena patted her shoulder. "It's okay. You can talk to us. I hope you know that."

I looked over my shoulder, ignoring the pain wafting through my body. Peter gave me a hesitant look before he walked around me, giving me a wide berth. He didn't want to be anywhere near me. That much was for certain. And honestly, with the way I looked, I couldn't blame him one bit. He walked over to where Rena was standing and exchanged places with her. He bent down, kissed Dani on the forehead, then took her hand softly within his.

"Okay, you ready?" he murmured.

Dani swallowed hard. "Ready for what?"

Peter sat on the edge of the bed. "Princess, can you please tell us what happened last night?"

8

———

DANI

I held his hand tightly, but I kept drawing a blank. What in the world was I supposed to tell my father about something like this? I mean, I sure as hell wasn't telling him the truth. I wasn't telling anyone the truth. The truth would stay between Max, me, Rupert, and the rest of the Red Thorns. It surely wasn't something I was telling my parents. The look in my father's eyes was desolate, though. My mother was practically begging me with the worried downturn of her lips. My father threaded our fingers together as he tucked a strand of loose hair behind my ear. And as I drew in a deep breath, I started with the truncated truth I had quickly concocted in my mind. Because I couldn't lie to my parents anymore. I felt guilty enough already that I had scared them so badly. Adding lies to that would do Max and me no good.

Especially since I wanted them to accept Max.

"Well, we were at Max's father's house. He has a pool in his backyard," I said.

Dad nodded. "Uh huh. Was there any rough-housing going on or anything?"

No. There were just thugs and business tycoons and gunfire and I watched a man die. You know, the usual stuff a college girl gets herself into.

I paused. "Not really. I mean, Max's friend Rupert was there. His father was there. I don't think John was with us, right?"

Max shook his head. "No. He wasn't. John doesn't swim."

Mom interjected. "Who's John?"

Max grinned. "My brother. He's got some lasting issues from a coma he slipped into due to some serious trauma a few years back that prevent him from doing things like swimming and riding a bike."

Dad's face hardened. "Seems like a lot of people get hurt around this guy, Dani. Are you sure he didn't--?"

I shook my head. "Dad, it isn't like that. Not at all. I'm telling you, Max is the one that saved me. It was just an accident. There wasn't anything that--"

Max cleared his throat. "It was my father."

My blood ran cold as my head whipped over to face him.

"Max, what are you doing?" I whispered.

He snickered. "Summarizing our eventful night. Just stand in my corner with this one, okay?"

Dad narrowed his eyes. "What are you talking

about? What the hell is going on? I demand to know what's going on this instant!"

Mom placed a hand on his shoulder. "Peter, calm down. We're only going to cause a scene if you don't calm down."

He shrugged Mom off. "I don't give a shit about the scene anymore. If it gets me answers, then so be it. You talk to me now. What the hell happened to my daughter?"

I panicked. "Daddy, stop. I'm telling you the truth. This isn't what--"

Max cleared his throat. "My father has always been a pain in the ass. We've had bad blood for years now, and your daughter got dragged into something that had nothing to do with her. That's what happened."

I stared at him. "Max, shut up. Now."

His eyes grew cold as he slowly looked at me. "You let me handle this."

Dad stood up. "What kind of bad blood? Did your father do this to my little girl?"

Max sighed. "Yes. He did."

Mom gasped. "What in the world? Did he try to kill our daughter?"

Dad roared. "That's it! I'm calling the police. I'm calling the police and having you arrested along with everyone else!"

I raised my voice. "Will you two just shut up and let him talk?"

Max took my hand within his as the door to my room ripped open.

"Do I have to start removing people from this

room?" the nurse asked.

I looked over at her. "No. I'm sorry. It won't happen again."

The nurse looked at me hard. "You know where that button is if you need it. But if I hear your voices again, all of you are gone. Got it?"

I nodded. "We got it. Thank you, Nurse."

"Uh huh."

But when she closed the door, the chaos didn't stop. It simply got quieter.

"You talk to me right now," Dad hissed.

Max nodded. "It's a long and involved story. But the gist of it is this: my father is not a good man. He deals with a lot of very bad people. He tried to rope me into something I wanted no part of. And when I told him no, he looked for any kind of leverage he could find against me to change my mind."

Mom gasped. "Oh, my gosh. Sweetheart."

Dad glared. "What did he do to my little girl?"

Max swallowed hard. "He bound her to a chair and lured me to his house. I swear to you, Mr. Young, your daughter's safety was the only thing on my radar. The reason she was under for so long was because she couldn't move. I continued refusing my father's advances and he pushed her in. I--"

I squeezed Max's hand as he blinked back tears.

"What did you do?" Dad growled.

I sighed. "He killed his own father to save me, Dad. That's what he did."

Mom paused. "You--killed your father to save Danika?"

Max nodded. "I did, yes."

I saw how hard it was for Max to look my father in the eye. But he did. And I was so proud of him. I felt like shit, though. I didn't know how in the world my parents were going to take this. I knew it wouldn't be good. I watched as Max and my father stared at one another for a long time. I saw how uneasy this made him. Both of them, really. And as I squeezed Max's hand, he drew in a deep breath.

"I'm not a fool either, Peter. I know what you must think of me. You're not alone in that position. I think of myself the same way, too."

I whimpered. "Max."

He looked down at me. "Gorgeous, this never would've happened had it not been for me. You know that as well as I do. I might not have put you in this hospital bed, but the things that come with my life did."

I shook my head. "This doesn't change anything. I care about you. I--I'm not going to let you take all of the blame for this. It's not entirely your fault. Your father's to blame here. It lies with him. None of this would've happened in the first place if he would've just left you alone."

"You know that's not how my father works."

"And that's somehow your fault? Come on, Max. Your father is a no-good criminal. A terrible father. A psychopath, really, who tried to kill his own son less than twelve hours ago."

Mom interjected. "Wait, is that why you look so bad?"

Max gritted his teeth. "More or less."

I reached up and cupped his cheek. I wanted to kiss him, to pull him close. But he wouldn't come to me. He wouldn't get anywhere near me. I knew my own father was to blame for that reaction. Having my father here was causing Max to back away from me. Especially with the negative emotion he was putting off.

"Daddy, can't you see? This isn't his fault. None of this is his fault. His father is a terrible, disgusting man. But you heard Max. Right?"

I looked over at my father to search for some kind of answer in his eyes before I heard people murmuring on the other side of the wall. Something was stirring outside, and Max squeezed my hand harder as he turned to look at the door. Then his head whipped back around to me. And as my father stood up, Max dipped his lips to my ear, lowering his voice.

"I want you to know that I love you and everything's going to be okay."

I furrowed my brow. "What?"

He kissed my ear softly, lowering his voice to a whisper. "I love you, Danika Young."

I shook my head. "What's going on? Why are you--?"

"Max Ryddle?"

I didn't even hear the door open. But when the hardened voice caught my ear, I knew exactly what was going on. I didn't even have to look to know that a police officer was standing in my fucking hospital room. Tears rushed my eyes. Max slipped his hand away from mine. And no matter how much I clamored for it, he turned himself around and slowly moved away from the bed.

Away from me.

"Max, no," I said.

The officer looked at him. "Are you Max Ryddle?"

He nodded, but he didn't say anything.

"You're under arrest."

I scoffed. "What? No! You can't arrest him, Officer. He did nothing--"

Dad placed his hand on my thigh. "Princess, just let the man do his--"

I slapped his hand away. "Don't you touch me. Did you do this? Did you call the police?"

Mom gasped. "Danika. Don't you ever hit your father like that again."

I drew in a deep breath. "Answer my fucking question!"

"Bambi."

My parents' eyes widened as I quickly turned to face Max. I watched the officer slap handcuffs on him, and not once did he resist. Not once did he fight. Not once did he try to plead his side of things.

"Please," I begged. "Max. Officers. Wait, this isn't right--"

Max's voice lowered. "Bambi. Gorgeous. Look at me."

Tears rushed down my cheeks as my gaze found his.

"Max," I whispered.

He nodded. "Everything is going to be all right. Trust me on that."

9

———

MAX

T*his isn't going to be anywhere near all right.*

It killed me to hear Dani sniffling as the two police officers walked me out of her room. I glanced over my shoulder and the faces on her and her parents would forever be etched in my mind. Her mother's face was stricken with horror, her wide eyes mirroring the shock in Dani's. Her father's face was filled with regret. Sorrow. Confusion. Anger. A hell of a first impression on the one man who meant the most to a girl.

Dani's face was filled with grief, determination, anger, and exhaustion.

I'll never forget that look as long as I live.

"You have the right to remain silent. Anything you say can and will be held against you in a court of law…"

Everything moved in slow motion. Everything felt like a blur. And I knew who had called the cops. I knew who had done this to me.

No wonder Peter was out in that hallway for so long.

A call to someone's boss didn't take that long. But a call to the police to feed them information did. I didn't feel betrayed, though. Not like Dani would if she ever found out. If anything, I understood. I understood his reaction, because it was the kind of reaction I would have had with my own daughter. Not that I'd ever have children one day. But sometimes I thought about it.

What it might feel like to lead a life that enabled me to have a family.

You're the reason for all of this.

"Watch your head," the officer said.

People rubbernecked around corners to watch me get hauled off. I flopped down against the hard plastic seat of the police cruiser and drew in a deep breath. And all the while, I thought about Peter. How dedicated of a father he was. How Dani didn't see that in him. I wished with all of my might to be there. To tell her that she really had something special with her father. Instead of bringing the demons down onto her shoulders--like mine always had--her father was protecting her from them. Protecting her from the monsters who lurked in the dark corners.

Protecting her from men like me.

Dani had a great father in Peter.

And because of that, I knew I'd never win him over.

I hoped Dani saw it that way one day. I hoped she didn't stay mad at her father forever. All he was doing was exactly what he was put on this earth to do: protect his family, provide for those who loved him, and to love the girls in his life with all his might. I knew Dani wouldn't see things that way right now, but eventually, I hoped she would. She had a father who wanted to love her. Who wanted to protect her. Who wanted to pull her out of harm's way instead of push her into it, like I had.

I wish I had a father like that.

My eyes fell out the window as the world passed us by. The cruiser inched away from the hospital, and it quickly fell away behind us. I couldn't think about Dani any longer. It made me sick to my stomach to think that I might never see her again. Because honestly? I wasn't sure what my future held any longer. I knew damn good and well the guys hadn't gone to my father's house to clean anything up. I knew damn good and well my father's cameras had captured most--if not all--of what went on last night. And I knew damn good and well it would take a fucking miracle from a lawyer I probably couldn't afford to pull me even halfway out of the hole I'd dug for myself.

Dani was alive, though.

And that's all that mattered to me.

I felt my anger bubbling, rising up the back of my throat. I felt the beast inside me rattling in its cage, begging for more, despite the poor condition of my body. In reality, the only person I was truly angry with was my father. He was the one who'd done all of this. He was the one who'd come after me. He was the one who'd tried to take out my entire fucking crew. He was the one who'd decided to gun for me because I wouldn't bow to his every whim.

I wonder if that man's still alive.

"So want to tell us what happened last night?"

I held my tongue as the officers started asking me questions.

"Come on, Ryddle. Does you no good not to talk."

"Just a bit. I mean, how in the world did that kind of carnage take place last night?"

I locked my eyes out the window on the passing landscape and kept biting further down into my tongue. I wasn't speaking to anyone without a fucking lawyer.

Though I wasn't sure how to obtain one if no one knew I had been arrested.

The officers stopped asking me questions once they figured out I wouldn't answer them. I kept myself tightly-lipped as we made our way for the precinct. I knew the rigamarole. I'd been through it a couple of times before, and multiple times with my men. Rupert was the worst of them, but he always found a way to wiggle himself out of things. I could only imagine what he had paid over the course of his lifetime in lawyers' fees. Maybe I could place a call to Rupert and have him call that lawyer of his.

Maybe I stand a chance that way.

Either way, I couldn't let the cops know what had gone on last night. I mean, they probably already knew I was involved. There was no way in hell they hadn't already been looking for me after finding my father's estate in the disarray we'd left it in. What I didn't know was what had happened to Rupert. I hadn't seen him since Dani and I were admitted. He hadn't been at my bedside. He hadn't come back in the morning. In fact, it hadn't even dawned on me that Rupert hadn't been around until my mind started wandering.

Is Rupert okay? Did he get caught up in all of this, too?

As the police cruiser pulled into the parking lot of the precinct, I closed my eyes. I lifted a silent prayer to a God that had cast me out a long time ago, hoping and praying that Rupert was all right. That he had managed to escape the police's interest. That he hadn't gotten caught up in the carnage my father had left in the wake of his death.

The praying stopped the second my door ripped open.

"Come on. Get out," the officer said.

They led me inside and everything went blurry. I registered nothing as they processed me. Took my fingerprints. Made me sign all sorts of shit and officially placed me in the system. The bars of the cell rumbled as they opened. But the sound didn't pull me from my trance. He shoved me into a holding cell with a few other men who looked just as bad as I did, and I moved into a corner, working my wrists to try and get the cuff stiffness out of them.

For the first time since being arrested, I actually took in my surroundings. There were five other men in this holding cell with me. And all of them smelled like various stages of rotting cheese. One man, sitting in the opposite corner from me, was clearly delusional. Or high. But definitely homeless. The man needed a shower. Possibly some food. He sure as hell didn't need to be sitting in a damn cell because he wanted a short, illegal release from the reality of his existence.

I hate the law.

"Oh, man. That stri-joint was great."

I nodded. "Glad to hear it."

The drunk man grinned at me. "Had thi-cutie patootie on my knee right here."

He slapped his thigh hard before he winced in pain.

"Shit, that hurt," he murmured.

I snickered. "Maybe don't do it again, then."

He nodded. "What was I talk--who--ah, fuck."

I watched the man as he realized where he was. In jail. In a holding cell. And not in that funky strip club of his. I wondered how many times he had 'realized' he was in jail, essentially.

I wonder if it even matters to him.

I looked at the man sitting on the bench in the middle of the cell and I crooked an eyebrow. He hung his head, almost in shame, as he sat there in his business suit. A nice one, too. Tailored specifically to him. He hiccuped before he started murmuring to himself. And between his slurred words, I caught 'wife,' 'kill,' and 'doo-ee.'

And something in my gut told me this wasn't this man's first DUI.

I leaned my head back against the wall and closed my eyes. This mess was only the beginning. That much I knew. And while I hoped my guys wouldn't try anything stupid to get me out of here, part of me wondered what they might try. Curiosity played through several scenarios that might go into busting me out of this place. But the rational part of me willed them all to stay the fuck away.

Because, despite the fact that I wasn't really sure my father had died, I knew there were still cogs turning in this bullshit nightmare.

If my father's alive, nobody's safe.

We had protocol for this kind of thing in the crew. If the president was to get killed or put away, then tradition designated that either the vice president or a former president would take over. And since I'd never designated a V.P. to stand at my side, that meant responsibility of the crew fell to John. Who would enlist Rupert to help him with things. What I needed to do, instead of dreaming about my escape, was trust that my brother had already taken steps to protect the Red Thorns and their families.

To protect Dani.

"What you in for? Huh?"

The homeless man's voice caught my ear and everyone turned to face me.

"Look pretty beat up for a night out on the town," he snickered.

I nodded. "Because I didn't have a night out on the town."

The man grinned. "You get into it with your girl?"

The drunkard slurred his words. "Shit, I've seen women do worse in my life."

The man in the middle sniffled. "My wife's gonna kill the hell out of me."

I nodded. "Probably."

I turned my back to the men and closed my eyes. I resisted the urge to sit down, lest they somehow think I was weak. The last thing I needed was for a bunch of men in this holding cell to perceive me as weak. Because I knew what happened in these places. People were cooped up for far too long and tensions ran high. People wanted out. Fights broke out and people got hurt.

The last thing I needed was another damn fight to bust through.

And the one thing I did need was lying in a hospital bed with parents poking and prodding at her a million miles a second.

I'm sorry I lied to you, gorgeous.

Because I honestly saw no way for any of us to get out of this all right.

10

DANI

I slowly panned my gaze over to my father. My eyes narrowed as he watched Max being hauled out of the room. He didn't even fight, didn't even attempt to protest the arrest. Did that not show my father the kind of man Max was?

"You didn't call work, Daddy, did you?"

His eyes fell to mine. "I did."

Mom sighed. "What did you do, Peter?"

He whipped around on her. "What any good man should do to his family. Something is going on, and it isn't right. That man has dragged our daughter--"

"--out of a fucking pool to save my life, Dad! Come on!"

He glared at me. "You curse at me one more time and I'm pulling you from the semester."

Mom gasped. "Peter. I've had enough of this. Rein it in now."

He balked. "Are you kidding me right now, Rena? Our daughter almost died! She did die!"

Mom nodded. "Yes. But she didn't. The entire reason why she's here and not downstairs with the M.E. is because of the man you just called the cops on."

I lifted my hand. "See? She gets it. Why in the world can't you?"

Dad held his hand up to me. "I won't hear another word of it. And if you so much as sass me one more time, you're done for the school year. You'll come home, recuperate, and we can re-enroll you next year. I won't stand for this."

"I'm not yours to control. I'm not a pawn. You can't force me to do anything."

Mom yelled. "Enough, you two!"

My back stiffened as Dad stepped away from my bed. I glared at him with heat rising behind my eyes before I shoved my elbow into the red button by my bed. Mom's eyes welled with tears. Dad hugged her tightly as Mom shook her head. And as a nurse came trolloping into the room, Dad spun around on her.

"Is everything all right? Do you need to take vitals or something?" he asked.

The nurse looked at me. "You rang?"

I nodded. "I want them out."

Mom took my hand. "No, honey. Please. Let us stay."

Dad narrowed his eyes. "Don't do this, Danika. Think about your education."

I snickered. "The only reason why you agreed to

pay for it was because I was following in your footsteps. I'm shocked you haven't held it over my head before now, since I changed my major without consulting you in the first place."

Then I turned to the nurse.

"When can I go?" I asked.

Dad interjected. "When you're healthy and ready to--"

The nurse lifted her hand to him, silencing his words.

"If your vitals are fine and your lungs still look clear, you're good to go."

I nodded. "Then get it done. I have somewhere I have to be, and I'd like to not put it off."

Dad growled. "You're not going anywhere."

I shrugged. "You want to know the difference between you and Max, Father?"

I slowly looked over at him and watched his face fall.

"The difference is that you love with control. And he loves with freedom. If anything, you're more like Max's father than the father you think you are."

Mom started crying. "Please don't do this. We're just worried about you. Talk to us. Tell us what you're going to do."

I nodded to Dad. "He lost that right for you when he called the cops instead of giving Max a chance."

The nurse piped up. "Let me get your vitals really quickly and then we'll get an ultrasound for your lungs. In the meantime, you two can wait in the waiting room."

My father stood his ground. "I'm not going anywhere so long as my daughter is in this bed."

The nurse nodded. "That's fine. I'll have you hauled out in handcuffs, then."

He balked. "But--the only thing I've done in this situation is worry about my daughter!"

"Security!" the nurse exclaimed.

Mom clapped her hand over his mouth. "Shut up before I leave you to the police. I've had enough of this."

I sighed. "Take her, too. I don't want to see either of them until I'm out of here."

My parents put up a good fight. A fight admirable of any parent worried about their daughter. But they had just made things worse without realizing it. Instead of treating me like the adult I was blossoming into, they were still treating me like some ignorant, idiotic eleven-year-old. And I wouldn't stand for it a second longer. It took two security guards to get my father out of the room. But, once he was removed, my mother wasn't far behind.

Then the nurses got to work.

After clearing my vitals and talking with the doctor, I was free to go. I checked myself out and accepted my clothes from last night. Clothes the staff had been kind enough to launder and dry for me. I knew I'd still have to battle my parents in order to get out of here. I knew I'd find them downstairs.

But right now, the only thing on my mind was getting in touch with Rupert. Or John. Or anyone that would help me.

We have to get Max out of jail.

The nurses wheeled me out the front doors in a wheelchair, as protocol stated. And, like I figured, my parents were there to greet me. Unfortunately for them, I was in a hurry. I had no time to waste on this matter. I needed to get into a cab, get my ass to Max's place, and figure out what the hell to do next.

But my father wasn't having any of it.

"Dani," he said.

I moved past him and held my hand up for a cab.

"Danika, talk to me."

I watched the cab pulling up into the roundabout circle as someone tapped on my shoulder.

"This is also yours," the nurse said.

I took my purse from her. "Thank you for everything you've done. I appreciate it."

"And remember what we said: no swimming for three weeks, rest and make sure you keep yourself nourished, and if anything pops up out of the ordinary--a fever, pain in your chest, shortness of breath-- you come right back to us. Understood?"

I nodded. "I understand."

My father kept rattling on in my ear as the cab stopped in front of me. I went to open the door, but his hand shoved it closed. I drew in a sobering breath as I tried to open the door again. But his hand was blocking my way into the backseat of the car.

"Dad. I'm asking you kindly to move," I said.

He shook his head. "Not until we talk."

I tried to open the door again, only for it to slam shut.

Mom took my hand. "Just talk to us. That's all we're asking."

I nodded. "Yes. And talking to you got Max arrested when he tried to save my life. I won't ever forgive you two for that."

Dad snatched my arm. "Danika. You're behaving irrationally. Please. Just sit down and talk this through with us. How long has this been going on? Where did you meet this man? Why did you think--?"

I yanked my arm free. "I would have answered these questions if you'd asked them before you arrested the man who saved my life. Now get the hell out of my way. I have to leave."

The nurse piped up again. "Do you need any help here?"

I looked down at my father's hand and he slowly removed it from the cab door.

"No. I've got it. Thank you," I said.

I peeked over my shoulder at my mother. "Don't bother following me, either."

My father growled again. "Danika Young, don't you get in that cab."

I ducked myself down into the seat. "Dad, if you actually wanted to help me, you would've tried to understand the situation rather than manage it. You have no idea what I've been through. Or what Max has been through to get me to this hospital in the first place. The two of you have done enough already. If you follow me, I'll have you arrested for harassment and defamation of character. Understood?"

I slammed the cab door before they had a chance

to respond. Then I commanded the driver to simply get me away from this place. I didn't want to be anywhere near my parents right now. Especially my father. I dug my phone out of my purse. Thank fuck it hadn't made it into the pool with me. As the cab driver pulled onto the main road, I felt his eyes on me in the rearview mirror.

"Got a destination in mind?"

I nodded mindlessly. "The nearest police precinct, please."

I dialed Rupert's number, but I got no answer. And of course, I didn't have John's phone number. I shoved my phone back into my purse and gazed out the window, my mind whirring a million miles a second.

"Actually, can you take me somewhere else first?" I asked.

The cab driver pulled over to the side of the road. "Where to, miss?"

I rattled off the address to Max's place and he whipped a U-turn in the middle of the road. If I wanted to find the guys after something like this, then they were in one of two places. They were either at the bar or at Max's. I had a pretty good feeling we were closer to the house than that bar. I wasn't quite sure where I was, but things quickly started to look familiar.

Like the fast food place Max adored getting burgers from.

Or the milkshake place he'd taken me to once at three in the morning after drinks.

"Uh, miss?"

I drew in a deep breath. "Hmm?"

"You sure this is the address you want?"

I turned my head forward. "Yes. Why?"

The driver pointed. "Look."

I craned my neck over the seat and my eyes widened. My pulse quickened and my palms began to sweat. Max's driveway was filled with cop cars, most with their lights flashing.

"Keep going," I said.

The driver nodded. "You want to head back to that precinct?"

I shook my head. "No. I've got one more place I want you to take me. Is that all right?"

"Long as you got a way to pay, I ain't askin' questions."

"I appreciate that, thank you."

Even in my panicked state, I had a growing hunch. Well, more like a last resort, really. I gave the cab driver the address for the bar and slid down into the seat. I couldn't even see the world passing by, and my only saving grace was this courteous driver who didn't have the kind of curiosity my parents did. I closed my eyes and drew in a few deep breaths. This place had to be okay. It just had to be.

I didn't know where the guys would be if they weren't here.

"I don't know about this place, either," the driver said.

I didn't even have to look up to see the flashing lights illuminating the inside of the cab.

"Bastards," I hissed.

I peeked over the edge of the seat and saw police

dragging leather-jacketed men out in handcuffs. Tears rushed my eyes as I ducked back down, mindlessly telling the driver to keep going. My stomach felt sick. It grew hard to catch my breath. I pressed my hand to my heart and felt it racing out of control against my palm. The house was gone. Men were being arrested in the bar. What did that mean for Max? And John? And Rupert? What did this mean for the crew?

What does this mean for me?

"Sure you don't want to go to the precinct now?" the driver asked.

I felt hopeless. "I don't know, really."

And the truth of the matter was, I didn't.

I didn't know what the hell to do now.

11

MAX

I jiggled my wrists, watching as my cuffs clanked against the table. They were threaded through a metal ring mounted to the table in front of me, which was bolted to the damn floor. It forced me to keep my hands on the table. Not that I wouldn't have had I not been cuffed in the first damn place. But, apparently, I looked like a man who needed cuffs.

So I had cuffs.

I wasn't sure how long I'd been sitting there. Or how long it would take for someone to get in here and start talking to me. All I knew was that I needed a phone call to contact Rupert. Or John. Anyone that might have been running the guys at this point. I needed to tell them to stand down. I needed to give the code word to tell them to disperse. They were in danger. In the pit of my gut, I knew they were.

And it made me sick to think about.

The door behind me opened and I sighed. Finally.

Someone to come relieve me of my boredom. I didn't bother craning my neck around. I didn't care who was actually coming in. All I cared about was the one phone call I should've already been afforded.

Guess guys like me don't have rights.

I watched a woman sit across the table from me before she lifted a briefcase onto the table. She popped it open before pulling out some paper, then slammed it shut. Her poorly-tailored tan suit almost matched her rust-colored hair, though I noticed gray coming through at the roots. She looked fairly young, though. In her face, at least. No crow's feet. No frown lines. No wrinkles in her brow.

What gives with the gray roots, then?

I watched as she tried to organize herself. She shoved her briefcase off to the side, and I watched it almost slide off the damn table. She placed the folder down and flipped it open, and I saw my mugshot paperclipped to the corner. Which made me even more curious.

"Who are you?"

Her eyes whipped up to mine. "Sorry. Just trying to get my ducks in a row first."

I nodded slowly. "Still doesn't tell me who you are."

She sighed. "Mr. Ryddle. My name is Jessica Hall. I'll be your attorney. Unless, of course, you have someone else at your disposal?"

Her tired eyes searched my face and I wondered how many other people she had seen before me.

"No, I don't have any representation."

She nodded. "All right, then. Let me take a quick look at your file, then we can talk. How's that sound?"

I shrugged. "Got all day."

She chuckled, but I didn't return the sentiment. So she cleared her throat and dropped her tired brown eyes back to my folder. She flipped the pages over, turning them around so I couldn't see what was on them. Every once in a while, she'd sigh. Heavily. Or click her tongue. A few times, she even shook her head. Which didn't fill me with the greatest of hopes.

"Not good, huh?"

Her eyes flickered up to mine. "We can determine that once I'm done reading. Hold on."

I licked my lips. "Like I said, got all day."

"Mm-hmm."

I went to lean back in my chair, but the cuffs stopped me. So I rested my forearms against the table. I was tired. Deep in the marrow of my bones, I was fucking exhausted. And this woman's sounds didn't do shit for my confidence. Ten years, at least. Probably more. This wasn't the first time I'd been arrested. This was simply the only time I'd made it this far in the judiciary process.

I'd say ten years, at least, for the shit that's already on my record.

I watched the woman gnaw on the bottom of her lip. After what seemed like an eternity, she finally closed the file. Her movements weren't as sharp as they had been when she first came in. She leaned back in her chair, tucking her hair behind her ear. And after crossing one leg over the other, she clicked her tongue.

"You're the youngest son of Ashton Ryddle."

I nodded. "Yes."

"And this is your fourth arrest."

I nodded again. "Yes."

She studied me. "Did you do it, Mr. Ryddle?"

I blinked. "Do what?"

She sighed. "What you say in this room stays between us. Lawyer-client confidentiality. But I need to know what kind of man I'm representing in order to do my job properly and see that you get the best deal out of all of this that you can."

I quirked an eyebrow. "What are you asking me, Miss Hall?"

She didn't flinch. "Did you shoot your father last night at his estate?"

"No."

"Do you know who did?"

"No."

She leaned forward, clasping her hands together. "Would your answer change if I told you your father came out of surgery this morning and doctors have confirmed he will survive with no permanent injuries?"

I felt my jaw flex. I fucking knew it. I knew my father would survive this. That fucking psychopathic devilish immortal son of a bitch! I tried to maintain my cool expression on the outside, but inside, I was fuming. I was fearful. I was worried for my men, and for Dani, and for anyone that might have been involved last night. If this woman was actually telling the truth, then we were all in danger. Dani. Myself. Dani's parents. Rupert. My men. John.

Anyone who had anything to do with me, even remotely, was in danger.

The woman nodded. "You don't need to answer right now, Mr. Ryddle. I understand loyalty. And I understand how clubs like yours work. You won't give up one of your men, so I'm not going to get you to try. But you should know that your men are already falling like flies."

I blinked. "I'm sure they are."

"It's important we get out ahead of this before it has a chance to spiral into something bigger. Your father's lawyers are already working. Quickly, I might add. And I must admit… I have the distinct impression that the sharks are circling. Are you a shark, Mr. Ryddle? Or are you bait?"

I grinned. "What do you think?"

"I think your father is a bad man. I think he's wildly lucky to be alive. And so are you."

"Anything else?"

She nodded. "I also think he has a lot to gain by dismantling your club. Am I wrong?"

I felt my heart pounding furiously. This strange woman with the premature gray roots had managed to make more sense of my father than I had in my entire goddamn life. And all of this by simply reading my file in front of me. What was she, some kind of wizard?

I could really use her on my side.

I mean, she looked tired and overworked. But there was a sharpness about her stare that promised intelligence. Not just the words flying from her mouth. And if I was a gambling man--which I was, on occasion--

then my gambling gut told me that I stood a chance with her in my corner.

So I braced myself.

"Well, Miss Hall, I suppose you're not wrong."

She nodded. "Good. Now we're getting somewhere."

I didn't know what this meant for me and my men. I didn't know what she meant by them 'dropping like flies.' My worst fears ran away with me, though. Had they been arrested? Where were they now? Was Rupert already in custody? What was he saying? John wouldn't be able to survive in prison. Not with the injuries he had. And I'd promised my men to keep them safe at all times.

If this woman was right about my father's survival, I could almost guarantee he'd already had them arrested.

Or much, much worse.

"So where do we go from here?" I asked.

She stared directly into my eyes. "We talk. You tell me what happened, honestly, and I tell you how I can help you--and your men--judging by what I've read in your file. Which, by the way, is extensive. The folder I pulled out is only one of four."

I can only imagine what you'll know after reading all of them.

"Guess I'm a popular man."

She leaned forward. "Or you've got a lot to go away for."

"Can't it be both?"

"Neither of us get anywhere with snark. I have two

hours with you, right now, unmonitored. It's illegal for them to record, listen in, or generally attempt to figure out what's going on with this meeting. I would hope you'd take advantage of that so I can better help you."

"Suppose I don't really have a choice, then."

She leaned back again. "Oh, you do."

I snickered. "Do tell, then."

She crossed her arms over her chest. "You can choose to not talk. Not tell me anything. Not accept my help. And that would lead to a cascade of reactions you'd be responsible for. Jailtime, for starters. You'd go away for a while. I might be able to get you a plea deal in exchange for information regarding your father. But something tells me you wouldn't do that."

I nodded. "You'd be right."

"After that, your men go down. One by one. I can't help them if you don't talk to me, and I can almost guarantee no state representative will step up to the plate for them. I was the only one that volunteered to take your case. It was passed around six times before it found me."

"Wonderful."

Her eyes grew stern. "You lose everything by not talking, and gain nothing but jail time if you don't. That's your decision."

I shrugged. "Sounds like a shit one."

"Well, we can't all be privileged in life, Mr. Ryddle. So what's it going to be? Are we going to have our meeting? Or are you going to dismiss me?"

12

DANI

"I want to see him. Now."

The cop sighed. "I know you want to. But you can't."

I blinked. "And why not?"

"Because that's protocol. No one can see an inmate."

"He's not an inmate because he's innocent!"

"And that will be determined by a jury, if anything goes to court."

"Has he had a phone call?"

The officer blinked. "Excuse me?"

"A phone call. I read up about things on my phone on the way here. He should've been granted a phone call. Has he been given one?"

He shrugged. "Not my area, so I don't know."

"Well, I know he hasn't been granted one because he hasn't called me. Now, you let me see him, or I'll have you--"

He grinned. "Maybe he just didn't want to call you. Ever think of that?"

This dumbass cop was giving me a hard time, and I wanted to throat punch him right in that massive Adam's apple he had protruding from his neck. I didn't want to be messed with any longer. Why did people think they could always fucking mess with me? I had to find a way to fix that. Later.

"I need to see Max," I said.

The cop shook his head. "You won't be seeing Mr. Ryddle for a while."

"What about a trade, then?"

He chuckled. "This isn't a negotiation. You can't see--"

"I was a witness to what happened at the Ryddle estate last night."

He blinked. "You were what?"

"You heard me. I was a witness. I saw everything. I want to make a statement, and I want to see Max."

He narrowed his eyes. "You can make a statement. Actually, you have to. It's your duty as a citizen to do that. But I still can't guarantee anything."

"You will let me see him or you get nothing!"

My voice cracked. I was borderline shrieking at this man. Hell, I half expected them to slap me in handcuffs and drag me off for getting so hysterical at the front desk officer. But I had to see him. This was completely unacceptable.

"Ma'am, why don't you go take a dip and cool down, okay? Because if you're going to give a statement, you're going to need to be in the right frame of mind. Which is not right now."

I glared at him. I wanted to smack him across his face, but something about his words felt off. *Take a dip? Cool off?* Why would he have made that statement to me? As I stood there, glaring at the grinning man, my gut began to tap at the inside of my ribs again. *Tap tap. Tap tap.*

I blinked. "I want to speak with someone else."

He shrugged. "There is no one else."

I hissed, "That's bullshit, and you and I both know it."

"There is. No one else."

I slammed my fists against the bulletproof glass. "Stop fucking with me and get someone else for me to talk to or I'm going to scream bloody murder and your boss will rain holy hell down on you. You got that?"

I tried to stand my ground as much as possible, even though my mind was working a million miles a second. *Take a dip.* Why choose those exact words? I hadn't given a statement yet. There was no way in hell anyone knew about me being there and being tipped back into that pool.

Unless Max has already given a statement.

I didn't know. Something didn't seem right about any of this. Including the officer behind that damn glass.

As his grin grew into a wide smile, I thought my threat might not work. Until there was a knock at the door behind him. His smile faded into an annoyed sort of frown before he got up and answered it. He murmured something to the person standing in the darkness, and when they stepped into the light I saw a female officer locking eyes with me.

She came over and sat down behind the bullet-proof glass before shooing the other officer away.

"Hello there, ma'am."

I nodded. "Hello."

"My name is Captain Riley. And I've heard there might be a disagreement taking place. I'm hoping maybe I can provide a solution that benefits all of us. How can I help?"

I leaned forward. "Can we speak someplace more private? I need to talk to you about what happened last night at the Ryddle Estate."

She nodded. "I'm sure I can make that happen."

"I also want to see Max."

"Max Ryddle?"

"Yes. You have him in custody here. I'd like to see him after giving my statement, please. That shouldn't be an issue, seeing as the gentleman before you informed me that he's still in holding."

"Is that so?"

"I read up on some things on the way here."

She nodded slowly. "We can try our best to--"

"You don't get my testimony unless I see him."

"You know I could technically swing that into a crime, right?"

I shrugged. "The only thing you have to do is let me see him. That's all I'm asking for. In my eyes, it's your issue. Not mine."

She didn't look too happy with me, but I didn't

care. If getting arrested and thrown in holding myself is what it took to see Max, then I'd make it happen. Because I wasn't going anywhere or doing anything until I got to sit down and see him. Talk to him before anything else happened. I needed to know what I could do, if there were any guys he wanted me to contact since it was very clear to me he wasn't being given the rights he was afforded as a U.S. citizen.

"Well?" I asked.

Captain Riley nodded. "Come through the door to your left with the orange handle. I'll wait for you in the hallway. You can follow me into a private room where we can take your statement."

I shook my head. "Not until I have some sort of physical proof that you're going to agree to let me see Max."

"You have my word, as an officer of the law."

I shrugged. "Cops are dirty all the time."

"Mine aren't."

"Want to bet on that?"

She narrowed her eyes. "What are you insinuating?"

"Nothing, since I don't know whether or not you're going to hold up your end of the bargain."

Her nostrils flared. "If I'm going to trust you, then you have to trust me. I'm trusting that you have more information about what happened last night. So if I'm going to trust you with that, then you have to trust me with this. Understood?"

I paused. "Fine. But, the officer that was here

before you? I want him nowhere near me, this testimony, or Max."

"And why's that?"

"Let's call it a hunch for now and live with it."

I heard the door unlock to my left and I rushed for it. And sure enough, Captain Riley stood in the hallway, waiting for me like she said she would be. I followed her into a room that had a desk and a computer. There was a window to my right and a plush chair sitting in front of the desk. The captain closed the door behind me before throwing the lock, and I wondered what I had just gotten myself into.

"Take a seat. I figured my office would make you feel more comfortable speaking to me, and only me," she said.

I nodded. "Thank you."

I took a seat in the chair across from her desk and waited until she sat down herself.

"So, Miss…?"

I cleared my throat. "Just call me Dani."

"All right, Dani. I want you to know that you can speak freely here. The only downside to my office is that no one is recording this conversation, so you will have to rely on me to translate and get it right. To make up for something like that, I'd like to record this on my work computer to have something in the system that backs up any testimony you might write down and sign. Are you okay with that?"

I nodded. "That's fine. Whatever you have to do."

She typed away at her keyboard. "Wonderful.

Okay. So what happened last night? Tell me everything from your point of view."

I sighed. "It was horrible, Captain Riley. But I need everyone to understand that Max Ryddle saved my life."

"Why don't you tell me how."

I launched into everything. How Max was supposed to pick me up from my dorm room for a nice night in and he never showed. How I worried so much I went out on the hunt for him. How Rupert told me to stay put, but I just couldn't. How I was kidnapped from my car and taken to the Ryddle Estate. I told her about how Max's father kidnapped me. Tied me to a chair. Pushed me into the pool and essentially let me drown.

"There are hospital documents to back up what I'm saying," I said.

The captain nodded. "We'll get them pulled. I'll have you write down the information once you're done."

"The only reason I'm here right now pestering you is because Max fought through those men. Five or six of them, before his father was shot. They didn't have a choice. That man would've killed his own damn son before letting him get to me. The only reason I'm sitting here is because that man was killed and Max jumped into the pool after me. And they still had to perform CPR for much longer than necessary before I came to. Max had nothing to do with this. The only thing he did was save me last night. Nothing else."

The captain blinked. "You said someone killed Ashton Ryddle."

Tears rushed my eyes. "Yes. And it's all my fault. If I would've just listened to Rupert and stayed put, no one would have come for me. I wouldn't have ended up in that situation and Max wouldn't have had to do the things he did last night just to save my life. If anyone is guilty here, it's me. For being an absolute idiot."

She furrowed her brow. "There's one major error in your story that really changes the place you're sitting in."

I paused. "What do you mean?"

"Ashton Ryddle is still alive, Miss Dani. He was rushed into surgery, where he came out just fine."

And I felt my entire safety net crumbling at my feet.

Now no one was safe.

13

MAX

I paced around in holding, enjoying the space I was afforded. All of the men that had been in here with me had come and gone throughout the night. And for once, I was alone. It wasn't my first time in a holding cell. But it was my first time alone in one of these places. And the more I paced, the more anxious I grew.

I need to get out of here and find Dani.

She wasn't safe. My lawyer promised me she'd get me out of this damn place, and I was banking on that. Because without phone calls, I felt like I was going stir crazy. I needed to figure out what happened to my men. I needed to get Dani somewhere safe.

Until my father could be eradicated, I had to make sure everyone I loved was okay.

My lawyer told me I might still be charged, which meant she had a lot of preparation to do in terms of a court case against my father. But she assured me she'd try with all of her might to get me out of here for the time being. I needed that time, too. I needed to be a free man. The only way I could ensure my father really went down for all of this was if I was running the show from the other side.

Heels clicking down the hallway caught my ear and I lifted my head. My incredibly tired lawyer was walking toward me, but the frown on her face told me everything I needed to know.

"They won't release me, will they?"

She sighed. "Not for another twenty-four hours. They want to hold you another day. I'm assuming to try and sweat out more information from you."

I shrugged. "I have nothing else to say. I told you everything that happened, and then some."

She nodded. "The good news is that once you get out, you're out until the supposed trial. Because I'm almost certain someone is going to try to pin charges on you. You know why."

Yeah. I did. They'd press charges against me because my father was a ruthless man who controlled half of this damn city and people always bowed to his every whim.

Fearful they might meet the same fate that almost befell Dani.

"But, setting all of that aside, Mr. Ryddle, you have a visitor. And she's been making some serious noise this morning."

I blinked. "A visitor?"

"Max!"

The second I heard Dani's voice, nothing else mattered. My eyes scanned the hallway, looking around as relief flooded my veins. Her voice sounded strong, and her footsteps sounded stronger. And when she finally came into view, I wished with all of my might that I was out of this fucking cell.

So I could hug her and kiss her properly.

"Dani!" I exclaimed.

She rushed to me and slid her hands through the bars.

"Max. I'm here. Holy shit, I'm here, handsome."

I slid my hands up her arms. "Gorgeous, what in the hell are you doing here?"

Tears dripped against her cheeks. "We don't have much time. But I need to tell you what's happening. Can't they let you out of here?"

My lawyer interjected. "Not for another twenty-four hours."

Dani groaned. "Fucking hell."

I brushed her tears away. "What is it? What's wrong?"

She sniffled. "Your father isn't dead, Max."

I nodded. "I know."

"You do?"

"Miss Hall told me."

"Who's Miss Hall?"

I nodded toward her. "My lawyer."

Dani looked over at the woman in the pantsuit before the two of them exchanged greetings. Then her worried eyes came back to me.

"Max, what do we do now?"

Even though her voice was strong, she still looked frazzled. I wanted nothing more than to scoop her into my arms and let her know everything was going to be all right. She already knew too much. She already had information at her fingertips that would get any of my men killed. And I didn't like that.

"I need you not to worry, gorgeous. Can you do that for me?"

She sniffled. "And I need you to remember that I love you after I say what I'm about to say. Okay?"

I felt my heart still in my chest. "Always."

She slapped my upper arms. "Don't fucking treat me like I'm some goddamn child, Max."

My eyes widened. "What?"

"I know what happened. I was there, remember? Stop shushing me and treating me with kid gloves. I'm in this, Max. I'm neck deep in this, literally and metaphorically. So I need you to listen to me. Okay?"

My lawyer started giggling to herself, but I blocked out the sound.

"Okay, Dani. I'm listening."

She nodded. "After I left my dorm, I went by your house, and it was crawling with police. The pub, too. I don't think the guys are available, even if you do get a phone call. I've got a really bad feeling about this, Max. Something more is going on. I can't explain how I know. I just--"

Miss Hall stepped forward. "What aren't you telling us?"

Dani looked at me before I nodded.

"She's okay. You have my word. But she's right. There's something that has you spooked."

She swallowed hard. "It might be nothing. But that cop at the front desk? The one I was yelling at before Captain Riley intervened?"

"You were yelling at a cop?"

"Will you focus? Damn."

"Okay."

"Did you tell anyone else other than your lawyer that I was pushed into that pool? That I'd, like, you know, practically drowned?"

Miss Hall spoke up. "I haven't filed any sort of formal testimony with the police yet, no."

Dani shook her head. "I fucking knew it."

I held her hands tightly. "What the hell are you talking about?"

Dani licked her lips. "When I was yelling at that police officer at the front desk, he literally told me to 'take a dip and cool off.' Take a dip, Max. Somehow, he knew I was pushed into the pool last night. He knew it without anyone knowing anything."

I paused. "That's a bit hairy to go on."

Miss Hall started scrambling around in her purse. "Not for me it isn't. Can you write that down on a piece of paper and sign it for me? I want to add it to the file I've got on this case."

I shook my head. "You mean to tell me--?"

Dani leaned in closer, whispering. "I think some of these cops are on your father's payroll. You have to be careful. Do you understand?"

I jammed my tongue into my cheek. "Shit."

As Dani scribbled it down for my lawyer, I raked my hands down my face. I mean, I should've seen this shit coming. He owned the rest of this town. Why the fuck wouldn't he own the police department, too? My father had always operated without a fear of consequences from the law. Back when we all still worked together, my men and I always seemed to skirt them in the nick of time without anything coming down onto our shoulders in the process.

How the hell had I been so blind to that fact?

I'm screwed.

For all I knew, he'd simply bury me in the prison system to keep me here. For all he knew, he had his paid minions trolloping around using everything in their power to hold me here until they could find a way to kill me. I felt the ground undulating beneath my feet. For the first time in my life, I felt physically sick to my stomach. I drew in a deep breath, trying to put on a brave face. And as Dani handed everything back to my lawyer, I felt her hands on my forearms.

Slowly, and softly, massaging me back to reality.

"We're going to get out of this, okay? You're going to be just fine," Dani said.

I wasn't sure I believed her, though.

If my father had free rein of Ann Arbor, everyone was screwed. This beautiful, thriving town would become nothing but a desolate wasteland being bled dry by my father. And if I wasn't there to stop him, he'd hop from city to city, doing the same damn thing. My father was practically impenetrable. No one had ever been able to get anything he did to stick in court.

He always weaseled his way out of situations like this one.

How the hell is that man still alive?

"Max?"

Dani's voice pulled me back to reality once more and I put my hands on her shoulders.

"Dani, I need you to listen to me. This is important."

She nodded. "I'm listening."

"I know this looks hopeless, and I know you're scared out of your mind. But my lawyer is capable. I have a very good feeling about her. And I trust her to bail me out of this."

Miss Hall sighed. "Aww, thanks. You shouldn't have."

Dani snickered. "No offense, but are you sure you want to put all of your eggs in that basket?"

Max quirked an eyebrow. "You sure that's a smart thing to say in front of a lawyer?"

Miss Hall laughed. "What are you two talking about? Sorry, I was checking my phone."

Dani grinned. "See?"

I shook my head. "Dani, you're not going to like what I have to say--"

"I know I'm not. So I'm going to beat you to the punch. I'm not leaving your side."

"You have to."

"Well, I'm not."

I gripped her shoulders tighter. "You are, and that's an order."

She scoffed. "You don't order me around. That's

not how this works."

"Fine, then I'll break up with you."

She paused. "You wouldn't."

My hands slid all the way down to hers before I took them in my own.

"Dani, this is dangerous. This is very serious. My father is a very, very bad man. I need you to keep your head down. I need you to stay as far away from this as possible. I need you to stay away from me."

Her lower lip quivered. "No. Please don't make me do this."

"You have to. Can you do this for me?"

"No."

"Well, I'm telling you that you have to. Until this is settled and until I know, without a shadow of a doubt, that you're safe, you stay away from here, and away from me."

Tears lined her eyes. "Max, please."

My hand cupped the back of her neck. "Come here. Come here, gorgeous."

I pulled her lips to mine and grew angrier at the bars separating us. I wanted to sink myself against her. I wanted to invade her and prove to her that I was doing this because I loved her. Not because I didn't love her. I had to keep her safe, and until I could get out of this place and check up on her myself, she had to be cautious. She had to take precautionary measures and listen to me, for once.

I reveled in the taste of her tongue before Miss Hall cleared her throat.

"Someone's coming," she murmured.

I reluctantly pulled away. "You've got this, gorgeous. Okay?"

I wiped a tear away from her cheek as her eyes met mine.

"I love you, Max."

I cupped her cheek. "I love you too, Dani."

Miss Hall butted in. "Sorry, guys. Pow-wow's over."

Feeling Dani slip away from my grasp caused me an anxiety I'd never felt before. Miss Hall kept guiding her down the hallway as Dani's sniffles grew more and more fervent. She kept peering over her shoulder with more tears streaking her face. And the sadness was enough to shatter my soul.

I'm sorry, Dani.

I turned my back to her as weakness took over. I wasn't physically able to watch her break down and be okay with it. Especially since I couldn't comfort her. The idea of Dani falling apart because of me didn't sit right. I felt bile creeping up the back of my throat again, threatening to show me just how weak I really was in this entire situation. I heard Dani calling out after me and my lawyer trying to talk her down from her furious high. And as a door slammed at the other end of the hallway, I felt tears percolating behind my own eyes.

I promise I'll make this up to you, gorgeous.

I took a seat on the bench in the middle of the holding cell. I had no idea how the fuck Miss Hall was going to get me out of this situation. Twenty-four hours my ass. These police would find some way to make sure I stayed here and rotted the rest of my days away. I pressed the heels of my aching hands into my eyes, trying to push the tears back. Because the last thing I needed was to be crying like a hopeless little bitch in this damn holding cell.

But fuck me, did my heart ever hurt.

14

DANI

T*he paint is peeling.*

The concrete beneath my ass was hard. The curve of the curb as doors slammed open and closed behind me were nothing, though, compared to how weird the paint looked. On the asphalt of the parking lot outside the police station, the paint was peeling right up from the road. Flaking off. Blowing in the wind. Brushing over my feet, as if to paint my shoes.

I'd never felt so numb inside before.

I didn't feel anything. The world passed by me like I didn't exist. Part of me didn't want to exist, either.

Not without Max.

How am I going to get him out of jail?

I wasn't an idiot. With his father alive, who knew when he was actually going to be free? Or if he'd ever be free again. I felt myself mourning for something I hadn't lost yet. I felt my heart mourning the loss of Max, even though he was still in my life. It killed me to feel that pain. To feel the tears burning as they rushed down my cheeks. I didn't have my car. I was running out of cash to have a taxi haul me around. I couldn't call my parents. I refused to call Hannah and listen to her rant of 'I told you so' the entire way back to campus.

Where is my car, anyway?

I looked back over my shoulder and watched as a man stormed out of the police station's doors. He looked about as angry as I felt. Well, as angry as I had been feeling. I wanted to go inside and ask someone what had happened to my car. But I didn't want to chance another encounter with that front desk officer. I knew he was in on all of this. I knew he had something to do with this bullshit that had transpired.

Maybe my car is still at the bar.

The more I wracked my brain for answers, the less I came up with. How had things gone so wrong? How had we ended up here, with Max in a holding cell they wouldn't release him from? There was an incessant buzzing sound in my ear that wouldn't go away. Like a damn mosquito flying around my head. I wanted to squash the invisible mosquito. I wanted the buzzing noise to go away.

How do I quiet the storm raging inside me?

I felt darkness falling over me. I hung my head and closed my eyes as I let it wash over me. And as I sat there, with tears falling to the chipping paint beneath me, I wondered if I should let it swallow me whole. I drew in ragged breaths. My hands began to tremble. I felt my heart breaking into millions of tiny pieces, threatening to be swept away by the storm raging through my body. I didn't know what to think. Or where to go. Or who to trust. Or who to call.

Until I felt someone sit down beside me.

"Hey there, Dani."

I turned my head. "John?"

He gave me a tight-lipped smile that seemed as weak as I felt.

"Wondered if I'd find you here."

My voice broke. "I'm so sorry I ruined everything."

He furrowed his brow. "What? No. Dani, you could never do that."

I sniffled. "I feel like I have."

His hand on my back was reassuring. Tears flowed down my neck in rivers as I struggled to catch my breath. John scooted closer and rubbed my back softly, trying with all of his might to console me. He even went so far as to wrap his arm around me and pull me in for a soft hug.

One I accepted with great pride.

"Benji ruined everything for us, Dani. My father, too. But not you. You were just in the wrong place at the wrong time. Okay?"

I closed my eyes. "I don't know what to do now."

He patted my back. "Come on. Getting you out of here is the first task."

I raised my head. "I can't leave Max."

"Well, you can't sit here, either. And I think if there's anyone he'd want you to be with right now, it's me."

He had a point. "Are the guys okay?"

"Let's get in my car first. Then we can talk."

He stood, with the help of his cane, then offered me a hand. I took it gladly, trying not to put too much pressure on him. I didn't want him to topple over, or break in two, or shatter. Like I felt my own body was doing. And as I stood to my feet, the two of us headed for his car.

"John?"

"Mm-hmm?"

"What does this mean for the crew?"

He unlocked his car. "Well, at this stage, I'm not really sure."

I opened my door. "What do you mean?"

He sighed. "I mean, I was arrested last night. Most of us were. But, the police don't have anything to hold me on. So I was released pretty soon after that. I'm sure they'll do their damndest to find something to pin on me, but in the meantime, I'll be working hard to get Max out of there. He's going to need all the help we can get, especially if we're going to piece the Red Thorns back together."

I blinked. "Were all of you arrested last night?"

He dipped down into the car. "Come on. We're burning daylight."

I didn't like the way he evaded my question. And I certainly didn't like the way he was fumbling with the keys to his car. His hand shook terribly, and when I gazed into his eyes I saw nothing but pain.

"John?"

He grunted. "Yep."

"Are you okay?"

He finally got the key into the ignition. "Yep. I just gotta--mmph."

I furrowed my brow. "What was that?"

I watched his back jump a bit before he groaned again.

"John, I think I should drive."

He shook his head. "I've got it."

I placed my hand over his wrist. "Please, John."

He sighed. "How the hell did things get so fucked up, Dani?"

I shook my head. "I don't know. I really don't."

I wasn't sure how long we sat there with John groaning and grunting in pain. It almost seemed like his back was spasming. His eyes grew unfocused. I saw the same kind of storm I felt inside of me rip-roaring behind his eyes. I smoothed my hand up and down his arm, hoping to coax him into letting me drive.

Then, finally, he looked over at me. "You drive standard?"

I nodded. "I can, yes. My father taught me when I was in high school."

"Good. You're driving. Come over here and help me out."

I scrambled out of the car and helped John to his feet. He was in obvious pain, and I wanted to get him home as quickly as possible. I walked him around the car and helped him sit down in the passenger's seat. Then, I rushed back around and practically threw myself into the seat.

"Ready?" I asked.

John eased himself back. "Whenever you are."

"I'll try to make this drive as smooth as possible."

"Just get us home. I need my--rah!--pain meds."

I cranked up the engine and sniffled for the last time. I eased us out of the parking space, but fucked things up trying to shift into first. The car jerked, causing John to yell out in pain. And as tears flooded my eyes again, I cranked the engine once more.

"I'm so sorry," I whispered.

John gritted his teeth. "Just get us out of here. Don't worry about me. I've got your car at my house."

"Wait, what?"

"Just go, Dani."

I took things slowly, but it made for smoother driving. I had practically memorized how to get to their place, so it required very little input from John in terms of getting us back. He lay back with his eyes closed, but I saw his legs jumping. The pain must be working its way down his body, and it broke my heart.

How could this possibly get any worse?

"You know, you're more than welcome to stay at the house. If you want."

John's voice caught my ear. "That might be a good idea. Especially with Benji still out there and all."

"Do you need anything from your dorm?"

I paused. "Honestly? I'm not sure. I packed everything up and tossed it into my car, but for all I know it might not be there any longer."

"We should go back and get you a few things, then. Just in case."

I peered over at him. "I'm going to have to pull a

U-turn, and it'll keep you away from your meds longer."

"You staying at the house?"

I paused. "I think it's best, yeah."

"Then get this over with and let's get to campus first. I'll accompany you upstairs just in case something happens."

I didn't like the plan, but I wasn't in a position to fight with him. So I eased the car around as softly as I could, growing more comfortable with the stick shift and the gears, and soon we were smoothly sailing toward my dorm room. Part of me just wanted to go back to the house. Even if my stuff had been stolen and this was the only outfit I had, it was better than what faced me on campus. Missed classes. Dropping grades. Possibly running into Benji.

Hannah.

"Oh second thought, maybe we should--"

John interrupted me. "You need clothes. I guarantee you that you've missed something you'll need in the heat of the moment when it came to packing up your stuff. Let's go back and give your room a good once over. Because once you're at the house, you're staying there until this is all settled. Understood?"

I nodded. "Fine by me."

I pulled the car up to the curb just outside my dorm room. I gazed up toward the window, watching the curtain already fluttering. Great. Hannah had already spotted me. Absolutely wonderful. I heard John's car door open before he gathered his cane, so I cut the engine of the car.

And together, we started toward the building.

I was glad for John's company, though it made me feel guilty to hear him stifling his grunts beside me. I kept stealing glances at him, and it seemed that every time I looked at him his limp got worse. I wanted to tell him to go back and wait for me in the car, but I knew he wouldn't listen. So as we rose up the elevator, I drew in deep breaths to settle my nerves.

"You good?" he asked.

I sighed. "Just nervous about seeing my roommate again."

"You two have a blowout or something?"

I snickered. "Or something."

The doors eased open at the top floor and I saw Hannah at the end of the hallway, standing by our front door. She gasped before she took off running toward me as I stepped off the elevator. John placed his hand against my back and I felt him gird me with his arm. As Hannah leapt at me, her arms wrapping around my neck, I felt her sobbing against my shoulder.

"My gosh, I was so worried about you, Dani."

And it took all I had not to push her away and brush past.

15

MAX

The walls of this damn holding cell were beginning to close in on me. I felt like I was going crazy. I felt like weeks had passed since I'd seen the outside world. When, in reality, Dani had only left me a few hours ago. I stretched my arms over my head and felt my back pop into place. I cracked my neck, feeling people staring me down in their drunken, stumbling states. Most of the people that came and went from the holding cell were nothing more than drunkards from the side of the road. There had been a couple of questionable-looking women in a profession I could only proclaim as 'salacious' that got locked in the holding cell next to us. And as their eyes raked over my body, their cat-calling started.

"Why don'tcha come over here and give me a nice look at those eyes?"

"How much you bench anyway, huh?"

"I like that leather jacket. You mind if I feel it?"

A cop slammed his fist against the bars. "Patricia! Diamond! Leave the man alone."

The two girls snickered as they went to sit down, but I didn't pay them any mind. They weren't bothering me because I sure as hell wasn't a stranger to things like that. I simply didn't indulge them anymore. I had the woman I wanted, and it was so damn frustrating that I wasn't out there taking care of her. Protecting her. Making sure she was staying out of trouble.

Fucking hell, I need out of this cage.

I got up and started pacing. It was all I could think to do. My holding cell quickly became the drunk tank on a random Monday morning. What these guys had been doing or where they had been found, only God knew. But I hoped my lawyer pulled a miracle out of her ass.

Or at least that these twenty-four hours go by quickly.

"Maxwell Ryddle?"

I slowly turned around as I watched a cop unlock the cell door.

"With me," he said.

All eyes were on me as he pulled my arms behind my back and cuffed me. He led me down the hallway before I heard one of the girls whistle at me again.

"Look at that ass!"

The cop snickered. "Shut it, Patricia!"

"Yeah, yeah, you and the rest of 'em, Bailey!"

I kept my mouth shut as the cop led me into the room I had been in previously with my own lawyer. I looked around for her, but she was nowhere to be found. The cop shoved me down into my seat before uncuffing my hands, only to cuff them to the table with that fucking metal ring attached to it. It forced me to hunch into a submissive position I would have rather died than actually do myself. But I didn't have a choice.

Just play nice until tonight.

Instead of the officer leaving, though, he clasped his hands behind his back and leaned over me, as if to cover me in his shadow. I furrowed my brow. I didn't know what the hell this man was doing, but I was over it. And as he started pacing the room, I sighed heavily.

I knew when to keep my mouth shut. But he wasn't making it easy on me.

"Maxwell Ryddle," he finally said.

I licked my lips. "I prefer Max."

He snickered. "I'm sure you do, *Maxwell.*"

I chewed on the inside of my cheek. "Should I be expecting my lawyer soon?"

He snickered. "You know, we've been waiting a long time to get something big enough to bury you for."

I watched a vicious smirk play against his lips. "I'm sure."

"You and your father. You're like two peas in a pod."

"I'm nothing like my father."

"You sure about that? Because the resemblance from where I'm standing is uncanny."

I sucked air through my teeth. "Why am I really here?"

He narrowed his eyes. "You're here because I brought you here, and that's all anyone needs to know."

Wonderful. "Off the books, huh?"

"Not necessarily."

I didn't know what the hell this guy was playing at, but I knew it wasn't good. I already knew he was bad news. In my father's fucking pocket. I'd still be back in that holding cell waiting for my time to be up if he wasn't being fed by my father. I wondered how much Ashton was paying him. Five grand a month? Seven? I'd known my father to pay someone as much as ten grand a month to do his bidding whenever he called.

I wondered what kind of deal this cop had with him.

"If you're going to interrogate me, I need my lawyer present," I said.

The man stopped pacing. "You see this uniform?"

"From a mile away."

His eye twitched. "This uniform should tell you I'm well-versed in what the law says."

And your countenance tells me you're well-versed in what my father says.

I nodded. "Right."

"Good. Glad we're on the same page. Don't feel the need to run me down on the law. You'll need your energy for other things."

I nodded. "Other things. Got it. Sounds totally legit."

The man slammed his hands down onto the table. "You want to mock me, Ryddle?"

"No, sir."

"You want to try to intimidate me? Threaten me? Make me play your little game?"

I shook my head. "No, sir."

He narrowed his eyes. "What kind of game are you playing right now?"

"There's no game. Just sitting here, waiting for my lawyer to be present before I start answering any questions you might have."

He chuckled. "Playing it safe, tough guy? I can appreciate that. But we need to know what happened at the estate. And time is of the essence."

I shrugged. "Get my lawyer here, and we can talk all you want."

"See, that's the thing. We're trying to call her, but she's not picking up. I'm sure she's swamped with better things to do than hover around your ass. So just tell me what really happened."

You aren't pinning anything on me, you piece of shit. "My lawyer has all those answers."

His eyes flared. "What the hell happened at your father's estate?"

I lifted my chin as the cop came barreling toward me.

"Talk, or I'll find someone to make you talk."

I felt my anger rising up the back of my throat, and I knew this man was trying to get me to lash out. Which meant I couldn't give in. I couldn't let him get the best of me.

God, please keep Dani safe for as long as possible.

The cop growled. "Answer me now, you piece of shit. Or I'll keep you in that holding cell until you rot."

God, I know you don't give a shit about me. But please, make sure Dani gets out of this alive.

"Answer me!"

I bit down onto the inside of my cheek to keep myself from lashing out.

Dani, just do ask I'm asking you to do. Stay as far away from this as possible. I'll come for you. I swear it.

The cop stood up slowly. "Fine. You don't want to talk to me? I think I've got someone who can get you to talk."

And as the man left the room, my mind fell to Dani. To her peaceful presence and her wondrous laugh and her serene smile. I fell into my happy place as the threats and the yelling and the problems continued. I easily lost myself in the memory of her, just to keep an even temper.

Praying that, one day soon, we'd be reunited.

For good.

16
____

DANI

I stood there as Hannah squeezed me tightly. I looked over at John and took in his confused stare. I felt Hannah sniffling. Her voice was filled with tears. And as I felt their wetness soaking through my shirt, I wiggled my hands in between us before slowly pushing her away.

"What--what are you doing?" she asked breathlessly.

I pointed. "John, our room is down at the end. Last door on the right."

Hannah paused. "What are you doing? Are you not back?"

I stepped around her. "I have to go."

She grabbed my hand. "Dani, please."

I ripped away from her. "Don't you even start."

John and I moved down the hallway as quickly as we could with Hannah hot on our heels. I barged into the room and started looking around, and I found that

John was right. I had left a great deal behind. I didn't have my books, or my laptop. I had none of my chargers, and I'd left a few toiletries behind as well. I reached for my swim bag and poured everything out. I shoved all of my wet clothes into a plastic bag to take with me, then wiped down the inside. And as John stood at the window, peering down at our car, Hannah piped up beside me.

"Where are you going again? Who is this guy with you?"

I shoved my things into the bag as John turned around with a kind smile on his face.

"I'm John. Max's brother."

Hannah's voice fell flat. "Oh."

I sighed. "I have to--"

Hannah gripped my arm. "Dani. Seriously. What in the world is this all about? Did you talk to your parents? They were--"

I slid out of her grasp. "I talked to them. They came to see me in the hospital this morning."

Her eyes bulged. "Hospital? Why were you in the hospital?"

"I was in the hospital because Max saved my life and took me there. Then, this morning, when it looked like things were going to be okay, my father decided to call the police and have him arrested because all he knows about Max is what *you* told him. So. Thanks for that."

Hannah blinked. "Dani. I didn't know where you were."

"And you won't ever again."

She sighed. "*Talk* to me. That's all I'm asking you to do. What happened? What do you mean he saved your life? How much trouble are you in?"

I zipped my bag shut. "I don't have time to talk about this right now. I have shit to do. John, you ready?"

I looked over at him and watched him nod. "Ready when you are."

I sighed. "Good. Hannah? I'd say it's been nice, but it hasn't."

I held tightly to my bag as John and I moved out into the hallway. He lumbered ahead of me as Hannah stood in our dorm room, frozen in her place. Good. Because I sure as hell didn't want her following us around. But I should have known it wouldn't last. Not with Hannah.

She had always been a persistent human being.

"Please don't go."

She wrapped her hand softly around my wrist. I looked down at our connection and her hand quickly fell away. But it gave me pause. Her voice sounded defeated. Her touch had been kind at that moment. And as John summoned the elevator with the push of a button, I turned to face Hannah.

"What do you want from me?" I asked.

Hannah shook her head. "I just want you to talk to me. Like we always used to do. We need to talk about this. I don't want to lose you, Dani. I'm so fucking confused about everything. I don't even know who you are anymore."

I snickered. "Really? Because I finally *do* know who

I am. And I like this girl. I trust her. She's stronger than I used to be and she's not going to sit around and cower in a dorm room. She's intelligent and bright. She stands up for herself and makes her own decisions. She knows what she wants, Hannah. And for the first time in my life, I feel like I really understand things."

"Well, I don't understand them at all."

"Good thing this isn't about you, then."

John piped up. "Elevator's here."

I sighed. "Max needs me, Hannah. Maybe when everything blows over we can figure this out. But…"

Her voice lowered to a whisper. "But what?"

I looked over my shoulder and John nodded his head. He held the elevator doors for me, and I knew it was time to go. I decided to give Hannah a hug. Just one arm, wrapped around her neck. And she clung to me. I mean, she dug her nails right into my back. As if she didn't want to let me go.

"But what, Dani?"

I cleared my throat. "We'll talk soon. Once this is all over."

"Dani, wait!"

I yanked myself out of her tight hold and made my way to the elevator. And not once did I look back. I didn't want to open up this conversation with Hannah. Mostly because I didn't have time. I knew the only place where I was safe was at Max and John's place. The only way I'd find resolution to all of this was if I worked in tandem with them. Which meant my classes and my life here on campus had to take a back seat.

I didn't even get out of the building before my

phone started ringing. It rang and it rang until I finally put it on vibrate. Even as I drove John and myself back to the house, it kept buzzing. And clattering. And thrumming. And vibrating. I knew it was Hannah. I knew she was trying to wear me down and get me to pick up the phone. It wouldn't work, though. I wasn't going to speak with her until this was all said and done.

If anything, for her own safety.

"You know, you don't need to cut everyone else out of your life to make room for men like us."

John's voice fell heavily against my ears as I pulled us into the driveway.

"And with how this is all going, you might need to keep people like your roommate close. We all need someone to catch us when we fall."

I shook my head. "The only person I need to catch me is Max. And I'm not going to let him down when he needs me. Not this time."

"When have you ever let him down in the first place?"

When I didn't listen to Rupert. When I jumped too quickly and got myself kidnapped. When I didn't go to him about Benji sooner. When I kept dragging my feet instead of giving in to Max sooner rather than later.

I sighed. "That's not the point. The point is, I can't focus on any of that right now. You might be right. But that doesn't overshadow the fact that the crew is falling apart and that Max is in jail. And right now, I can't afford to entertain some conversation I've had with Hannah four times already simply because she doesn't get it."

He nodded. "One of those people that 'doesn't get it' until you start obeying their every word?"

"Yep."

He snickered. "I'm very familiar with those kinds of people."

I cut the engine. "I want you to know that I hear what you're saying. It's just that, right now, I'm in prioritization mode. And the priority right now is Max and this crew. Everything is in upheaval. It needs to settle first."

"What about your classes?"

I shrugged. "What about them?"

"Oh, come on. Don't tell me school isn't important to you any longer. I mean, you packed your books, for crying out loud. What are you going to do?"

I sighed. "Email my professors. Tell them I've had a family emergency. See what I can work out with them. But even if I have to repeat my semester, it'll be worth it if Max and the guys come out of this okay."

He nodded. "So long as you know what you're doing and that what you're doing comes with consequences."

I snickered. "Yeah, thanks. But I'm well-versed in how this works by now."

He chuckled. "You ain't seen nothing yet."

The two of us shared a small moment of laughter before he opened the door.

"Now, come on, Bambi. Let's get you inside. That's what they call you, right?"

I giggled. "You can call me whatever you want, John."

He reached for my bag. "Sounds like a plan, Stan."

I paused. "You're not really going to call me Stan, are you?"

He grinned. "Guess you'll just have to wait to find out."

17

MAX

The slamming of the bar doors jostled me awake. My wrists throbbed with pain and my head felt like it had been leaning against a brick wall this entire time.

Because it has been, idiot.

I groaned as I sat upright. I tried to blink away the sleep as I heard bootsteps coming for me. I cracked my neck and stood up. I felt the officer's hand come down against my arm before he twisted it around my back. Fucking hell, I wasn't sure my wrists could take anymore handcuffs.

Definitely got more respect for women who bust those out for their men.

Without a word spoken, the officer led me out of the holding tank. I walked in a mindless haze as he shoved me into yet another private room. I looked up at the cameras as I flopped down into the chair. I went along with the motions as he uncuffed me, only to re-cuff me to the table. I placed my forearms against the cold metal and leaned my head against my tired muscles. I missed my bed. I missed John's coffee. I missed my house and my men and my bike.

And my woman.

"Mr. Ryddle."

Miss Hall's voice made me raise my head. "I was wondering who summoned me in here."

She furrowed her brow. "Who did you think it would be?"

"For starters? The cop who had me in here yesterday before he yelled at me and threatened me with a good time."

She paused. "Who did that to you?"

I shook my head. "Don't worry about--"

She dropped her briefcase from her hand. "Who did that to you, Max? You're my client, and that's illegal."

I sighed. "Just sit down and talk to me. It's been a hell of a time in here, and I'm exhausted."

She glared at me before she composed herself. She nodded at someone at the door, who then closed it loudly behind me. I forced myself not to jump, even though the clang of the door startled me. I was much too tired to be in control of my faculties, and the last thing I wanted to do was show that this place was wearing me down.

Because that's what these damn cops wanted to do.

"I've done some more research into your predicament," she said.

I nodded slowly. "Great. What did you find?"

She sat down in front of me. "Well, your father's lawyers are working overtime. So I've been doing the same thing. But I first want to ask how you're holding up in here. Especially with the information you just gave me."

I shrugged. "My wrists are pretty sore."

"Anything else?"

"My head hurts."

"I can see about some Tylenol for you. Have you gotten a phone call yet?"

I shook my head. "No."

"I'll be talking to them about that, too. They should at least be offering it to you."

I shrugged. "I'll take my men being safe at this point."

She reached for her briefcase. "Which brings me to some of the things I've dug up."

I sighed. "I know, I know. I have a feeling my guys are taking some heat for this, too."

She placed her briefcase on the table. "Yes. They are. There have been multiple arrests, both at your house and at a bar. Over a dozen at this point."

"My brother--"

She pulled out files. "--is safe and sound at home, as far as I'm aware. Though I can't say the same thing about your friend Rupert. Things aren't looking good for him at all, Max."

"Fucking hell."

"I'm sorry to be the bearer of bad news. But his fingerprints are all over the gun that matched ballistics from your father that the police found at the estate."

I blinked. "That gun wasn't left at the estate. We took it with us."

She paused. "Oh?"

"Rupert had it with him when we drove away."

She grabbed a pen. "Interesting."

"So someone is fucking with us? On my father's end."

She nodded slowly. "Seems like it. But please. Keep your voice down. I know when I'm part of a conspiracy. And believe you me, you're wrapped up in one. Someone is making sure you go down for this, Max. They're rushing. They're working within the time constraints of the law. Which is why they're holding you here for twenty-four hours. That's within their right, but if the police don't charge you, they're supposed to release you."

"Time kind of blurs in here. You got any idea when that twenty-four hour point is?"

She looked at her watch. "Four hours from now. But I know they sent out a request to hold you for a maximum of ninety-six hours since you're accused of aiding and abetting, as well as attempted murder."

I groaned. "Okay. So what happens after the ninety-six hours?"

She folded her hands together. "Either they charge you or they release you."

"Great."

"In cases like this, Max, it's best not to let charges be laid. Okay?"

"Trust me, I got that much."

She leaned in close. "And between you and me?

I'm not a very expensive lawyer. I haven't worked any big cases. I think that's why I got the call to represent you. You know how I said this passed through many, many hands before it got to me?"

I furrowed my brow. "You think someone orchestrated that."

She nodded. "I think *they* think I'm going to be easily bulldozed or manipulated. But, let me assure you, I have no intention of letting your father ruin your life over something you didn't do. Okay?"

Relief washed over me. "I appreciate that. Thank you."

"Now. Let's go over everything from the beginning. And don't you dare leave a shred out from your point of view."

"Again?"

She nodded. "Again."

I leaned up as far as I could and rolled my shoulders back. I had a crick in my spine that felt like an air bubble pressing against my existence. I wanted to pop it so badly. I wanted to rid myself of it. And as I sat there, struggling, I felt my frustration mounting. I couldn't even pop my fucking back right in this position. I wanted nothing more than to simply stretch my hands over my head.

Prison is going to eat me alive.

"Max."

My eyes whipped back to Miss Hall's. "Sorry. Yeah."

She poised her pen over an empty notebook. "I'm ready when you are."

I drew in a deep breath and started from the beginning. Recounting everything to her that happened to me that night. From being kidnapped to being tied up in one of my father's warehouses to being beaten by Benji and some goons. How I escaped, the car I used, the phone call I placed to Rupert. I left no detail out. And when I was done, half of Miss Hall's notebook was filled with scribblings.

"All right. Ready for me to read it back to you?" she asked.

I quirked an eyebrow. "Do you really need to do that?"

She nodded. "This is your official record. I want to make sure it's right. I'll read it back, we'll fix what we need to, and then you'll sign it. And once it's signed, there's no going back on your word. Understood?"

"Understood."

"Good. Now, sit back and relax."

I blinked. "You serious right now?"

She snickered. "Sorry about that. Force of habit."

"Uh huh."

She crossed her legs. "Ready to begin?"

I nodded. "Ready when you are."

And as she started reading my words back to me, I stopped her to fill in the blanks. Give her more information as it came to me. Even if we had to sit here for the rest of the twenty-four hours, I didn't give a shit. If this was what it took to get me out of here and back into the world, I'd do it. If this was what it took for me to get back to Dani, I'd do it. Time, and time, and time again.

Until we got it right.

18

DANI

I wrung my hands together as I paced the living room of Max's house. I kept drawing in deep breaths trying to calm myself. Every inch of my body was hyper-focused. I felt like I could see musical notes and smell colors. The world blended and ebbed and flowed before bursting into its smallest pieces and making me even more anxious. I heard John typing away on his phone while he sat on the couch, his cane propped between his knees. And as I turned to face him, he looked up at me.

"Relax. They'll be here," he said.

I scoffed. "That's what I'm worried about."

I wiped my palms off on my jeans and rushed into the kitchen. I needed another bottle of water. My mouth felt like cotton and my stomach felt like a desert and I needed more water. More, and more, and more of it. I ripped the fridge open and reached for the bottle I had already opened. And after grabbing John one, I booked it back to the living room.

"John, I don't know if this is such a--"

The front door crashed open and I jumped. The bottled water tumbled from my hands and crashed against my bare foot and I hissed with pain. I jumped around, trying to shake the pain out of my big toe. The front door slammed closed again and it brought me back to reality. I whipped around and gazed at the beast of a human being standing in the doorway of the living room.

Then he moved towards John.

Max's brother stood from the couch and shook the giant's hand. The man was clad in dark, thick leather and his boot strikes fell heavily against the carpeted floor. It felt like the entire foundation of the house creaked beneath him, groaning, and grumbling, and cursing the weight that had flooded the house. John patted the man's arm before his eyes fell to me. And as he adjusted his jeans, he nodded at me.

"The rest are right behind me, little lady."

I swallowed hard. "How many?"

He shrugged. "Thirty, give or take."

I felt like I was going to pass out. The room started swirling around me as John and the giant got to talking. Their voices muffled as my ears muted themselves and my head spun on my shoulders. Thirty of them? Seriously? Were they all as massive as this man was? I didn't remember thirty men. I remembered a handful, sure. But thirty?

A rumble off in the distance caught my ear and it

forced my eyes out the window. I rushed to it, pulling back the curtain as I peered outside. John and the giant were still talking as I searched for a source of the sound. And as it grew louder and louder, I saw dots appearing on the horizon.

Dozens and dozens of black dots.

"Sounds like a lot more than thirty," John said.

The massive man snickered. "I mean, give or take, sure."

My jaw dropped open as the Red Thorns blazed a trail straight for Max's place. The roar of thirty-plus motorcycle engines rattled my ribcage and pushed all other sounds out of my mind. All I knew was that roar. All I felt was its trembling sound. All I heard and all I tasted and all I smelled were those bikes.

The exhaust.

The motor oil.

The growl of gears shifting.

One by one, the men pulled up and parked. They stuffed the driveway full and pulled behind the house. Some of them parked on the curb while others took a spot right on the front lawn. I counted thirty-four bikes in all, which meant thirty-four massive brutes stacking this house from corner to corner.

I felt a hand come down against my shoulder.

"Shit!" I jumped before I whipped around and found John frowning at me.

"You have to keep your cool. If they see you panicking, they're going to think there's something to panic over."

I paused. "Isn't there something to panic over?"

He blinked. "Good point."

By the handful, these men pushed their way into the house. With the door wide open and spitting out mounds of muscle and leather, the house quickly filled with the smell of musk, sweat, and the inside of some guy's boots. They all nodded their heads at me before shaking John's hand. I shoved my own hands into my pockets to keep from wringing them in front of me. They were already growing sore and red. The last thing I needed was to rub them until they blistered.

I needed a way to dispel this nervous energy, though.

A sharp whistle pierced the chaos of men and they all turned to John. He flagged them down with his free hand as he leaned against his cane with the other. Then, without a word, he beckoned to me.

And the wall of thick-muscled men turned to face me.

I couldn't see anything. All of these men were much taller than me, and I felt like I was staring at their crotches more than their faces. I walked over to a chair in the corner and stood on it, trying to seem more even with the crowd. I cleared my throat as they all looked at me, waiting for me to feed them more information.

At least they don't look angry.

"We all know Max is in trouble," I said.

"What?" one guy asked.

"Speak up, Bambi. Can't hear ya."

"Yell like this!"

The guys laughed and the sound almost drowned

me in its vibrance. I clenched my teeth, girded my core, and drew in a deep breath.

"We all know Max is in trouble. Right?" I asked.

The men nodded, signaling that they'd heard me. And the more I continued to speak, the more my nerves dwindled.

"Right now, we are the only thing standing between him and his father. There's corruption in the police precinct where he is being held. His father's minions have him right where they want him, and I know they won't stop until Max is buried up to his neck in litigation and charges."

My eyes danced around the room and I noticed something. Not only did I have their undivided attention, but they were nodding along with me. Really, truly listening to me. Intent on hearing what I had to say. They weren't snickering or rolling their eyes. They weren't correcting me or trying to interrupt. It was as if they regarded me as one of their own. Deserving of the respect they gave one another, including Max.

I knew these men would help me. Fearlessly. And my worries about whether or not Max would be all right quickly melted away.

"Gentlemen, I saw it with my own eyes. I heard the discrepancies with my own ears. And Ashton Ryddle is going to use everything he can as leverage against Max. Against all of us, really. We have to move quickly if we want to get Max out of there legally. And at this point? Legally is our best option if we don't want to be on the run for the rest of our lives."

The giant spoke. "What do you suggest?"

I swallowed hard. "We have to turn the story around. We have to finish Ashton Ryddle before he finishes Max."

A chuckle trickled across the room and I felt my strength falter.

"And how do you plan on doing that, Bambi?"

"If he has the cops in his back pocket there ain't shit we can do against him."

"He runs this town, Bambi."

"I'm surprised he hasn't already killed--"

I tightened my fists in my pockets. "Don't you even say it."

My growl silenced the men as a few of them nudged one another.

"And no, he doesn't. Ashton Ryddle wants us to think he owns this town. But the truth of the matter is that the rules of this place have been lying under the surface waiting for our call to action all this time."

The men stared at me with apprehensive glances as I gathered my thoughts.

"Look, we rule this town. The Red Thorns have been here much, much longer than Ashton Ryddle. Yes, that man might have founded this crew. But Ashton Ryddle wasn't Ashton Ryddle before this club was founded. That man made his dark fortune off the backs of this crew. You guys are the reason why he stands in the position he does, and all because he played every single person in this room for fools."

The men looked around at each other as hope filled my chest.

"And I think it's about damn time we shook those

chains from our wrists, put our boots down, and took this damn city back. I think it's about time we pushed Ashton Ryddle out of this place. I think it's about fucking time you guys got your due around here!"

"Yeah!" they exclaimed.

"I think it's about time we rose up from the shadows he pushed us into!"

"Yeah!"

"And I sure as hell think it's about time to get Max out of jail!"

"Hell fuckin' yeah!"

The guys started clapping and whistling. I peeked through the crowd at John and saw a massive smile spreading across his face. He held his hands out as if to say *Look at what you've done. Look at what you've rallied.* And as the men high-fived one another and chest-bumped each other into walls, John let out another piercing whistle, settling the crowd down one more time.

"If we do this, gentlemen, we do this right. If we take back this city, we do it right. For Max, for ourselves, and for the future of our families. If we really do this, we're going to put Ashton Ryddle exactly where he belongs. Behind bars, for the rest of that fucker's life. This is it, gentlemen. This is our call to action. So are we going to stand by? Or are we going to stand up?"

19

MAX

Of course I was being held for the full ninety-six hours. Why the hell should I have expected differently? The only thing that made me nervous was that I hadn't seen my lawyer yesterday. Ever since our Monday meeting where she gave me the rundown of how this might pan out, I hadn't seen her. Or heard from her. I hadn't gotten a phone call, I was lucky if I got snacks for meals, and I felt my mouth running dry.

I could drink that fucking pool right now.

While I shouldn't have expected anything different, I had been hoping my lawyer would get me out of here sooner rather than later. Time passed by much too slowly, and I had been interrogated over a dozen times. But at least the cops were playing hardball now. Not once did I sit in an interrogation without her present. Which is what frustrated me about not having another private meeting with her.

She was here for the interrogations. Then she'd

leave before those assholes released me from the damn table.

What if she's working for him, too?

The thought had occurred to me more than once. And it wouldn't have shocked me one bit. The way these cops looked at me, the way they jeered at me and the things they asked in these interrogations, I knew without a shadow of a doubt at least half of these fuckers worked with my father. Miss Hall gave me knowing looks, too. Nothing got by her, I was quickly coming to find out.

I had to keep convincing myself that she was on my side.

And I didn't like that.

I watched the torturous clock on the wall slowly tick down. Every time the door at the end of the hallway opened, I jumped. I didn't want to tell my story another fucking time to a bunch of cops I knew were just getting paid off by my father. I didn't want to recount everything and relive what happened to Dani and rehash that nightmare to assholes who were only going to turn it around on me. Who were going to use it against me.

Who were going to toss me in jail for the rest of my life over it.

I ran my fingers through my hair. I talked myself through some deep breaths. If I had to be interrogated again, at least I'd see my lawyer again. And maybe I could talk her into having another meeting with me before I was ultimately released. I raked my hands through my hair. I felt someone approaching my cell.

Sounds around me were muffled as I slowly lifted my head, trying to fight through the hopelessness I felt burrowing into the marrow of my bones.

Then I heard the iron bars rattling open.

"You're free to go, Max."

Miss Hall's voice piped up behind me and I shot to my feet. I whipped around, staring at the tired, grinning woman. On either side of her were two very displeased-looking officers. And as Miss Hall stood there with her grin continuing to grow, she folded her hands in front of her.

"Don't tell me you love this place so much you want to stay," she said.

I blinked. "I'm free to go?"

She nodded. "Yep."

"Now."

"Uh huh."

"Right this second."

The cop piped up. "Get out or stay in. But make a choice."

My lawyer dismissed the officers with a flick of her wrist. And as they grumbled to themselves, they started back down the hallway. I was more confused than ever before. But she didn't look as if she was joking.

"I should still be in here for--"

She cut me off. "Another eight hours. I know. Trust me, this might not be a good thing. As you can see, the police aren't happy about it at all. Which means I'm sure you can wager a guess as to why."

Yeah. This isn't my father's doing.

"So you didn't do anything?" I asked.

Miss Hall shrugged. "I haven't presented them with anything they don't already know. Nonetheless, you're free to go."

I stepped out into the hallway before I felt Miss Hall pat my back. I looked down at the small woman, and she gave me a hearty smile. Together, we started down the hallway, with every cop giving me the dirtiest look they could muster.

Once Miss Hall opened the door that led me into the main lobby, I heard an all-too-familiar sound.

Bikes.

My spirits lifted as I made my way to the glass double doors. I shoved myself through them, only to be met with the roaring sound of what could only be described as the entirety of my crew. There were a sea of faces. Men I had grown to love. Men I had come to respect. Men I regarded as family. As my best of friends. As those I could lean on in times of need. My heart stopped in my chest. The guys all revved their engines, applauding me as I walked out of those doors a free man.

Then, the person standing at the front of the pack removed their helmet.

"Dani?" I asked.

She tucked the helmet underneath her arm. "I wondered how long it would take you to get out here."

I stepped off the curb and headed straight for her. She smiled up at me as I wrapped my arms around her, picking her up against my body. She giggled as I held her close. She wrapped her legs around me, her face hovering above mine. And as I gazed into her eyes, my heart filled with delight.

"You're a wild woman, you know that?" I asked.

She snickered. "No. I'm *your* wild woman. And it's about damn time we got out of here."

I growled as her lips crashed down against mine. My crew erupted into applause and laughter as a few of them revved their engines again. Holy fuck, it felt like it had been ages since I'd tasted the woman I loved. Her tongue fell against mine and I felt her sucking on my lower lip. The guys whooped and hollered, and the sounds only seemed to egg Dani on. I set her back down onto her feet and fisted her hair. I tilted my head off to the side as her free hand fisted my leather jacket. I wanted to ravish her. I wanted to rip her clothes off and bury my face between her breasts while my cock sought out its home.

But I settled for claiming her in front of my guys.

I had to force myself away from her as one of the guys walked up. He nodded at me as he handed me my helmet, and I searched for my bike. Snake parted the group with his skinny ass, pushing my bike to the forefront. And after passing it off to me, he hopped into a sidecar Colter had attached to his bike.

Usually used for his wife, but it would do in a pinch.

"Yeah. Let's get the hell out of here," I said.

I thrust my helmet into the air and the deafening roar of their cheers made me laugh. Dani led me over to my bike before we both hopped on, and I groaned at the feeling of her arms wrapped tightly around me. It felt like I'd been in purgatory for years. Finally released from captivity and experiencing life for the first time again. I slid my helmet over my head as her hands gripped my leather jacket. I felt her tense against me, and I grinned to myself. Her legs flexed as I kicked up the kickstand. I revved my engine in a very distinct pattern, signaling to the guys to all follow me.

We took off toward home.

Thirty-four bikes rumbling down the road. Speeding through yellow lights, kicking up burnt rubber around corners, and marking our town with our presence. I took the long way home. I wanted everyone to see us. I wanted my father's minions to know I was out and coming for them, whether they were ready or not. I wrapped around and headed for the house. I pulled into the driveway and felt my men parking in any free spot they could find. And after I slipped off my bike, I pulled my helmet off my head.

Only to find Dani's beautiful eyes staring up at me.

"What in the world is this all about?" I asked.

She hooked her thumb in the belt loop of my jeans. "Nothing special. You know, just letting your father know he has to go through all of us to get to you."

I sighed. "Dani, I appreciate all this. But it's reckless. It's-"

"Dangerous?"

I nodded. "Yes."

"Impulsive?"

"Very."

She smiled. "Good."

I blinked. "What?"

She snickered. "Max, you know as well as I do that we'll be harder to break if we stand together. And your father needs to know that he's messing with the Red Thorns, not just Max Ryddle. Not just his son. As soon as he finds out you were released he's going to take action. And we're going to be there when that happens."

I paused. "We?"

She nodded. "We're in this together now. Whether you like that or not."

She was remarkable. The most amazing woman I had ever come across in my life. And as I slipped my arm around her, I pulled her in for a kiss. I slid my tongue along the roof of her mouth and heard her helmet clatter to the cement. I nuzzled my nose against hers as one of my guys scooped it up, handing it back to me.

Then I gazed around at my guys and smiled.

"So, I'm going to need all of you to wait outside here. I need to use my house. Privately."

Dani blushed as the guys revved their engines and pumped their fists in the air.

"Did you really have to announce it?" she said through her giggles.

I grinned. "Would you really have it any other way?"

She shook her head as I pulled her off my bike, helping to steady her on her feet. I hung my helmet on the handlebar of my bike, and together, we started into the house. I held her hand tightly as we walked inside.

I wasted no time in leading her down the hallway. Into my bedroom we went, bypassing everything to get to the shower. I needed a fucking shower. As hot as I could stand it. I needed to feel clean again. I needed to wash that damn holding cell and all of the interrogations from my body. I needed to scrub until the memories were gone.

While holding Dani closely against me.

20

DANI

The steam of the shower filled the bathroom as I closed the door behind me. Max had been eager to run himself a hot one and get in. He moved like lightning. Hard to catch, hard to see. But the glimpses I caught were powerful and beautiful. I saw his shadowed form moving behind the curtain, and I drew in a deep breath as the sounds of the bikes on the front lawn quickly faded away. I kicked off my shoes and slipped out of my jacket. I heard him groaning with relief as I eased my shirt over my head. I smiled at how happy he sounded. How he hummed to himself and filled the bathroom with a smell I had quickly attributed to him.

Mint and oak.

"You coming, or what?"

I giggled. "You gonna be patient, or what?"

His head peeked out from beyond the curtain. "Get in here before I punish you for that sass."

I winked. "And if I don't?"

He growled playfully and I quickly shed the rest of my clothes. I hopped in with him, practically launching myself into his arms. The heat of the water battered against my back and I hissed. But I didn't let it bother me. The only important thing was that I had him back. Max was back in my arms, and in this house, against my body. He was okay. He wasn't hurt. He hadn't been injured while in that holding cell.

That was all that mattered to me.

"I'm so happy you're okay," I whispered.

I looked up at him and found him staring at me.

"We're not out of the woods yet. If anything, we're standing at the edge of the forest now."

I nodded. "I know. I know. I just…"

I ran my hands down his chiseled chest before I leaned my forehead against it. He wrapped his arms around me, pulling me close as my ear settled against his heartbeat. Well, near his heartbeat. Damn it, I was so much shorter than him. Still, though, I could hear it. Feel it. And the sound brought tears to my eyes.

"I'm so glad you're alive," I whispered.

He reached for something behind me. "Come on. It's time we get you cleaned up, too."

I wanted to protest, but I decided to go along with it. I felt his washcloth caress my skin as bubbles popped and tickled me. I melted against him as he swirled them along my body, sliding the washcloth up and down my spine. His hands landed on my ass, and the bubbles made me giggle.

"Gotta hold still if I'm going to wash every crevice, gorgeous."

I sighed. "My God, I missed you calling me that."

He kissed the shell of my ear before he backed me into the hot streams of water. I felt the soap washing away from my body before he turned me around. He wrapped one arm around my shoulders, and I felt him kissing my neck. My cheek. Even the top of my head. His other hand slid around my body, coating me in cleansing bubbles.

"Gotta get up under here, too," he murmured.

I gasped as he swiped the washcloth beneath my breasts.

"Mmm, gotta make sure these hip bones are clean, too."

I moaned. "Max."

He nipped at my neck. "Patience, gorgeous. Patience will do you well right now."

His hands meandered, making my muscles jump. His lips kissed me softly, bleeding warmth through my veins. I felt him traveling farther downward. Sliding that washcloth over my thighs. Between my legs. Sliding over my lower lips with a featherlike softness.

"Max," I groaned.

He chuckled. "Patience."

I scoffed. "I've had enough patience. Eighty-eight hours' worth of patience."

He paused. "You were counting?"

I turned to face him. "Of course I was counting. And every minute without you was agonizing."

His eyes darkened as the washcloth fell from his

hand. I knew that look. I'd seen it before. I'd dreamt about that look the entire time he'd been locked away. His hands reached for me, gripping my waist tightly. Pulling me into him as my desire for him rose. I watched his pupils blow wide with lust. His hand slid through my soaked hair, fisting it as his eyes held mine captive.

"You're the best thing that's ever happened to me. And whatever I have to do to get you out of this, I will."

His lips fell against my own and I lost myself in him. In the fierceness of his kiss and the tight grip he had on my hair. I groaned at the feel of his stiffened girth pressing against my stomach. Eager for me. Waiting for me to spread myself so he could devour me whole. I raked my hands along his skin, relishing his growl. I grabbed at every part of him I could find before my hands settled against his ass cheeks. The thick, taut muscle rolled against my palms. I felt my pussy wetting itself as water bashed against us. Max's tongue invaded me. Marked me. Pushed me to heights that made my ears ring.

Then his lips fell to my neck.

"Max. I have to feel you. Please, I can't take it anymore."

He bit into my shoulder. "Let me taste you first."

"Max."

"You heard me."

I whispered, "I'm begging you, just this once."

His head lifted and my eyes fluttered open. My half-hooded stare met his dancing gaze, his eyes bouncing between mine. I felt tears rush my eyes. Tears I had held back for what seemed like weeks. And as he picked me up against him, relief flooded my veins.

"Thank you. Thank you so much."

He pinned me against the wall. "I'll give you what you want if you answer one thing for me."

"Anything. Anything to feel you."

His cock teased my entrance. "Are you scared, Dani?"

I froze. "What?"

"You heard me. Are you scared?"

"Of what?"

"Of this. Of everything. Of what we're about to do."

The weight of his question fell heavily against my shoulders. But it didn't stop me from answering him honestly.

"More than I could ever imagine. But it's easier when I'm with you," I said.

His lips captured mine as he eased himself inside me. And the electricity that flooded my brain sparked colors behind my eyelids. I wrapped my arms around him as I felt his pelvis sink against my own. And as his hands planted into the tile wall, he slowly pulled back.

"I missed you so much," he murmured.

He slammed into me and a moan of ecstasy bubbled up the back of my throat.

"I couldn't stop thinking about you," he grunted.

He pulled himself back before plunging into my depths, pulling groans from the tip of my tongue.

"Max, oh fuck."

He growled. "And holy hell, did I miss you saying my name like that."

He peeled my hands from around the back of his head before pinning them against the wall. My head fell back, opening my neck to him as his tongue lapped up my pulse point. I shivered against him. I felt my walls clamping around his cock. And as he slowly stroked me, the torture was more than I could stand.

"I need to come. Max. I need to--I need--"

"Patience," he whispered. "Let me relish you for a second."

I sighed with anticipation as my forehead fell against his. He held me up, stroking me softly before swiveling his hips. I felt his tightly-wound curls raking against my clit. Against that swollen nub between my legs that made me jump. I squealed, making him chuckle. He swiveled his hips again and my pussy held him tight within its vice grip. He grunted as he pulled back. He eased himself back home before swiveling those hips of his.

And the combination made me yearn for him.

"Max. I can't take it. It's so--you're so--"

He kissed my cheek. "When I've had my fill of you, you'll come. And not a second more. Understood?"

I nodded quickly. "You can have all of me, Max."

Time melded together as hot water flooded our bodies. I felt his muscles rumbling beneath my fingertips as he released my wrists, allowing me to explore him. His movements were slow. Strong. Filled with intent and purpose. I clung to him, burying my face into the crook of his neck. And as he washed over me, the words fell from my mouth in an effortless chant.

"I love you. I love you. I love you so much."

I felt myself spiraling. I felt his body pressing deeper into mine. As the water slowly faded from hot to lukewarm, he snapped his hips against my own. The sounds of skin slapping skin filled my ears. I clung to him, digging my nails into his taut muscles. He growled and groaned. He chanted my name and pressed his lips against my ear. Goosebumps ran along my skin, puckering my nipples and making my clit ache for more attention.

Then I heard Max's voice in my ear. "You're perfect for me. For my life. For my future. And I'll do whatever it takes to keep you safe."

Tears rushed my eyes. "I love you."

"My God, woman, I love you, too."

His words threw me over the edge. I felt my entire body lock up as I threw my head back. Max pulled me away from the wall, catching my head on the palm of his hand. And as he continued to buck his hips, I felt myself bouncing on his cock while he held me against his gorgeous form.

"Max, Max, Max. Yes. I'm coming. Max. Don't stop!"

"Here. I. Come."

With one last grunt, my back crashed against the wall. His lips found mine as he swallowed my moans and my groans. I felt my walls massaging him as his dick pulsed deep inside me. He swiveled his hips, stroking my clit as my toes curled and my legs jumped.

Then everything spiraled into darkness.

"Dani, can you hear me?"

My eyes fluttered open and I found myself looking up at the ceiling.

Huh?

"Gorgeous, I need you to look at me. Can you turn your head?"

I lobbed my head to the side. "Max?"

He sighed. "Thank fuck. You scared me for a second."

I furrowed my brow. "What--?"

He cupped my cheek. "You passed out on me. I thought maybe your head bashed against the wall or something."

"No. I don't--I mean, my head doesn't hurt. My body does, though."

He chuckled. "Sounds like I did my job right, then."

I blinked. "Did I pass out during...?"

"I won't tell anyone if you won't."

I narrowed my eyes. "Why do I get the feeling you're going to tell someone anyway?"

"And wear that shit like a badge of honor? Hell yeah, I am."

I snickered. "You're crazy, you know that?"

He kissed my forehead. "And you're everything to me, you know that?"

My heart warmed with pride. "I know. I hope you know the sentiment is mutual."

He nodded. "I do, yes. But seriously. You okay?"

I giggled. "I mean, I can't really move right now. I

feel like I'm being weighed down by cement. But I also haven't slept well these past couple of nights, so that might be contributing to it."

"Well, let's get you tucked in then. I'm starving, and it sounds like you need sleep."

"What if I'm starving too?"

He grinned. "Then I'll heat you something up when you wake up. That's what."

My eyes fell closed as he pulled a warm, soft blanket over my naked body. And as I turned onto my side, I felt Max bend over me. His lips kissed the shell of my ear one more time, then he whispered those magical words that lulled me right to sleep.

"I'll be here when you wake up, gorgeous."

And for the first time since Saturday night, I fell asleep without my worry of Max looming over my head.

21

MAX

I watched her lying there, spreadeagle on my bed. The second I moved away from her grip, she slid along the sheets. Inching closer. Pressing her hand against my back. Sliding it up and down my leg. Enticing me, in her sleep, to try and come back to bed.

I couldn't, though.

The second I stood up, she made her home against my mattress. With her head burrowed into my pillow, her arms spread out and her legs straightened. She had my comforter entangled between thighs I wanted to kiss. She had her hands twisted into sheets when I wanted them twisted into my hair. But I couldn't sleep in with her this morning. I couldn't stay.

I had things I needed to do.

She needed the rest. And I wanted her to sleep. I had a feeling she hadn't gotten a good night's rest in days, and that was important for anyone. Much less a woman like herself who had a lot of decisions to make.

Like with her parents. And her education. And what to do if things went south with her family. I kept bouncing back and forth between what was right and what was selfish. I knew the right thing to do was break up with her. Leave her. Let her progress through the rest of her life and make something of herself.

Then again, I'd tried doing that with Benji.

Look what that got me.

I rifled through my dresser and pulled out some clean clothes. I pulled the jeans up my legs gingerly and muffled my grunts as I tugged my black shirt over my head. Fucking hell, I'd hurt for weeks. That much was certain. But I wouldn't take the pain medication they'd given me.

I couldn't let anything alter my focus.

There were things that needed to be done and issues that needed to be addressed. I needed to figure out where the fuck Rupert was, for starters. He hadn't been with the crew when they rolled up yesterday. Which meant he was still in custody somewhere.

Or worse.

I also needed to figure out what the fuck my father's plan was. Because if he really wasn't dead, we had much bigger problems than where Rupert was located. My greatest fear was that my father had Rupert. The thought made me shiver to my core. As I turned around, gazing at myself in the mirror above my dresser, I took in my bruises. The stitches along my left cheekbone. The ligature marks around my neck and the bloodied scabs on my knuckles.

I look like shit.

A light flashed in the mirror and I slowly turned around. Dani's phone had been silently going off at all hours of the night. As I walked around to her bedside table, I peeked down just before the light dimmed. A rock settled into my gut. I tapped her screen, just to make sure I'd read it right. And I had.

She had eight missed calls from her father.

Not just from her father, though. She had even more missed calls from Hannah. And her mother. Twenty-three in all, and not one of them had been answered. I frowned as another call silently rolled in from Hannah. I watched the screen light up and dim. Light up and dim. Should I pick it up? Answer for her? Let her roommate know that Dani was simply sleeping, and I'd make sure she called back once she woke up?

You know damn good and well you can't make Dani do shit anymore.

I grinned at the thought. She really was coming into her own. Commanding my men and owning her sexuality and bringing me to my knees with just one kiss. She was more in control than she thought. And the only upper hand I had in all of it was playing on that part of her that didn't know just yet.

God help me when she figures it out, though.

I smiled at the thought as I gazed down at my sleeping woman, her shoulders rising and falling with her steady breaths. I wanted to wake her up with my cock. I wanted to make love to her before I went anywhere. But things were weighing on my mind and I needed to talk to John.

I bent down and pressed a soft kiss to the back of

Dani's head. She shifted around and yawned before spreading her arms out even further. Still seeking me, even though she was dead asleep. Every step away from her side felt agonizing. It was torture to my heart and my soul. But my mind was more focused than ever before. There was one end goal. One thing I wanted to accomplish once we got through this bullshit.

I want my father gone.

I slipped out of the bedroom and closed the door behind me. And as I made my way to the kitchen, the sounds of several footsteps at once caught my ear. I froze, clenching my fists as my heart leapt into my throat. I paused my movements and stilled my frenzied mind, watching as multiple looming shadows appeared against the kitchen floor.

John poked his head around the corner.

"Coffee's up when you're ready. Some of the guys are still here, so I'm gonna whip up something for breakfast real quick."

I cleared my throat. "Yeah. I'm coming."

He paused. "You good?"

I shook my head softly. "Yeah, yeah. Just--worried about Dani."

"You looked in a mirror lately? You should be more worried about yourself."

I grinned. "That bad, huh?"

"You're gonna need two cups of coffee to wake up, let's just say that."

I stifled my chuckle as I walked into the kitchen. Standing there, in every corner and along every wall, were my men. Tall and short. Broad and lean. Their hands were on their weapons, waiting. Protecting us even in the dead of night.

I owe them my life.

We all got coffee while John whipped up some toast and eggs. Then we gathered around the kitchen table. John and I sat with a few guys in front of us, the rest standing around the table as if they were looming over us. I groaned over John's coffee. I hadn't had a decent cup of caffeine in fucking days. It felt so great that I refused to communicate until I had gotten through two mugs.

After pouring my third one, John finally spoke.

"We've got some bad news."

I clicked my tongue. "I'm well aware of the fact that Dad's still alive."

John blinked. "Wait, what?"

My eyes peered over at him. "What?"

"Dad's still alive?"

I furrowed my brow. "That's not what you were about to say?"

John turned fully toward me. "Are you fucking telling me our father survived?"

"What the hell were you about to tell me?"

My brother sighed heavily. "Rupert's been charged with attempted murder."

I felt my anger boiling over. "Shit."

How the fuck were we going to reverse something like that? Especially when it was fucking true. I didn't know how we were going to dig him out of this mess. I mean, shy of my father admitting what really went down at the estate, I didn't know what the fuck to do.

The only way out of this I saw for my best friend was to convince a jury that, had he not taken that shot, my father would've killed me, Dani, and him. Just to get what he wanted.

But a jury would never know that if my father kept quiet what happened that night.

"You know he's not the sort of man to bend over and accept defeat," John said. "But it's not going to be easy, either."

I leaned back. "The only shot we've got is getting Ashton to give up the truth."

Even the guys chuckled at that statement as John quirked an eyebrow.

"Okay, I'll bite. How do you figure we pull that off?"

I rubbed my stubbled jaw. "We'll have to trick him."

Now the guys were holding back snickers that should've gone along with bigger guffaws. I mean, even John rolled his lips over his teeth.

"Trick him? Really, Max?"

I nodded. "Yes. Trick him. Convince him we have something he wants."

"Something he wants. Like…?"

I shrugged. "I don't know. It's just a beginning idea. But if we can convince Dad that sending Rupert to jail isn't going to be good enough, we might catch him in another act."

John paused. "You want to convince Dad he has to kill you? Are you crazy?"

I smiled. "What if we convinced him that he's got a

chance to kill me? You think he won't take it? I mean, really?"

"He's in a hospital bed recovering from a gunshot wound to his gut, Max."

I shrugged. "So he'll send someone in his place. Someone who wants the job done as badly as he does."

He blinked. "You're not saying…?"

I nodded. "Benji."

The guys fell silent around me as John fell against the back of his chair.

"You know damn good and well Dad will leave it to Benji. Especially since he succeeded in getting me tied up in that fucking warehouse. That'll be proof enough for Dad that he can get the job done. Especially with emotions running high."

John sighed. "Dad never was good at separating his actions from his emotions."

"Exactly. He sees that as a strength, but we can easily turn it into a weakness."

"How does that get Rupert off the hook?"

I shrugged. "I don't know. But if Benji's caught trying to take me out, you think he won't sing like a bird for the cops?"

"If Dad doesn't kill him first."

"This is Rupert we're talking about. We've got to do something."

"You don't think I know that, Max? I just don't want to go around trying to get people killed on some long-shot idea that might not work."

I smiled. "Got any better ones? Because I'm all ears if you do."

The room fell silent as my guys looked around at one another. No one had a better idea because there was none. This was our last shot. Our last chance at bringing down my father for good. And the only chance we had at freeing Rupert from these fucking charges. My brother pinched the bridge of his nose and shook his head. John sighed.

"He's not going to trust a little fuck-up like Benji with something like this, Max. There's too much risk for fallout."

I licked my lips. "Which is why we play directly into Dad's--"

"If he gets caught--"

I interrupted him. "Dad will have taken precautions. You know how calculating he is."

"And yet we're planning on using his emotions against him? You're talking in opposites."

"No, you're just not listening."

"If Benji gets caught, Dad's going to scrub everything, cut that cord, and let our cousin flail. That's what he *does*, Max. Dad will let that asshole rot in jail and he won't shed one tear for it. Benji is the no-risk option."

"Which is why we have to use this moment. Think about it, John, just for a second. Listen to me. Benji is no-risk. You just said it. Dad's other men aren't like that, though. They're not as desperate. They're not as emotional when it comes to all of this. Benji will want me dead badly enough to do whatever Dad tells him to do. And it will mess with both of their judgment."

John shook his head. "This is complicated and

diluted. We're hinging this on some other-worldly force we can't control."

I snickered. "And when has Dad ever been a force we could control?"

Silence fell between us as I reached for another piece of toast.

"I'm right about this, John. I know I am. Dad's got a raw nerve exposed right now, and it's directly linked to Benji. Does it have other ways it could spin that aren't good for us? Yes. But so does every other fucking situation with that man. This is the best option we've got, even if it isn't good. With the hand we've got and what's at stake, this is our play. Even you can't deny that."

John blinked. "There really isn't another way?"

"Let me finish my coffee and you think about it. Then we can talk."

I sipped my coffee and kept eating toast. The men around us looked at each other but stayed silent. All eyes and focus were on John as he murmured to himself and slid his hands down his face. I had to admit, he was trying. I gave him props for that, too. Benji had been John's little project. While it was my job to uphold John's wishes, it was John that originally denied Benji entry into the club. Denied him a chance at being a prospect. In my brother's words, "He's got too much to offer this world to be running around with a bunch of bloodthirsty men."

I knew John wouldn't like any plan that put Benji in harm's way.

"You're right."

My brother's voice pierced the air before my eyes panned to his face. I watched him heave the heaviest, most burdened sigh to ever come from any man's lips.

"You're right. There's no other avenue to exploit. And now that we've tried taking Dad out once, he won't stop until we're both dead."

I nodded. "I know."

"Which means it's us or him."

"I know."

He reached for his fork. "So how do we make this happen? How do we orchestrate this?"

I placed my hand on my brother's shoulder, trying to provide him with some sort of comfort.

"We lure Benji out of hiding. Right now, he's hunkered down somewhere. Waiting for some sort of signal, no doubt. We lure him out. Make him think I'm an easy target. With Benji's incessant need to get in good with people, he'll never be able to fight the temptation to take me out in order to show Dad what he's made of. And once we've got him right where we want him? We get him to admit who he's working for."

John nodded. "And why."

I nodded. "Exactly. Who, when, where, and why."

"Which will hopefully get Rupert off the hook for these bogus-ass charges."

"And put Dad away for good."

22

DANI

The first thing I smelled was a lack of him. His cologne was fading away. And the cool sheets on his side of the bed startled me awake. I quickly rose up, whipping my head around to see if I could find him. But when Max was nowhere to be found, I threw the covers off me.

"Max?"

My feet hit the floor and I hissed at the cold. I stumbled around, trying to get my bearings. It was morning. The sun was trying so hard to peek through the blackout curtains in his bedroom. I made my way over to the bathroom and flipped on the light, straining to see if he was in there.

"Max, where are you?"

I turned around and read the room. At least, I tried to. I rubbed my eyes, clearing them of their crusted sleep, and that's when relief washed over me. The drawers on the dresser hung open. A shirt had been cast to the floor. A pair of socks lay in the corner, as if they had been tried on before someone said 'nope, no thanks.'

Max is up for the day.

The room didn't look disheveled. It didn't look as if someone had a fight or was hurt, in any way. I drew in a deep breath, trying to get the trembling in my hands to go away as my legs found their strength. I was still on edge. Even after falling asleep next to Max last night, I still felt worked up. I had to find a way to calm myself down, to ground myself again.

Max is fine. I'm fine. Everything's fine.

Except for his father still being alive.

Something lit up in the corner, though, and it caught my eye. I wandered back over toward the light, only to find my phone flashing on the bedside table. I saw my father calling, and I picked up the phone. I ignored the phone call to check and see if Max had sent me anything. Or called of his own volition. But the numbers that reflected back at me raised my eyebrows.

"Thirty-seven missed calls?" I murmured.

My phone started flashing again with my father's name popping up. I sat myself on the edge of the bed. At some point in time, I'd have to talk to them. I couldn't simply cast them out, like I had Hannah. They were my parents. And I knew they'd pester me until kingdom come if I didn't answer the phone.

I braced myself for the inevitable.

"Morning, Dad."

I heard him sigh with relief. "My word, thank heavens. Dani, where are you? Are you all right?"

I resisted the urge to hang up. "I'm fine, Dad."

"Okay. Then tell me where you are. I'm coming to get you."

"I said I'm okay."

"I get that. Now I'm coming to get you."

"No, you're not."

He sighed. "Danika, don't make me fight with you in front of your mother. She's already worried sick enough as it is."

I shrugged. "Then don't fight me. I'm fine. I'm safe. That's all that's pertinent to this situ--"

"Where are you? You tell me right now. Or I'm having someone ping your phone."

"Dad, if I tell you where I am, you'll send the cops to come get me or something. I'm fine."

"Now's not the time for jokes."

I snickered. "Who in the world said I was joking?"

A long pause settled over our conversation before I heard my father clear his throat.

"Then when are we going to talk about this?"

I shrugged. "Well, I'm kind of in the middle of something. So I guess we can talk about things once I can get my head above water."

"Not funny."

"I wasn't trying to be. I just woke up and haven't had my coffee. Spare me the irony of my statements, please."

"Drop the attitude and maybe we'll talk."

I rolled my eyes. "I'll find room in my schedule to

pencil you and Mom in so I can give you a play by play of my personal life."

His voice grew stronger. "That's it. I've had enough of this attitude of yours, Danika. I swear, you didn't even give us this much trouble as a teenager!"

"Don't make the joke that this is me making up for it now. Because it's not."

"Well, what else are we supposed to think?"

"That I'm finally coming into my own and proud of the person I'm becoming."

"You can't possibly be serious."

I nodded. "As a heart attack."

The phone call went silent again and I had an idea of what was going on. Dad was either muting his side of the phone and relaying information to Mom, or I was on speakerphone and he kept muting his side of things every time Mom kicked up. I pinched the bridge of my nose. As I sat there on the edge of the bed, I suddenly felt wide awake. Not the kind of wake-up call I wanted to make a regular thing in my life. But at least my focus was coming back.

Which would make this conversation with my father much more productive.

"Dad?"

I heard something click on his end. "I'm here, princess."

"I know you're muting the phone and talking to Mom."

He paused. "Well, you've practically got her in bed with grief. It's about the only way I can communicate with her right now."

"Tell her I'm fine. I'm okay. I'm with people who have my best interests in mind, and--"

"Please let me come get you. Let me see you, Danika."

I shook my head. "No."

"And why not?"

"Because I don't want to see you. And that is just as important as your wanting to see me. You don't get to demand my time, nor my presence. If I don't want to see you, that is within my right as a human being. You don't own me, Dad. And for the longest time, you've assumed you do."

"This is insane. We can talk about this when I come--"

I stood to my feet. "You're coming nowhere. I'm not telling you where I am because I don't want to see you. I'll get in touch with you when I want to. But until that point, there's nothing you can do about it. You have no control over this situation, so get used to it."

"You listen here and you listen good. I'm not going t--"

"No. You listen to me for once. I'm tired of everyone in my life thinking *they* know what's best for me. That they know better than I do for my own life. And I get it. I get that I scared you. Even if you don't think I get it, I do. And I didn't mean to do that. I'm sorry, Dad, that I frightened you so badly. But I'm done with letting other people make decisions for me. Even if those people think they have my best interests in mind, I'm done with it. I make the calls in my life, and if that means making some serious mistakes along the way? Then so be it. I should have the right to make those mistakes, whether you approve of that idea or not."

He chuckled bitterly. "Danika. This is madness. Your mother and I are staying at the Hilton in town. Please come stay with us. You'll be safe here. We won't even extend our stay. Just come stay with us until--"

"Daddy. Listen to me."

"Stop interrupting me!"

"No, you stop attempting to override my decision! I'm safe. S-A-F-E. Now that I know where you and Mom are staying, of course I'll come see you. But I can't do that right now. I have things I need to do first."

"Are you even going to tell me what things you're talking about?"

I bit my bottom lip. "I'll tell you later. I promise, Dad. But right now, all I'm asking you to do is trust me and give me some space. I know it's hard. And it's unfair. I get that, too. But it's also unfair what you did to Max at the hospital. And to me."

"Danika, I made the best decision I could have as a father."

"I needed him, Daddy. Not you. Not Mom. Him. The man who saved my life. And you took him from me and you sent him off to jail without knowing the full story of what happened. You did that even though I told you, repeatedly, that he was responsible for me being alive in that hospital instead of dead at the bottom of a pool."

"I--Danika, it--you just--can't you just try to see

things my way for a second? My little girl--my only child--was in a hospital bed. With bruises on her skin. And this massive man comes in with this gruff voice who looks like he just got hit by a train and dragged for miles, and I'm not supposed to think he had a hand in what happened to you?"

I shook my head. "Not when I'm looking you dead in your eyes and telling you he saved my life."

"Cut me a bit of slack here."

I shook my head. "No. And I'll tell you why I'm not going to do that. I'm not going to cut you any slack because my entire life has been centered around what you and Mom have wanted for me. When I first declared my major? It was because you wanted me to declare that specific major. When I switched majors? Mom ended up directing me to some HR degree because she thought I'd be good at it. And it's always been that way with us, even during school. I did after-school activities and sports you guys wanted me in. I decorated my room the way you guys wanted it. I displayed things about my life the way you guys wanted them displayed. And through all of it, you never asked me what I wanted."

He paused. "Did you not like swimming? Did you not like theater?"

"Liking it or not liking it isn't the point. The point is that you never asked, Dad. Neither you nor Mom did. No one gave me a choice. It was suggested, and it was my responsibility to accept."

"You didn't have to, Dani."

I snickered. "Remember back in middle school?"

"What?"

"Humor me for a second. Remember back when I was in middle school? When a slot on the History Debate Team came open my seventh grade year?"

He paused. "I do."

"You remember how hard Mom tried to get me to join?"

He sighed. "Dani, that was--"

"Do you remember, Dad?"

"Yes, I remember. And I know where you're going with this."

"Good. Then this will cut the conversation short. I told Mom I didn't want to do it, and she threw a fit. Got you involved. And the two of you sat me down and essentially told me I'd regret not doing the History Debate Team. That I was too young to understand the consequences of my decisions, and that you had already called the principal of my school to let him know I'd be trying out. Remember that?"

"Dani, please. It was only one time."

"And sometimes, Dad, once is all it takes. One lesson being learned at the exact right moment is all it takes for something to really stick. And that stuck with me, Dad. You and Mom completely disregarded what I wanted for my life at that moment and you used the age excuse with me then. Just like you are now. I'm not going to let you get away with it. This is my life, which means these are my decisions."

"I can't fight with you anymore. Just please, tell me where you are."

I shook my head. "I love you guys, but I have to go."

"Dani, plea--"

I hung up the phone before flipping it over. I slid the battery pack out and placed the pieces back onto the bedside table. I didn't want to take any chance that my parents might actually get so desperate as to have someone track my damn cell phone. At this point, I couldn't put anything past them. My heart felt heavy. My soul felt as if it were still being weighed down in that pool by that chair. I looked down at the clothes I'd fallen asleep in and took stock of how wrinkly they were. So I decided to exchange my shirt for one of Max's.

Before following the smells of coffee into the kitchen.

I felt all eyes on me as I schlepped into the room. I made my way to the coffee pot and plucked a mug from the cabinet. I picked up a piece of toast and shoved it into my mouth. Some of the other crew members were lined up against the walls with their eyes facing the table. That meant they were talking. Deliberating. Trying to figure out the kinks to this plan. And as I carried my coffee to sit next to Max, I draped an arm around his shoulders.

"So! Is everyone on board, handsome?"

John paused. "Wait, she knows?"

I sipped my coffee. "I'm actually kind of hurt you think I'm not in the know, John."

Max chuckled. "She knows, yes."

I kissed the top of Max's head. "Didn't answer my question, though."

I gazed into the eyes of every man lining the walls of the kitchen before I sat next to the love of my life.

"Is everyone on board?" I asked.

23

MAX

"Mmph."

"Ugh."

"Fuck, come on."

"Ergh, shit!"

I took the bag from Dani's hands. "Take a breather, gorgeous. I've got it."

She took it back from me. "I'm not a child. I've got this."

"I'm not saying you're a child. I'm saying you've matched me, bag for bag. Take a break."

She wiped at the sweat on her forehead. "What? Think I can't keep up?"

"Dani."

She sighed. "I'm sorry. I'm sorry. It's just…"

I stopped hoisting bags into the back of the rented truck before I cupped her cheeks.

"Gorgeous, I know you're fully capable of stepping

up to the plate. You've proved that to me more times than I can count. Okay?"

She nodded. "Okay."

"You're tired. There's nothing wrong with that. Go get some water, take a breather, then you can get back at it. Okay? No one's going to think anything bad about you just because you're winded."

"I know. I know. It's just--"

I ran my thumb along her lower lip. "Shhhh. You need to trust that I understand a bit more than you give me credit for. And I promise you, whatever's going through your head right now, that's not what's actually happening."

After watching her nod softly in my grip, I placed a kiss to her sweating forehead. We'd been lugging these massive bags into the back of the truck for well over an hour now. And it shocked me that she hadn't taken a break up until this point. I knew Dani was on edge. I knew she was overly concerned with how people perceived her right now. And in some respects, I understood.

But she needed to learn how to rein her emotions in during times like these.

I watched her make her way back into the house before I picked up another bag. I lugged it into the back of the truck, listening as the chassis groaned. The bed wouldn't be able to haul much more than this. And we still had to unload them at the other end. I wiped my face off with my shirt before I dusted off my hands. The street behind me was lined with motorcycles. Lined with my men, ready to jump at the drop of a hat if someone rolled up onto us.

I just hoped this worked.

"You sure he's going to buy it?"

John's voice sounded behind me and I turned around.

"Yeah, I really do. Benji's strong suit isn't his wits. He's going to be pissed after what I did to him in that warehouse. So if he thinks you're offering him redemption, he's going to jump at it."

My brother pointed to the bags. "And all of these are necessary?"

Dani walked out of the house. "If you tell me we've tossed those bags onto that truck for no reason, I'm having someone's head."

A few of the guys chuckled as a grin crossed my face.

"I'd like to see you try that, gorgeous."

She handed me a bottle of water. "Play your cards wrong, and you just might."

I smiled as she winked at me, then I cracked open the bottle. The glorious cold liquid dripped from the opening, and it was all I could do not to choke myself on it. I guzzled it down, completely unaware of how much I had exerted myself up until this point. The bottle crinkled as I continued sucking it back, barely giving myself room to breathe.

Then, with a growl, I tossed the bottle into the bed of the truck as well.

"Hey, now. Don't go ruining all of our efforts," Dani said.

I snickered. "I would never."

She smirked. "Uh huh."

John piped up. "So someone want to run me through this plan one more time?"

Dani turned to face him. "Which part do you want to hear?"

John snickered. "All of it, maybe?"

She licked her lips. "I know it's not as thorough as everyone would like it to be. Myself, especially. But I trust this is going to work out. Do you trust me, John?"

My brother peeked over at me. "She being serious?"

I shrugged. "Do you trust the girl?"

Dani corrected me. "Woman."

I winked. "Hell yeah, you are."

Dani rolled her eyes. "John, do you trust me?"

He sighed. "Yeah. Yeah, I do. But this is also Max's only shot at getting out of this as a free man."

Dani nodded. "Which is why it's worth the risk to me. Remember, John, you need to tell him we're running. That we're leaving town. Getting out of Dodge for good. And you need to make sure Benji understands it's because of him. That's the important part. It's the only thing he'll believe, because he's just as egotistical as your father."

I jumped in. "He'll follow us if you make sure he understands we're leaving due to his treatment. Benji won't want to leave anything unfinished. If my father has rubbed off on him that much, we play this like we'd play our father."

John chuckled breathlessly. "Playing our father. Sounds like a cause of death on my tombstone."

I sighed. "It'll only be a matter of time before Dad's paid goons catch up with us, too. As long as Benji makes it to us first, we'll be good. He'll talk. But, if Dad's paid idiots find us with him, this might get complicated."

My brother nodded. "Got it. Make sure it's all about Benji, and that he makes it to you guys first. I can do that."

Dani smiled. "We knew you could."

John paused. "You're sure he's going to be at the hospital?"

I hoisted one last bag into the bed of the truck. "Positive. There's nowhere else for him to go. He's got no one else at his side but Dad right now, and we know Dad's still recuperating in that hospital bed. Benji isn't going to be at school. He can't come to any of our clubhouses without risking his own life. And he can't go to the estate because it's still a crime scene. He'll be at the hospital, either talking to Dad or waiting to see Dad. It's a safe place to corner him."

John paused. "If we don't want Dad getting to you guys first, are you sure we don't want to lure him away from the hospital?"

Dani cupped my brother's cheeks. "John, you need to take a breath with me. Okay?"

I watched the two of them draw in deep breaths together, and out of the corner of my eye I saw some of my men on their bikes doing the same thing. Their chests expanded as their eyes closed. They were breathing with Dani, as if she were silently commanding them.

Hell, those men never listened to me like that at all. And it was inspiring.

What a woman.

"All right, John. Ready?" she asked.

He nodded. "Ready."

"You're the one who's going to the hospital. Max and I are getting on the road. When you talk to Benji, follow our stipulations. And when you do, that's when he leaves the hospital and comes after us. We're banking on the hospital holding back your father from placing phone calls or leaving or generally fucking this up. Okay?"

He nodded fervently. "Got it. It's all sorted out in my head now. Sorry."

She patted his cheeks. "Such a dirty word. You have nothing to be sorry for. It's complicated, and diluted, and risky at best. You need any other clarification?"

I stood in awe of her as she talked my brother through the bare bones of the plan with poise and confidence.

"No, no. I'm good. Thanks," John said.

Dani dropped her hands. "Wonderful. Okay. Max, do we need any other bags in the trunk?"

I shook my head. "Got the last one in while you were doing your focus thing. We're good to go whenever John is."

She smiled. "John?"

"Yeah?"

"You gonna be able to do this?"

He paused for longer than I liked. "Yeah. I'm going to be able to do this."

Dani giggled. "Great. Fantastic. Max? I'm going to go get cleaned up a bit more, then I'll be ready. You need anything while I'm inside?"

I shook my head. "Just need to talk with my brother while you're gone. Then I'll be ready."

I watched Dani disappear back into the house before I walked over to my brother. I slung an arm around his neck, pulling him in for a brotherly hug. I closed my eyes and cherished the moment, because I knew it might be the last time we ever saw one another. If shit went south with this little operation of ours, I didn't know who the hell was getting out alive. It'd be every man for himself at that point, and we'd actually be forced out of town.

I wanted to make sure I left no stone unturned.

"I love you. I hope you know that," John said.

I patted his chest. "Yeah, I know. And I hope you know I do, too."

He nodded. "Yeah, I know."

I sighed. "Don't you dare do anything stupid. You got it? I'll do my part. You do yours. And I'll see you on the other side."

"So long as you keep up your end of the bargain. If we're not doing stupid shit, neither are you two. Got it?"

"Trust me, I more than got it."

"Good."

He wrapped his arms around me in a massive hug

and I had to close my eyes. I swallowed back the knot forming in my throat as John clapped my back. I hugged him tightly, holding on to him a few seconds longer than I normally would have. And after I heard the front door of the house open again, I released him.

Before Dani came to stand at my side.

"Ready?" she asked.

I looked into John's eyes. "You ready?"

My brother nodded. "Ready when you guys are."

I clapped his cheek. "Good. Because I'm ready to end this."

I hugged my brother one last time before I wrapped around the back end of the truck. While John opened the passenger door for Dani, I hopped behind the wheel of the massive vehicle. I let Dani and John say their goodbyes before she climbed into the seat. And as she buckled her seatbelt, John's words made me chuckle.

"You take care of my little brother now, Bambi. He's fragile, though he doesn't like to speak of such things."

I chuckled. "Fragile. You wish."

Dani giggled. "I promise I'll take good care of him. You just take care of yourself. Okay?"

John's eyes found mine. "She's one of us, through and through."

I grinned. "I know."

I cranked up the massive diesel engine and heard it roar to life. John closed Dani's car door and I watched him in the mirrors as he retreated to the guys lining the curb with their bikes. I backed out of the driveway and straightened the truck out in the middle of the road, keeping my eyes on the guys.

I felt something warm and comforting squeeze my knees.

"This will work, Max. I promise."

Dani's voice sounded so soft, yet so reassuring. And it brought me a great deal of hope.

"I know, gorgeous. But, more than that, it has to work. Our futures depend on it."

She patted my knee. "Try not to put that kind of pressure on yourself just yet."

Easier said than done.

I looked each and every one of my guys in the eyes as we idled in the middle of the road. I chose to ignore the way Dani's hand trembled against my knee with nerves and the soft break in her voice as she swallowed hard. I already felt it in my chest. The tension of this moment. The desperation in the eyes of my men as they looked to our truck as a source of their own hope. We were playing with fire. All of us were. I looked over at Dani, and the confidence in her posture washed over me.

I'll do anything to keep you safe.

I wanted this to be behind us once and for all. I wanted my father and Benji out of the fucking picture so we could all get on with our lives. I was tired of the torture. Tired of being bossed around. Tired of eating ramen and scrounging for change in the couches because someone else was in charge of the jobs we took. The money we made. I wanted better for my men. I wanted better for myself.

And damn it, 'better' felt too close not to reach for it.

With my father out of the picture, I could love Dani without fear of losing her. I could hold her at night without fear of someone attacking us in the middle of it. I could go to campus to visit her without fear that someone had gotten to her. Like Benji at the pool. Or my father, creeping in the shadows next to her dorm. With this behind us, Dani and I had a future we could strive for. A future where our love wasn't overshadowed by my father's insanity and lust for blood.

That alone was a future worth putting everything on the line.

"Ready?" Dani asked.

I raised my head high before I nodded.

"Let's go, gorgeous. We've got a future to preserve."

Then I sped off down the road, listening as motorcycle engines revved and sputtered, as if the guys were clapping for us, cheering us on. Sending us off into a better world fit for the two of us.

Soon.

Soon, my life could be everything I dreamt of and everything I felt was impossible for my world.

Once my father and Benji were gone for good.

24

DANI

"Which ones have our stuff in it again?" I asked.

Max pulled the truck up to our motel room. "The ones in the back seat. The ones in the bed of the truck are filled with random things. You know, to make it look like we're hauling more stuff than we are."

I nodded. "Just making sure we didn't have to dig for them or something. I'm exhausted."

"Me, too."

I stared at the door to our room. "You think four hours out of town is enough?"

He opened his door. "We're about to find out, I guess."

"Doesn't give me much hope, handsome."

He snickered. "Well, if you're looking for hope, you shacked up with the wrong guy. Because I don't deal in hope."

I looked over at him. "Oh, really? And what is it you deal in?"

He grinned. "Certainties."

I rolled my eyes at his pompous attitude, but I was a bit jealous as well. He seemed so calm. So cool. So collected, despite everything going on around us. I wished I felt that way, too. On the outside was a curt frown and unfocused eyes, which matched my mood on the inside. I was worried. Fearful of the future. Concerned that this would all blow up in our faces.

Or that Max would actually wind up dead.

The door behind me opened. "I got your bag. Just grab the key. It's in the cup holder."

I reached for it. "Got it. I'll go unlock the door."

I slid down from the truck and went to unlock the door. Max walked our bags in before going out to lock the truck back up. I watched his eyes pan around, as if he were looking for something. Or possibly keeping one eye in the distance.

Reminding me of the trouble following on our heels.

"You gave them the fake name, right?" I asked.

Max stepped inside. "Yep. Didn't even bat a lash when I said Monroe."

I nodded. "Good. A third of this is already done, then."

I closed the motel room door and locked us in. I pulled the blinds closed before tossing the key onto the small round table in the corner. Making my way to a random chair, I sat down on the edge . I couldn't relax. I wouldn't relax until all of this was said and done.

Flopping onto the mattress, Max let out a satisfied groan that made me even more jealous of him and his collected demeanor.

"Enjoying yourself over there?"

He lifted his head. "I'd enjoy it more if you were with me."

I snickered. "Sorry, but this love factory is closed until we can get through this insanity."

He sat up. "Oh, really now?"

I pointed at him. "Don't you dare."

He grinned. "Don't I dare what?"

"I'm serious, Max. That's the furthest thing from my mind."

"And what if I could change that?"

"I told you no. I mean it, too."

He held up his hands. "Okay, okay, okay. Just teasing you a bit."

I snickered. "Not really a teasing kind of time right now, you think?"

He shrugged. "If anything, I think it's a great way to blow off some of the stress we're feeling right now."

"Blow, huh?"

He smiled. "Well, you know."

I rolled my eyes. "Down, boy."

"You know I can never resist you."

"Which is why it's all the more important for me to resist you. So stay over there."

He took a step toward me. "And if I don't?"

I quickly stood up. "No, Max. Please."

His face fell. "What's wrong?"

"Really?"

"Yeah, really."

"Take a look at the situation we're in and answer that question yourself."

He held his arms out for me. "Come here."

I sighed. "I don't wanna."

He grinned. "Come here, gorgeous. Come on. You know you wanna."

"Ugh."

I walked to his towering form and felt his comforting arm blanket my body. I closed my eyes and drew in his scent, feeling my body meld against him. I sank into his muscles, letting him pull me close. He sat back down onto the bed, pulling me into his lap. I wrapped my arms around his neck and straddled his pelvis. As his hands ran up and down my back, he placed soft kisses against my temple.

"Everything's going to be okay," he murmured.

I sighed. "I wish I knew that for certain."

"Well, I do. So trust me."

"What if he really does kill you, Max?"

He scoffed. "Benji? Hell, no. That asshole had me tied to a chair and he didn't do it. No way he'll go through with it now."

"I'm sorry I'm not any stronger than this."

"Dani, look at me."

My eyes found his. "Yeah?"

He gripped my chin. "You've been nothing but strong since this entire thing began. If there's anyone in this situation that's been strong, it's you."

I shook my head. "I don't feel that way."

"Those who are truly strong usually don't."

I peeked over his shoulder at the digital clock. "How long do you think we'll have to wait for him?"

His hands settled onto my hips. "Probably not more than an hour. Benji won't let a minute go to waste. Especially if it means proving something to my father."

"And if he consults your father before he comes?"

He barked with laughter. "Then my bet is on thirty minutes."

I swatted at his chest. "That's not funny."

"I know it's not funny. But the answer to your question is that we won't be waiting very long, either way. Both of them are going to want to end this quickly. And while we're out of town, to boot. It's the perfect time for them to jump us. They won't waste another second if they don't have to."

"I'm worried, Max."

He kissed the tip of my nose. "I know you are, gorgeous. I'm worried, too."

"You are?"

He nodded. "Yep."

"You don't look nervous."

He snickered. "I've had my entire life to perfect the art of never looking nervous. You've only been in this for a couple of months. Cut yourself some slack."

"I've aced midterms in shorter amounts of time."

"But have you ever fought for your life and come out the other side still breathing? Because that's what this is right now. This isn't college. This isn't school. This isn't a test. This is do or die."

My shoulders slumped. "I know. I know. Trust me, I get it."

"Come here, Dani. I've got you."

I let him pull me back to his body before he tucked my head against his neck. I sighed heavily, reveling in his warmth as he slowly lay down. I relaxed on top of him, feeling his heart beating against my own. His hands softly explored me, never breaching my clothes as they languidly slid around.

And me?

Well, my stomach was one big knot of nerves.

I felt my confidence slipping away. Now that we were on the brink of fighting our way out of this, I felt terrified. I didn't feel strong, like I had in that alleyway. I didn't feel empowered, like I had talking to all of those men that night. I didn't feel headstrong, like I had when riding with those guys over to the police station.

Now I just felt like Dani.

Little, sheltered, pointless Dani.

"Max?"

"Hmm?"

"Does it bother you that I'm scared?"

He stroked his fingers through my hair. "No. It doesn't."

"So if I were to ask you what we might do if this doesn't go the way we planned, what would you say?"

He gripped my hair softly. "I'd say you're looking too far into the future. And pulling your focus away from a present like this is almost always fatal."

"So what if I asked you about being abandoned?"

He paused. "What?"

I lifted myself up. "What if we're completely abandoned out here? What if Benji comes with backup or something and we're completely outmatched? What if--?"

He sat up quickly. "Shhhh, sh-sh-sh-sh-sh. Slow down."

I shook my head. "What if I've brought you out here to do nothing but die?"

His forehead pressed against mine. "Then I die with happiness in my heart."

"Don't say shit like that."

"It's true, Dani."

He fisted my hair and pulled my head back softly so he could gaze into my eyes.

"You make me the happiest I've ever felt. And if this is where I die, I die knowing damn good and well I loved someone with my whole entire being."

I sniffled. "Max, please."

"You know as well as I do that we're not alone out here. But even if we were--and even if something did go wrong--I'm not going to let anything happen to you. Understood?"

"Don't die because of me. Okay?"

He chuckled. "You don't get a choice in that. Because if the choice is my life or yours? It's mine in a heartbeat."

My eyes watered. "I can't live without you. Don't make me do that."

"At the expense of your life? That's not a choice I can make. But I promise you this. Are you listening?"

A tear streaked my cheek. "Yeah. I am."

His eyes grew stern. "Nothing bad is happening to us tonight. Got it?"

I nodded. "Got it."

"Good."

His lips pressed against mine, but my mind was elsewhere. How in the world did he know for sure things would be all right? It boggled my mind, the kind of confidence he had about this situation. I felt his tongue slide across the slit of my lips and I gave him entrance. I invited him in as my head fell to the side, finding more distraction with every stroke of his tongue. I collapsed against him. His back crashed to the bed. And as his hands migrated beneath my jacket, I pressed my hands into the mattress.

Before pushing myself up.

"Max?"

"Yeah?"

"Does it worry you how much has changed in the past few days?"

He cocked his head. "How do you figure, gorgeous?"

I licked my lips. "I don't know. I mean, just a few weeks ago I was nothing but a normal college kid. Following my same old routine, day after day. Over and over again. Classes. Swimming. Time with Hannah. Studying. Always alone, and always so on edge."

He cupped my cheek. "You're not alone anymore, Dani. And you won't ever be. Not as long as you have me."

I sat up, still straddling his body. "That's the thing. I mean, so much has changed, you know? The way I feel. The way I see my life. And my future. Even the way I see myself has changed. I was afraid of everything, Max. And I mean every fucking thing that crossed my path. But now?"

He propped himself up on his elbows. "Now, what?"

"Now I feel… gigantic."

He grinned. "Good girl."

"I feel strong. And useful. I'm bracing for a fight. A war, really. And all of it because I found something worth fighting for in my life. Worth completely tanking myself over, if that's what it required of me."

"I don't ever want you to tank. I only want you to be happy."

"And that's the thing, Max. I am happy. For once, I'm happy about my future. I'm happy about my present. Not just content. Not just going through the motions. Not just getting through it. I'm enjoying it. I'm enjoying life. I'm enjoying you."

He smiled. "I see what the guys meant by 'speech maker.'"

I furrowed my brow. "What?"

He snickered. "The guys said you were a speech maker."

"Whoops."

"Not a bad thing. They were very impressed."

"Really?"

He nodded. "Really, really."

I smiled softly. "You said we had about an hour, right?"

He quirked an eyebrow. "Yes…?"

I grinned. "Well, what if I told you that I'm feeling a little better about things now?"

He sat upright. "Hmmm, well then. I'd tell you we've still got some time to kill."

"Poor choice of words, Casanova."

He shrugged. "Not good with them like you are. I'd rather show my efforts instead of explaining them."

"Really now?"

His face came closer. "Very much so."

I bit down on my lower lip. "Then why don't you show me what you might like to do in order to pass the time, big boy?"

He growled softly before he wrapped his arm around me. He whipped me around, causing me to squeal as my back settled against the mattress. I gazed into his heated eyes. His hand slid along my body, tracing my waist and the curves of my hips. I shivered against his touch as my nipples puckered against my bra. And as his fingers unbuttoned my jeans, he licked his lips.

"I love you, Dani."

I felt a tear streak the side of my face as I cupped his cheeks.

"Make love to me, Max."

I brought his lips down to mine and he fell against me, pinning me to the mattress with his strength and his command. I spread my legs wide to accommodate him, our tongues dueling for battle as he rolled against me. I felt his cock growing. Thickening. Pressing hard against my clothed slit. And as his lips released me, the words breathlessly fell from my lips.

"Make me forget about all of this."

He nuzzled my pulse point on my neck. "Your wish is my command."

25

MAX

I felt her heart rate speed up against my nose. She sighed so gently. So tenderly. And as her back arched for me, I pressed my lips softly against her skin. This woman set me on fire. She gave me a new passion for life. A new lust for adventure. If it hadn't been for her and her efforts, I'd still be behind the bars of my own mind. I slid on top of her glorious body and felt her legs spread for me as my lips ventured further downward, kissing the valley of her breasts. I wanted to strip her all the way down. I wanted to feel her soft skin against my own. But I didn't want someone rolling up on us while we were completely naked and bared to one another.

The idea of someone catching Dani vulnerable like that made me sick to my stomach.

Her hands threaded into my locks of hair and I growled against her clothed stomach. I let my hands slide along the expanse of her body as I knelt on the floor between her legs. I grabbed her ankles, pulling her closer to the edge. She giggled with delight as her nails softly scratched my scalp, sending shivers down my spine. I nibbled her inner legs as I unbuttoned her jeans. She groaned and jumped for my viewing pleasure as I slowly worked her zipper down. My hands slid down her legs before I removed her shoes. Then I looped my fingers into the belt loops of her jeans.

"Lift," I commanded.

Her hips rose high in the sky and I pulled them down over her pert little ass. Her cotton panties were stained with her wetness, and it only made my cock harder for her. I slid her pants to her knees before she fell back against the bed. I kissed up her soft skin, reveling in her smoothness. Her womanly scent tugged at my soul. I felt my heart skip a beat as I pressed a kiss against her clothed pussy. She gasped softly. I felt her roll, just to get more friction where she wanted it the most.

So I decided to give in.

I pulled her panties to the side and lapped up her slit. I gathered her juices on the tip of my tongue, listening as she grunted. My tongue breached her lower lips and she jumped. I felt the tip of my tongue tickling her clit, and she whimpered. I swirled around that swollen nub of hers, going as slowly as I could and watching the way her body reacted.

"Max," she moaned.

I growled as I wrapped my lips around her pulsing clit. Her legs slid over my shoulders before her thighs clamped around my cheeks. I loved it when she did that. When she threatened to drown me in her soft excess. I wrapped my arms beneath her legs, letting my hands creep up to her breasts. And as I massaged them softly, I pressed my tongue against her clit.

"Max! What the--shit!"

I grinned as her surprise orgasm took her. Damn it, I read her body like a book. The way she reacted. The way her body built up its pleasure. I knew exactly how to stroke her. How to lick her. How to make her tremble in my wake. I licked her slowly through her storm of pleasure. I felt my cock leaking against my jeans and I released her breasts in order to pull it out. I sighed with relief as I stroked my girth. I cleaned up the mess I left behind as my precum lubed my length.

But I wasn't quite ready to get up yet.

If this is our last moment together, I want to make it the best.

"Max, oh-oh-oh. I--I don't know if I can--"

I kissed her lower lips softly. "I know you've got one more for me, gorgeous."

She whimpered. "It's so sensitive. Just--fuck!"

I pressed my tongue back against her clit as I stroked my dick. She bucked wildly against me, her body jiggling and flushing for my viewing pleasure. Her juices dripped down my neck. I let her overwhelm me as I squeezed my cock tight, trying to stave off my own burst of pleasure. I groaned as my balls grew heavy. I felt them protesting the lack of release as I started stroking myself again. I edged myself as I felt her legs quivering again. I felt her hands growing tighter in my hair as her juices flooded my cheeks. She was close. I knew she was. I felt it. I smelled it. I breathed it all in. I squeezed my cock one last time, wanting nothing more than to fill her with my seed.

"Max! Yeah!"

"Come for me," I grunted.

"Yes. Yes. Yes. Yes. I'm coming. I'm coming. I love you. Holy fuck, I love you so much."

I opened my mouth to receive her offering. I swallowed all of her down before I shot up to my feet. I couldn't take it a second longer. I had to seek relief. I had to fill her. I had to feel her throbbing walls wrapped around my cock. I reached down for her legs and pulled her farther to the edge. She gasped for air as her skin flushed a deep shade of red. And me? Well, I tossed her ankles over my shoulders before I lined myself up with her entrance.

"Can I be on top?"

Her words were so breathless, I almost missed them. The fog of pleasure clouding my judgment almost caused me to plunge into her much too soon. As her soft voice pierced the carnal growl ricocheting through my head, my eyes met hers.

"Is that what you want?"

She nodded. "More than anything."

"Then of course."

Whatever she wanted tonight, she'd get. I slid her legs off my shoulders before she turned around, kicking her pants off her ankles. I watched her wiggle her way out of those panties as a grin settled against my cheeks. A satisfied grin as I watched excitement spread across her face. Normally, I wouldn't allow something like this. I wanted to be in control. Always.

But I trusted Dani.

And I trusted her enough to let me rest for a little while.

I slid out of my own boots and pants before climbing onto the bed. I lay down, my head propped up on a pillow as she straddled my hips. Her hands pressed against my chest. She leaned in for a soft kiss that made the entire world outside fade away. She licked at my lips softly, tasting herself on me with a contented sigh.

Then I felt her pussy lips rolling against my dick.

"God, you always feel so good," I murmured.

"And to think, you're not even inside yet," she whispered.

My hands slid down her sides. Her tongue pressed against mine as I parted my lips, allowing her entrance. I gripped her ass cheeks and lifted her up, positioning myself at her entrance. I felt my tip breach her walls and my girth slide against her wetness. She moaned against my lips and I felt her fingertips curling into my chest. As our hips bottomed out together, I sucked on her lower lip.

"Holy fuck," I grunted.

She pressed herself upright as she looked down at me. She cupped her clothed tits and massaged them, her head falling back in pleasure. My hands slid around to her hips. I gripped them tightly, moving her exactly as I wanted. Side to side. Up and down. Swiveling, so I could feel her juices dripping down my balls a little more. My toes curled. My heart ignited with desire. I saw something burst behind Dani's eyes. A power I'd never seen before.

It thrilled me and intoxicated me. It made me curious and filled me with wonder.

Then she smacked my hands away from her hips before her palms fell back to my chest.

"Dani, what are--holy fuck!"

She giggled as she ground against me, taking the whole of my cock inside her body. My eyes bulged and my hands fisted the sheets as she bounced wildly against my pelvis. Her juices splashed against my skin. Her moans and groans filled my ears. I pressed my heels into the bed, bucking hard against her. Meeting her thrust for thrust. I knew I wouldn't last long. Not with her walls gripping me like they were.

"That's it, Max. Come with me. Fill me up. Make me yours, forever."

I gritted my teeth. "I love you. Dani, you're the--best--I--shit--holy fuck, I'm gonna fill you with everything I have."

Feeling her command my cock in ways I'd never felt pushed me to the clouds. It was all too much for me, this powerful woman taking my pleasure into her hands. I couldn't stand it. I loved this woman more than anything. And the tighter she clamped down against me, the more my balls pulled into my body.

I'd rather die than see her in harm's way a second longer.

"Oh, Max. I'm so close. So close. So close. Yes. Yes. Yes. I love you. I love--Max!"

I sat up, wrapping my arms around her. "I love you

beyond compare, Danika Young. You're my entire world."

My voice broke as my cock exploded. I held Dani's body close against mine as we both fell back to the bed. With her body quaking against mine, I bit into her shoulder. Growling, and salivating, and grunting as threads of arousal shot from the tip of my dick. I felt her walls accepting me, pulling me further into her breathless body as my balls emptied themselves. Pump after pump after pump.

Until the two of us went limp in a heap of sweat.

I closed my eyes as Dani rested against me. I felt her heart rapidly beating against my chest as my hands trembled. My arms fell limp against the mattress. Even my legs gave way. My cock dwindled, naturally pulling out from between her legs. And when it did, a gush of fluid rushed against my skin and soaked the bed beneath me.

"Sorry," she whispered.

I chuckled. "Nothing to be sorry for."

"Oh, fuck yeah. That was marvelous."

I smiled. "I'm glad you enjoyed it."

Dani slid off to the side and I turned to wrap my arm around her waist. We shuffled out of the mess we had created before her leg slipped between mine. I held her close as we lay there, listening to the dead of night outside our motel room. With one ear turned toward the road, keeping tabs on any sound that came our way, I kept the rest of my attention on Dani.

And the way she wiggled that naked ass of hers against my tired dick.

"You might want to be careful with that," I murmured.

She snickered. "And if I'm not?"

I spanked her thigh softly. "You might just get punished, if you don't want to listen."

She moaned softly. "Sounds like fun."

I kissed the shell of her ear. "You have no idea what 'fun' is with me yet."

She wiggled tighter against me and I held her as tightly as I could. I closed my eyes and drank in the moment, committing it all to memory. The smell that hung in the air. The way she'd looked taking command of my body like she did. The way her face twisted up every time she orgasmed. The way she tasted on the tip of my tongue. The way she shivered and shook, opening up to me and snuggling tightly against my body.

Still seeking me out.

Even in her tired state.

"I love you," I whispered.

She giggled. "I love you, too, Max."

I kissed her shoulder. "No matter what happens, never forget that. Okay?"

She paused. "Okay. I won't."

"Good."

I felt her shuffling around in my arms until she twisted herself around. But her eyes didn't meet mine. Instead, she tucked her head into the crook of my neck, seeking any way out of this situation. It broke my heart. As much of a strong front as she had up, I knew she was petrified. And all because of me.

"I promise you I'm getting you out of this," I murmured.

She kissed my neck. "I don't want out if you're not at my side."

And my fear was that she meant every word of that statement.

Because if a woman like her wanted to die at my side, it made my job harder trying to save her life.

26

DANI

Every time my heart skipped a beat, I had to take in a shaky breath. But my heart wasn't skipping because of Max. I mean, my legs were shaking because of him. My hands were trembling because of him. The weakness I felt in my gut was because of him. Not my heart skipping beats, though.

Those were nerves.

"Breathe with me," he murmured.

I nodded softly. "Okay."

I felt his chest expanding against my own, so I drew in a breath through my nose. I let it in slowly, focusing on my chest meeting his in the middle. I felt our hearts intertwine. I felt his hand venture to the dip on my waist. And as he clamped his thighs down against my leg, he whispered, "Now, out."

I heard him counting mindlessly and I followed every order. I breathed in when he did, and out on the counts he created for me. I felt my heart settle back into place, but only for a moment. Because the second I stopped the breathing techniques, it would happen again.

"It's okay. I've got you, gorgeous."

I sighed. "I don't know what's wrong with me. I can't--"

He wrapped his arm around my back. "You're nervous, Dani. It's normal to be nervous in circumstances like this."

Yeah. No shit.

I wondered if Max felt the same way I did. I mean, I didn't feel his heart skipping beats. But that didn't mean he was all right. I pulled my face out from the crook of his neck and found his eyes. He winked at me, and it tickled my cheeks. Only for a second, though. I let my fingertips dance over his body. They gravitated up his torso and along his shoulder until I felt them touch down against his cheek. He felt safe. He felt like home. And the idea of having that ripped from me gave me more anxiety than I knew what to do with.

"On the count of three. Ready?" he asked.

I nodded. "Okay. I'm ready."

"In through your nose. One, two, three. Out, two, three. In, two, three. And out, two three."

A sound at the head of the bed startled me and I jumped. I pushed away from Max and leapt up, standing with my feet planted into the mattress. My knees were bent. My hands were up. I had my fists balled up as I started clocking all of the weapons I could see.

The lamp on the table to my right. The knife in the pocket of my jeans on the floor. The--

"Dani," Max said curtly.

I swallowed hard. "Are they here? Is this it?"

I felt his hand against my shin. "Dani, get down here. Everything's okay."

"What was that sound? It was very loud. Is there someone in the room next to us?"

"Remember the plan, Dani. Your fear is clouding your mind. Push through the fog and remember."

In, two, three. Out, two, three. In, two, three. Out, two, three.

I felt my fists relaxing as I slowly sank back to the bed. Max wrapped me up in his embrace as he sat up, his back falling against the headboard. He pulled me into his lap and pressed my head against his shoulder. And as the adrenaline coursing through my veins slowly ebbed into nothingness, I closed my eyes.

"The guys," I murmured.

He kissed my forehead. "Exactly. The guys. Don't be startled about sounds on either side of us. You know who's there."

I breathed out hard one last time before I opened my eyes. Good. The guys were here. That meant we weren't alone. I felt my nerves abating a bit, but not much. I mean, just because some of the guys were holed up in the rooms beside us didn't mean Benji wouldn't come with backup. And lots of it. For all we knew, he'd roll up with an army and we'd only be six or seven strong.

Please let this work. Please let this work. Please let this work.

"Are you cold?" Max's voice pierced my thoughts.

"What?"

"You're shaking. Are you cold?"

I shook my head. "No. I don't feel cold."

He pulled the comforter over us anyway. "Here. Just try to hold still and focus on your body."

"Kind of hard when death might greet us at the door."

He paused. "Have you spoken with your family at all?"

"Yeah. I have. I mean, since we've gotten out of the hospital, yes. I talked with Dad this morning."

"How did that go?"

I snickered. "I asked him for space and he practically cursed me for it."

"I'm so sorry for putting you in such a bad spot with your family."

I shook my head. "It's not your fault, Max. I made these decisions of my own volition."

"I'm not so sure about that."

I peered up at him. "What do you mean?"

When he didn't look back at me, I started moving myself. I straddled his lap. I sat up, feeling our naked pelvises pressing against one another again. I cupped his cheeks, making his eyes look deeply into mine. And as he heaved a heavy sigh, I stroked his face with my thumbs.

"What do you mean by that?" I asked.

He chewed on the inside of his cheek. "I just get the feeling that--"

"That…?"

He rolled his eyes. "Sometimes I wonder if I've forced you into this life with me. If maybe you thought you'd lose me if you didn't come along with me. So you did it just for that reason."

"What if I did?"

His face fell. "Did you?"

"I don't want to lose you. Ever, Max. Why is that a bad thing?"

He shook his head. "I should've known better. I should've known better than to have forced you into something--"

"Now, wait wait wait wait wait."

His eyes closed. "I forced you into this, didn't I?"

"Max, look at me."

"I don't know if I can."

"I'm telling you to look at me."

His eyes slowly opened. "What?"

I snickered. "How did we go from me sticking by your side so I wouldn't lose you to you forcing me into this? Because I'm pretty sure the only person who's pointed a gun at me is your father."

I felt him tense. "My father did what?"

I blinked. "Max. He got me into a chair and tied me to it. How do you think he did that? Because he sure as hell wasn't going to put his hands on me. Not without a fight."

He shook his head. "You're insane, you know that?"

"And you know you wouldn't have me any other way."

"I'm worried that I've forced you into this."

"You never once held a gun to my head and told me to make this decision or die. If anything, you've done everything you can to convince me that I'm better than this life. And look where it's gotten you."

I slid my pussy against his cock, rocking against his body. He grunted with joy, his eyes flashing with fire.

I grinned. "It's gotten you right where I want you."

He smirked. "Where *you* want *me*."

"Exactly."

I pressed my lips against his softly and his arms cloaked my back. I felt his cock slowly coming back to life beneath me as he quickly rolled me over. I giggled before his tongue filled my mouth. I felt him rake it along the roof of it, puckering every hair against my body. I wrapped my arms around his neck, feeling how ready he was to slide back inside me. And as my legs parted for him, his lips fell to my neck.

"You know, I'm not exactly the sort of guy that parents want their daughters to end up with."

I giggled. "Who I end up with--oh--isn't up to them. And I'm--shit."

He nibbled my shoulder. "You're what, gorgeous?"

I sighed. "Ready for you."

"Uh uh uh. Tell me what you were going to say."

He poised his cock at my entrance, but didn't push forward. Even if I bucked, he pulled back. Teasing me. Taunting me. Hanging me off the edge. My eyes fluttered open and my nails dug into his back. His eyes blew wide with darkened desire as I licked my lips, ready to accept the whole of him again.

"I was going to say that I'm tired of living a life where every choice I have is made by me for other people."

He kissed the tip of my nose. "So what's your next decision, gorgeous?"

Better now than never. "I'm going to drop out of school."

"What?"

I bucked against him, ready to make love to him once more. But he pulled away. And not just pulled away, but he sat back on his haunches, with his cock falling back into place as my words completely demolished the mood.

"Max?" I asked as I sat up.

He blinked. "Say that one more time."

I swallowed hard. "I'm dropping out of school."

"One more time."

I smiled. "I'm dropping out of school."

"That's what I thought you said."

I studied his face. "Why don't you look happy with me?"

"Because I'm not, Dani. Why the fuck would you drop out of school?"

"Because I don't want to be in HR. I don't want to be some human resources officer or whatever for the rest of my life. Just like I didn't want to be a pharmacist like my father."

"Then find something else. You're smart, Dani. Incredibly smart. Why the hell would you throw that away for something like this? For someone like me?"

Confusion washed over me in waves. What the hell

was this man talking about? He looked disappointed with me, which wasn't the reaction I was expecting. I watched him turn around. He turned his back to me and sat on the edge of the bed. And it wasn't until he started tossing my pants and my shoes to me that I understood what he was doing.

He was getting dressed.

"Max, what in the world?"

He stood. "You're not dropping out of school."

I snickered. "Did you not hear a thing I just said?"

He whipped around to face me. "You're not dropping out of school, and that's final."

"Isn't this the kind of thing you pulled with Benji? Not allowing him into your crew? And look where it's gotten him. Look where it's gotten you!"

He pointed at me. "You're different. You're not like him. You're not like any of us. You can choose a different degree. You can choose any path you want."

"Which is why I choose this."

"Any path but this one."

I pulled on my shoes. "Great. So I can make any decision but the one you don't want me to make? Funny. You're starting to sound like literally everyone else in my world."

"Maybe they're right."

"And maybe you're not the man I thought you were."

His back straightened. "You want to try saying that again?"

I stared him down. "If you really can't see where I'm coming from right now, then you're not the man I thought I'd fallen in love with. You're not a man at all. And I'd proclaim it from the rooftops if necessary."

He blinked, but he didn't say anything.

"I don't want to work in HR. I don't want to be a pharmacist. I don't know what the hell I want to be. All I know is that this is the normal track for people. High school, college, career. But it's not what I want for my life. All of this with you? It's made me realize I want more than mediocrity. More than average. Meeting you made me realize I never want to settle, Max. I want to change what feels right."

He blinked. "And what's that? What feels right to you?"

I didn't skip a beat. "You, Max. You feel right."

He shook his head. "Dani, I can't--"

I took his hands in mine. "You feel like home. You feel like goodness. You feel like every dream come true and every good future that could have ever come my way, all wrapped up into one. You are my future. You and whatever this life brings for us. And if--out of all this--you're the only thing left? Then I've still gotten exactly what I wanted."

"I can't let you lose everything."

"If I lose you, I lose everything. Life isn't about degrees and societal norms and social classes. It's not about parties and events and massive dinners and holidays. Life isn't about any of that shit. Life is about who you love and how you spend time with them. It's about having them in your life through thick and thin. Always. You're my everything. Not school. Not my parents. Not some bullshit roommate who thinks she's my friend when she really knows nothing about me at all."

"Your family and your friends are important."

"But not as important as you. And if you think for one second you can stop me from dropping out, you're mistaken."

He growled softly. "I don't like this."

I shrugged. "That's your prerogative. But when all of this is done, if I still have you, I'm going to be just fine."

"You deserve better than fine."

"Then I'm going to be fantastic. Perfect. Set for life. However you want to phrase that."

He sighed. "I love you too much to watch you lose everything."

"Funny how you think I had everything to begin with."

He shook his head before he pulled me against his body. He wrapped his arms around me, holding me tightly as my hands slid up his torso. They fell against his heart and I felt it beating rapidly. I placed my ear against it and sighed with relief, listening to it beat with strength and fervor and passion.

Then Max kissed the top of my head.

"I love you, Dani."

I smiled. "I love you too, Max. No matter what comes our way. Okay?"

He kissed my head again. "No matter what comes our way, gorgeous."

27

MAX

As I stood there, holding Dani in my arms, I saw lights flash against the wall. I whipped around with her still in my arms, listening as she gasped. She pulled away, but I pulled her back. I clapped my hand over her mouth as she started talking. And as my eyes peered through the blackout curtains over the window, she pulled my hand away from her mouth.

"Door. Now. I'll stay on the bed," she said.

I nodded as she pulled away from me. I watched her in my peripheral as she sat on the bed, away from the window and out of sight. She scooted up to the headboard, curling into a ball to try to keep from being seen. Playing right into the plan we had established.

It took a few seconds to get my feet to move.

I was worried about the fear gripping my gut. I'd never been this scared in my entire life. The idea that one bullet could end my entire future made me quake in my boots. And I had to find a way to gain control of my fears.

In, two, three. Out, two, three.

I silently timed my breathing as I reached the door. I peered through the peephole, trying to figure out what the fuck was going on. I looked back over at Dani and saw her staring at me. She looked as if she were about to move, so I held out my hand, silently commanding her to stay put.

The lights on the vehicle that drove up hadn't turned off yet. I peeked back through the peephole, just to make sure I had my bearings. I heard the softest footsteps on either side of me, with my men prepping themselves in the adjacent rooms. It was the only thing that gave me hope as I studied him on the other side of the door. That short stature. Those broad shoulders. That ratty-ass leather jacket and those black jeans with holes in his pants.

Benji.

Benji was on the other side of the door.

He walked with a limp and his arm was cradled against his stomach. But I saw he was packing heat. On both hips, actually. The bruises on his face and his split lip filled me with pride, but also regret.

Because I should've killed that asshole when I had the chance.

A rush of nerves poured over me as my hand fell to the doorknob. I reached my other hand out for the wall and softly drummed my fingers against it. I held my breath as I flipped the lock, sliding the door chain out of place. I turned it slowly and tried my best to control my movements. Because I sure as hell didn't want to betray how anxious I was about this plan.

Then, as the door eased open, my eyes fell upon a massive black SUV still shining its fucking lights against the window of our motel room.

Benji grinned up at me as I looked down at him. Then the sound of a door opening caught my ear. My eyes traveled over the top of his head and I watched as three other men get out of the vehicle. I studied them as they slammed their doors, obviously wanting to announce their presence. They buttoned up their suit jackets and made their way for the sidewalk, sunglasses covering their faces.

I didn't recognize them at all.

Then another car pulled up.

Time to start the game.

"You got something you want to say? Or should we just start shooting?"

Benji snickered. "Really, Max. Is that any way to greet family?"

"Just answer the question."

"Or I could simply draw my weapon and put a bullet in your chest."

I heard Dani moving, and it filled me with relief. As Benji smirked up at me, I clocked her sliding off the bed and pressing herself along the wall. I prayed my cousin couldn't hear the soft rapping of her fingers against the plastered wall before she slipped into the bathroom. And the second I heard that door click behind me, I threw caution to the wind.

"Come and get some, then, I guess," I said.

The second he lunged at me, I slammed the door closed. I heard his entire body hit it full force before the sound of crunching cartilage sounded in my ear. My smile practically split my face in half. I flipped the lock and backed up, moving to the dresser. I opened the first drawer and pulled out my shotgun as someone slammed against the door. I stuffed my pockets with ammunition and loaded the damn thing as Benji struggled to get the door open.

The sound of a muffled pistol sounded before the doorknob became nothing but a piece of useless metal on the floor.

"Gotta pick the right lock first!" I exclaimed.

Benji snarled. "When I get my hands on you, you're dead, Max. You hear me? Dead!"

I stuffed a pistol into the back of my jeans and flipped my jacket over it. And just as the door came crashing in, I leveled my shotgun. The door slammed against the wall, with the corner embedding itself into the plaster. Benji strode in with a muffled pistol pointed directly at my face, so I decided to return the courtesy.

I raised my shotgun to his eye level as I backed closer to the bathroom door.

"Well, well, well. What do we have here?" Benji asked.

"A dead man, soon enough."

He snickered. "And yet, I'm pretty sure you're going to be the dead one in a minute."

"If you wanted me dead, you would've already shot me."

"See, that's where you're wrong, Max. Because

unlike your father, I enjoy watching people squirm. Especially people who tried to keep me down all these years."

I shrugged. "Sorry for assuming you had more potential. I guess even presidents get it wrong sometimes."

His hand started trembling. "I never took you for the running sort, Max. But I suppose love makes men do stupid things."

I stood in front of the bathroom door as a disgusting smile swept across his face.

"Hello, Bambi. Enjoying the bottom of that bathtub?"

Fuck.

I heard the bathroom door open behind me and I prayed to any god listening that nerves weren't clouding Dani's judgment. I needed her to remember her part in this plan. I made sure to take my place between her and Benji . But it worried me when I didn't feel my leather jacket creeping up my back.

Come on, Dani. Take the fucking gun.

Benji seemed oblivious to her behind me. "Your brother showed his true colors tonight, you know."

I nodded. "I'm sure he did."

"He chose the winning side. Want to know why?"

I shrugged. "I'm sure you'll tell me anyway. Pompous men always do that."

He chuckled. "He knows your ship is sinking. He knows your father is going to change the way the game is played. And he knows he can cash in if he's on the right side. See, Max? Money rules all. And your father has a great deal of it. How does that make you feel?"

"I guess relieved. Because I sure as hell don't want to put up with cowards like John."

His eyes ran down my body. "At least one of you has some self-preservation skills."

"He's a coward and nothing more. Just like you."

"You're the one who ran, Max. Who's the coward now?"

The suited men behind him chuckled, and I gritted my teeth to keep from firing back.

"What has my father offered you anyway, Benji? Hmm? What the hell is so important that it's worth turning your back on the people who treated you like family? The people who are family?"

"That's rich, coming from you. Because when I tried to make myself family and pledge your pathetic little crew, you denied me. Time and time again. Doesn't really sound like family, does it?"

"All I wanted was the best for you. You've got smarts, Benji. You could've gotten yourself a degree and really made something of yourself instead of scraping the bottom of the bucket of what this life has to offer. That's what I wanted for you. And instead, you decided to get selfish. To throw it all away, and for what?"

He chuckled bitterly. "For family, Max. For loyalty. For camaraderie. But you don't care about any of that shit, do you?"

"I've always cared about you, Benji. About family. About life, and love, and loyalty."

"Yeah, only when it suits you though, right?"

"Stop twisting my words and--"

He cocked his gun. "All you wanted to be was right, Max. That's all you ever care about. Being seen as some big man with big plans and big dreams. And always, always right. That's why you pushed college so hard. Because to you, this life was a fallback. Because you had nothing else to give this world. Well, you know what? I chose this life. Even though I had another road to take, I chose this one. It wasn't a fallback for me. It wasn't a last resort just to stay alive. I love what I do and the people that surround me. I don't let my want to be right cloud my judgment. You do, though. All you care about is being right instead of being *in* the right."

I hated how true his words were.

"Max. Let's be honest for a second. Can we be honest?"

"I'd rather you shoot me."

He chuckled. "All right, honesty it is. You and your little crew are nothing but a bunch of posers. You have no power. No wealth. You haven't had jobs in months. You've got nothing. You *have* nothing. You're flies compared to your father. No, no, no. You're the larvae of flies. And that man's offering me more money than I could even dream of. He's offering me a life. A *real* life."

"Killing people and making ties with one of the foulest men on the planet is a real life for you?"

He shrugged. "If I have to get my hands dirty to

earn it, I'm fine with that. Plus, I don't plan on staying by your father's side forever."

"So what? You're going to be his part-time enforcer before you take his place?"

He grinned. "You won't be alive for it, so what does it matter?"

"I mean, you've been flapping your lips this entire time. Might as well fill me in on the rest before you splatter my brains against the mirror. Right?"

"You think you can taunt me, but it won't work. I know how this ends. I've seen it."

"Seen it, huh? I wonder how my father would take to partnering himself with someone who has hallucinations. Guys, did you know he hears voices?"

He pressed the pistol to my forehead. "Shut up!"

I finally felt Dani lifting up my leather jacket. "And here I was thinking all you were good for was a punching bag."

"Your father sees potential in me. Not my fault you didn't."

"All he sees in you is a dumbass that's easy to take advantage of."

Benji hissed, "He's building a fucking empire, you ungrateful piece of shit. One sliver at a time. He knew he could pay the police off to broaden his operations. But he also knew that if you caught wind of what he was up to, you'd expose him. And you can't build an empire from prison."

I shook my head. "What the hell have you gotten yourself into, Benji?"

His smile grew positively maniacal. "There's a lot of money in drug smuggling, Max."

And there it was. The entire reason Benji was doing this. The entire reason my father had been hunting us down. Hunting *me* down. All for some measly drug-peddling. It had taken John over two years once he took over the Red Thorns to get us out of the drug game. And it still took me the better part of a year to really clean out the crew and get rid of the guys still dealing behind our fucking backs.

I should've known. I should've fucking known.

"You have no idea what you're getting yourself into, Benji."

His eyes grew wide. "With your father's expansion, he'll have control over this whole region. And his reach will grow, mark my words. Others will come. Others will want a home only your father can provide. A home they'd never find with you. Then there won't be a damn soul to stand between him and his kingdom because you and your little deer will be six feet underground. And all by my hand."

I pressed my shotgun into his gut as his eyes sparkled with something unrecognizable. An evil and a greediness I'd never seen anywhere. Not even in my father's eyes.

"Any last words?" he asked.

I nodded. "Yeah, I do."

"Then let me have them. I promise I'll deliver them to someone that I think will care."

"I take it this is where you say, 'which is no one.'"

He snickered. "Guess you aren't as stupid as you look. So got those words for me?"

"Yeah. I do."

I felt Dani's warmth back away from me and I grew worried as to what she was doing.

"Come on. You really don't want to keep me waiting, Maxxy-poo."

I grinned. "You talk way too much."

28

DANI

I drummed my fingers on the outer wall of the motel on the other side of the tub. Hoping and praying someone heard me. Then I quickly stepped out from around Max and held up my hands.

"Please! Don't shoot."

Benji's eyes stayed locked with Max. "Truth be told, I can't believe you're still here, Bambi. Maybe you aren't the doe-eyed waste of space I thought you were."

As much as I wanted to lash out at him for the insult, I let it roll off my back. Benji had said enough in the last few minutes to get both Max and Rupert off the hook. As well as throw Benji in prison for a very, very long time. All I needed was to keep people from firing any guns. Because if gunshots rang out, that destroyed everything. There were supposed to be precautions in case Benji came in with guns blazing.

But he hadn't. He came here to say what he needed to say first.

And we got it recorded.

Just a few more seconds, Dani. Stall him.

Benji's eyes returned to Max. "Any last words, you two?"

I shrugged. "Only a few."

Max hissed. "Dani, shut up."

I snickered. "Funny that you think you can make me shut up."

Benji grinned. "Cute. Now, what is it?"

With my arms hanging slack at my sides, I rolled my shoulders back. I felt the pistol I'd taken from Max's belt band pressing against my side. I wasn't sure if anyone could see it. Part of me hoped they did, but part of me hoped they didn't. So without wasting any more time, I launched into the only plan I'd quickly formulated in my head.

"You made a mistake," I said.

Benji blinked. "I take it you're going to tell me what I've done?"

I nodded. "Yep. Your mistake was coming after us."

He feathered the trigger. "Desperate people say desperate things. Why do I get the feeling you're only stalling for time?"

I shook my head. "Nope. We knew you'd come. We counted on it, actually. And now? Here you are. Just like the pawn we thought you were."

Max grumbled, "That's enough."

Benji's hand trembled. "Let the woman finish. God, you're always such an asshole, Max."

I drew in a deep breath. "Did you really think Max would run? I mean, really. Truly. Running from a fight. Has he ever done that? Did you really think he'd do that?"

Benji's eye twitched. "Tell your girl to shut up."

Max shrugged. "I'm pretty sure she's already showed you that she doesn't listen to me."

I smiled. "It's kind of true. Max likes to portray that he's got me on a leash. But his ass is mine for bailing him out of all this stuff."

Benji hissed. "You didn't bail him out of shit."

I shrugged. "That's cool if you think that. But if you shoot Max? You'll never know how I got him out of that holding cell eight hours earlier than intended."

Benji's eyes finally snapped my way. "What?"

"You're curious, aren't you? How I knew when the crew needed to be at the police station. How Max got out of jail sooner than instructed. How I figured out that Max's father had half the damn police department in his pocket. You want to know all these things, right? So you can report back to Mr. Ryddle like a good little puppy?"

"Seriously, gorgeous. That's enough."

Benji feathered the trigger again. "Let the woman speak."

I smiled. "Thank you, Benji. Now where was I? Oh, yes. I was telling you exactly how I knew everything I needed to in order to get Max out of that holding cell."

"Spit it out or eat lead, sister."

"Wow. So very impatient. I'm sure Mr. Ryddle wouldn't like that one."

Benji whipped his gun over to me. "Tell me!"

Max jumped in front of me again. "You keep that thing pointed at me, asshole."

I peered from around Max's body and grinned. "John did everything we told him to, Benji."

He blinked. "What does this have to do with--?"

"Oh, I'm back to our current predicament. Where you said John was a coward? I mean really, Benj. Keep the hell up."

"Dani."

I patted Max three times on the back. Signaling to him that we still needed time. Just like the signals we'd talked about on the way to the motel.

And he shut up.

"Benj--can I call you Benj?--John did everything we asked him to. He's good, too. Right? And you did exactly what we thought you'd do. You came right here, putting yourself in harm's way with a gun you barely know how to wield. And where's Mr. Ryddle?"

Benji swallowed hard. "I'm just fine with guns, thanks."

"I don't know, dude. The shaking of your hand doesn't make me very confident."

Max snickered. "You and me both, gorgeous."

Benji roared. "Shut up and tell me what the fuck's going on!"

I smiled. "Your loyal and stunning chief is lying in a hospital bed, safe and sound. While you're out here doing all of his dirty work. Taking all of his bullets. It's really a shame that you're going to take the fall for him. But hey. You had it coming, you asshole."

Benji's eye twitched yet again. "I think I'm going to enjoy splattering your brains against the wall first, Bambi."

And as his gun moved back to me, Max started yelling.

"Now! Now! Now! Now!"

Sirens wailed and lights flashed. I heard tires squealing in the parking lot as something crashed against metal outside. I smiled brightly at Benji as his suited men started yelling at one another, shouting commands and scrambling to get into places to defend themselves. Benji peered over his shoulder and Max took the opening. He wrestled with the lanky man, scrambling to get the gun out of his hand.

"Come on, you piece of shit," Max growled.

Benji looked up at me. "You bitch!"

I giggled. "Don't get all nasty because I outsmarted you, dickhole. Also, the police heard everything. They know you were sent to kill Max. And me. They know you had a hand in my kidnapping."

Max grunted. "A little help here, gorgeous."

He forced Benji's hand to the floor and I saw him trying to pull the trigger. So I raised my boot and stomped down onto Benji's wrist. He cried out in pain as police swarmed the motel room, and I kicked the gun into the bathroom.

"You want to know what they also know?" I asked.

Benji growled. "I'm going to kill you. I'm going to slaughter you all!"

I dipped down to meet his eyes. "They know you're on Mr. Ryddle's payroll. They know you're his right hand man. Which means you're going to jail for life, sweet cheeks. All because you put your trust in the wrong damn person."

Benji spat at me. "If you think I can't make moves from prison, you're sorely mistaken."

I bopped his nose. "I'll be waiting then, *Bambi*."

Max chuckled as he ripped Benji from the floor. He was flailing and bleeding and screaming and cursing. Making a massive scene as Max tossed him into the arms of the S.W.A.T. officers clearing the room. I watched the suited men get hauled out in handcuffs. I listened to them read Benji his rights as Max wrapped his arm around me. I wrapped my arms over my chest and tucked myself tightly against his body, seeking his comfort and his warmth as Benji slung insults and threats around.

"You stupid little asshole. I'm going to get you both. You mark my words and watch me! By the time I'm out of prison, the two of you will be dead, I tell you. Fucking dead!"

Max snickered. "Good luck with all that solitary confinement you're racking up for yourself."

Benji shrieked. "Fuck you! Ashton was going to kill John as well. He wanted you *both* dead. He knew you'd stand in his way when his business grew and other criminals started flocking here. He ordered the hits on you, Max. He orchestrated the attack outside the club when he hired you for security detail. Your client was supposed to get hit and his sons were supposed to come after y--"

Max shook his head. "Can you shut him up?"

The S.W.A.T. officer shrugged. "Why? We read him his rights and he's feeding us more information. Far as we're concerned, he'll give us enough to go after your father as well."

Benji started panicking. "Wait, what? No, no. I didn't mean all of that. I mean, all I meant was--"

I clicked my tongue. "So which is it? Are you the mastermind? Or is Ashton?"

Benji tried spitting at me again. "I'd rather die than tell you any fucking thing, you piece of shit."

Max tsked. "Such foul language from a college student. I mean, really, Dani. What is he thinking?"

I giggled. "I don't know. But I like this hole he's digging. Maybe he'll get it all the way down to six feet before your father decides to off him in prison."

The S.W.A.T. officer scolded us. "All right, you two. That's enough. Don't give us a reason to arrest you guys as well."

I held up my hands. "I'm as innocent as they come."

Max muttered under his breath, "Over my dead body."

I nudged him playfully as another S.W.A.T. officer rushed into the room. She pulled off her helmet and stared at Benji, her nose softly wrinkled. The look in her eyes said, *Really? This is him?* But the stance of her body said, *Come at me and you're dead.*' Then she turned and locked her eyes with mine.

"Well done," the police captain said. "I have to admit, I'm not sure my people could've pulled that off better than you two."

I nodded. "Anything to help the department. I'm assuming this means Max is off the hook?"

Max butted in. "And Rupert?"

The captain nodded. "Once we get this man booked and in a holding cell, your friend will be released. It's more precautionary than anything else. We want to make sure there's absolutely no threat before we release him. And once we do, we'll provide a police escort back to his place."

I grinned. "You don't have to bother with that. We've got thirty-four men ready to escort him back to his place."

Max pulled me tightly against his body. "Thank you for the offer, though, Captain."

She nodded. "The offer's there should you change your mind. Now, time to take out the trash."

I saw Benji's eyes grow wide and I had to stifle a laugh. Man, he looked absolutely ridiculous. Leading this kind of lifestyle, yet not ready for the consequences of his actions. His glare quickly turned into a look of panic, and I couldn't help the words that fell from my mouth.

"What's the matter, sweet cheeks? You look like a deer in headlights."

Max chuckled. "Yeah, Bambi."

I nudged him. "Hey, I kind of still like that name. Let's not try to taint it too much."

He winked at me. "Whatever you want, gorgeous."

Benji struggled against the officers as they hauled him out of the motel room. I watched him peer over his shoulder with one last glare before they turned the corner and fell out of sight. I peeked out the door and finally saw what made such a booming crash. And as giggles fell from my lips, Max joined me with his own chuckles.

The massive S.W.A.T. vehicle had slammed straight into the black SUV that hauled those men here in the first place.

"I suppose that's one way to get the job done," I murmured.

Max rubbed my back. "You were amazing. You know that, right?"

I looked up at him. "I'm amazing because you believe I am. Without you, though--"

He fisted my hair. "Don't you even say it. You know damn good and well this was your plan. I helped with the bare bones, and you filled in the details. Without you, this wouldn't have happened."

"Thanks, handsome."

"Great stalling tactic, by the way. I approve."

"I figured you'd like it."

"How did you know we needed more time, though?"

I nodded into the bathroom. "I kept hearing someone on the other side drumming their fingers against the wall. And when the drumming stopped, I figured we were okay at that point."

"How did I not hear the drumming?"

I reached up, stroking the shell of his ear. "Guess you've heard one too many loud booms in your lifetime."

He snickered. "You're damn right about that."

With Max guiding me along, we walked over to the window and pulled back the blinds. With my head leaning against his chest, I watched as the captain stuffed Benji into the back of a cop cruiser. The three suited men were driven off into the night with sirens blaring and lights flashing every which direction. I watched the S.W.A.T. team speaking with other police officers before everyone parted ways. As the cars all cleared out, the captain turned back to face us.

Before starting her way back into the motel room.

29

MAX

Everything happened in such a blur I was almost taken aback. Almost. While I'd been part of shady, underground situations, I'd never been part of a police bust before. A part of me worried that something Benji might reveal would take us down again. Put me back in cuffs or put Rupert back behind bars. The only thing that kept me grounded was the feeling of Dani pressed against my body. Her head softly leaning against my chest. I stared out the window, my eyes following the cruiser that escorted Benji away from this fucking place.

Then the captain came back into the room.

"I don't know how to thank you two enough," she said.

Dani giggled. "Well, for starters, you can guarantee that neither myself, Max, nor any of the Red Thorns will be arrested after we helped you with something like this. A lot of us put our neck on the line to make this work. The last thing I want to see is it backfiring in our faces like that."

Captain nodded. "You've got my word on that. I've already drawn up deals for all of you to sign. Because I sure as hell am not going to be pissing off the men who have had direct contact with Ashton Ryddle."

I licked my lips. "I'm assuming you'll want some of us to testify?"

Captain sighed. "If it comes down to it, I'm hoping so. I've been building a case against Ashton Ryddle for years. And do you know how hard it is to pin down a man like him?"

Dani laughed bitterly. "Yeah. I think we have an idea."

I snickered. "I've got more than an idea, honestly."

The captain shook her head. "I mean, nobody takes me seriously with it. Any time the name 'Ryddle' comes up in anything--any report, any testimony, any story--cops just run for the hills like little fire ants. But this time? This time I have enough to make it stick. And it's because of you two."

I nodded. "Trust me, we were more than glad to help."

Dani wrapped her arm around me. "Just as long as it's worth our while in terms of our safety."

Captain chuckled. "It will be, I promise. I'm not going to drag my feet on that paperwork, either. Thank you for working with me to close this once and for all. I couldn't have done it without you. And I'll see to it that everyone is compensated accordingly."

I looked down at Dani. "I'll be okay with Rupert out of jail and making sure my woman's safe."

Dani looked up at me. "And I'll be okay with making sure my men are safe. All of them."

I quirked an eyebrow. "Something I should know, gorgeous?"

She giggled. "You didn't think you were the only one who cared about the Red Thorns, did you?"

I lowered my voice. "We're technically not supposed to say anything like that around cops."

The captain laughed. "I'll let it slide this one time. Just make sure to keep your noses clean, yeah? This is a fresh start for all of you. Make it worth something, all right?"

I nodded. "You've got my word on that. Especially if my father's going to be off the streets."

The captain placed her hand on my shoulder. "You give me a few days, and you've got exactly that."

I held my free hand out for her to shake. And when she did, Dani did the same. Finally, it felt like I had some sort of closure in this situation. But something still tickled at the back of my mind.

Something I couldn't explain.

I clicked my tongue. "Captain, by any chance, is my father--?"

She smiled. "Already in police custody. While he recovers in the hospital, of course. When my men confirmed for me that they had what they needed on their recordings, I ordered your father's room to be guarded at all times. He's cuffed to the bed, he isn't allowed anywhere without two police escorts, and he'll be headed straight to the station once he's discharged from the hospital."

I sighed. "Thank you. That's a relief."

Dani rubbed my back with her hand. "When will the court dates start, do you think?"

Captain shrugged. "Things like this can take some time. With a name as infamous as Ashton Ryddle, though, I assume things will get pushed up. Timelines will be obstructed to deal with this particular case. And it will get messy, you have my word on that."

I snickered. "Trust me, anything involving my father is messy, no matter how you go about it."

The captain rolled her eyes. "Don't I know it."

I heard worry creep into Dani's voice. "How messy, do you think?"

The captain sighed. "I'm bracing for this to be the messiest case I've handled up until this point. I suspect Ashton will attempt to throw us everything he's got. Fight until he's got no reason to fight. And men like him always have a further reach than anyone expects."

I narrowed my eyes. "What are you trying to say?"

She shrugged. "All I'm saying is, if you two don't have a vacation planned, it might be a good time to take one. At least until this all blows over."

Dani murmured, "Sounds like a bit more than a vacation."

I held her against me. "Got any suggestions on where we should end up?"

The captain grinned. "You two got passports? I hear Bora Bora is great this time of year."

Dani giggled breathlessly. "We'll think about it."

I nodded. "Yes. We'll think about it."

The captain licked her lips. "Suit yourself. You two got a way home?"

I nodded to the truck. "We rented a truck to get us out here. And since that S.W.A.T. vehicle of yours didn't crunch it to bits, we've got ourselves a way back into town."

She barked with laughter. "Yeah. Connelly gets a bit high-and-mighty with that steering wheel. But I figured, why not? Anyone else is in that vehicle, we gotta pin 'em somehow."

Dani snickered. "Well, thank you for missing the truck."

Captain saluted us with two fingers. "Anytime."

I held my hand out one last time. "Thanks for everything, Cap."

She shook my hand. "And thank you two. For everything. But, seriously, think about getting out of town. At least until the trials start to strike up. That goes for all of you guys that have tangoed with Ashton. Might do you all some good to get some fresh air anyway."

"I'll definitely take it into consideration, thanks."

I gazed down at Dani and she smiled up at me. For all the trembling her body kept doing, she sure as hell had her fight face on. I was more than proud of her. For once, I felt as if I was the one not taking the reins. Not shining in the presence of darkness. All of this had been her. From helping me concoct the plan to placing the right kind of calls. Hell, even the truck rental was her suggestion. Not mine.

"We did good, gorgeous."

She winked. "We did good, handsome."

Cap interjected. "Oh, and one last thing."

Dani and I both looked at her as she dug around in her pocket. Before pulling out a square white card, of course.

"If either of you need anything--whether it's related to this case or not--you give me a call. Got it?"

I took her card. "You have my word."

Dani nodded. "Thank you. We appreciate it a lot."

Cap slid her helmet onto her head. "And we appreciate you two."

"Oh, oh, oh. Just one more thing," I said.

Cap turned her back to us. "Don't worry. Your friend Rupert will be released as soon as I get back to the precinct. So if there's nothing else..."

I shook my head. "Nope. Definitely not anything else."

Cap peered over her shoulder, looking at us through the visor of her helmet. Had I been able to see her face, I knew she'd be smirking underneath that thing. It looked positively badass. She put her hand in the air and waved at us as she walked out of the busted motel room, her shoulders squared off strong and her stride filled with confidence. I led Dani over to the door as we stood there, watching her climb into the passenger's seat of the massive S.W.A.T. battering ram they called a vehicle.

Then they backed up and drove away.

Leaving us alone with all the carnage.

Dani sighed heavily. "Holy shit."

I let out the breath I had been holding. "You got that right."

"So do we head back to your place? Do we get another room? What do you want to do?"

I grinned. "You mean you don't want to stay in this room for the night? I mean, it's already booked and paid for."

"Absolutely fucking not."

I threw my head back with laughter. "Just wanted to make sure I wasn't assuming something I shouldn't have."

"Yeah, yeah, yeah. You just like living on the edge, you weirdo."

"Hey, you're the one still here, helping me out with all this shit."

She scoffed. "What do you mean, helping? This entire damn thing was my idea."

I rolled my eyes. "And I'll never hear the end of it."

"Not if you want to get laid, you won't."

"Ugh. You drive a hard bargain."

"Takes a hard one to give a hard one."

The bark of my laughter filled the room as Dani's giggles soared on the foundation I provided for her. I wrapped my arms around her and pulled her close, kissing the top of her head. What an insane human being she turned out to be. And she was damn near perfect.

No, she is perfect.

I kissed the top of her head before I released her. I walked over to my small suitcase in the corner and picked it up. Dani dug through the mire and the chaos of the motel room until she found her bag of belongings. Then together we headed out to the truck.

Dani tossed her bag into the back seat. "Is it bad of me to think that I'm still shocked this all went off without a hitch?"

I tossed mine on top of hers. "Nope. Because I was just thinking the exact same thing."

"How many times do you think we do that during the day?"

"Do what?"

"Have the same thoughts."

I climbed into the driver's seat. "I don't know. I'd imagine more times than we figure. Why?"

She climbed in next to me. "Care to figure out what's on my mind now?"

I looked over at her and watched a carnal darkness roll over her eyes. My cock pulsed to life as I closed my truck door, slamming it with purpose. I leaned over and captured Dani's lips, letting my tongue slide against hers as she cupped my cheek. So long as I lived, I'd never get enough of this woman. She'd never cease to amaze me, and she'd always have my heart.

So long as I lived.

"Mmmm, I think I know exactly what you're thinking, gorgeous."

She nuzzled my nose. "Good. Because I'm starving."

"For this meat, huh?"

She blinked. "No, crazy. For a cheeseburger. Duh."

I paused. "Seriously?"

She smiled brightly. "Then maybe some dessert. Like a milkshake."

"Poured over your body, I hope."

She bopped my nose with her finger. "Be a good boy, and you can cover my body in anything you want."

"Mmmm, yes ma'am."

I captured her lips, reveling in how wonderful she tasted. But she was right. If I was hungry, she *had* to be hungry. The tiny little thing. I slid my fingers through her hair, gripping her tendrils softly. And after pulling her face away from mine, I lost myself in her gorgeous brown eyes.

"Thank you."

She furrowed her brow. "For what, Max?"

"For saving me. For planning this all out. For working a fucking miracle and somehow saving my guys in the process."

"Our guys."

I smirked. "Right. Our guys. Thank you, Dani. For bringing your intelligence into this scenario. Because without it, I don't know where the hell we'd be."

She smiled. "Well, now we're even. You save my life, and I save yours."

30

DANI

The four-hour drive back to Max's place tasted like victory and smelled like paradise. The cheeseburgers we picked up along the way filled the cabin of the car as we chowed down and wiped our faces with cheap paper napkins. The minutes ticked by as we sped down the highway with the windows rolled down and the classic rock station blaring. It was the freest I'd felt in a very long time. And seeing Max relaxed for the first time since I'd met him was something I never thought I'd witness.

"I like this side of you, handsome."

Max snickered. "What side of me?"

"So cool, and calm, and relaxed."

"What? I'm like that all the time."

I blew a raspberry. "Yeah, right."

He took the exit we needed. "I'm always calm. That's what makes me tick."

"Calmness makes you tick?"

"Yeah. Why not?"

"I'm pretty sure that phrase doesn't mean what you think it means."

He clutched his heart. "Your words. They hurt. Oh. I never thought I'd see the day when you lorded your college degree over my head."

"Well, newsflash, hot stuff, I don't have a college degree yet. And I won't. Ever."

"Yeah, we still need to talk about that."

I shrugged. "We can talk. That's fine. It won't change my opinion, though."

His hand fell against my knee. "I've got ways of persuading you."

"Max."

"Dani."

"You can't make me do something I don't want to do."

"Then I guess you'll just have to truly convince me that you really don't want college in your life. Because I don't believe that shit for a second."

I settled my hand on top of his as we finally got back into familiar territory. It was a few minutes past two in the morning, and the grease in my stomach had finally settled. I felt my eyes drooping, a need for sleep overcoming my body. I had finally come down from my adrenaline high, and all I wanted to do was slip off into dreamland for a few hours.

"Holy shit. Rupert!"

The truck slammed into park and my body lurched. I heard a door rip open before heavy footsteps scuttled across the ground. I had to blink the sleepiness away for a while before the dark world came into focus. And when I saw John on the porch with a smile on his face, I quickly found Max. Embracing Rupert.

In front of the truck.

I drew in a deep breath as I unbuckled myself. I heard the sound of motorcycle engines revving in the distance. Dozens of them. As if to say 'goodbye for now' one last time. I hopped out of the truck and walked over to Rupert, my arms opened wide for the redheaded, bearded man in the beanie. He patted Max's back as laughter fell from both of their mouths. I eyed Rupert and he quickly pulled away, then scooped me up into his arms. He twirled me around, making me giggle before he set me back down. And as I rubbed his arms, I let my eyes dance over his body.

"You don't look hurt. Are you hungry? I think there's a pizza joint that's still op--"

"Bambi, look at me."

My eyes panned up to his face. "It's really good to see you, Rupert."

He smiled. "It's good to see you, too, badass."

I blinked. "What?"

Max placed his hand on my lower back. "Yeah, Dani. You're a badass now. Deal with it."

I shook my head. "I don't--I don't know how--"

Rupert released me from his grip. "Don't go getting all coy on us now. John told me the plan. He told me everything that was supposed to happen, and whose idea it was all along."

John limped up to us on his cane. "Yep. Oh, and a woman S.W.A.T. captain told us to send her regards to you two. She said 'Hopefully this proves you can trust her.'"

I drew in a relieved breath. "It sure as hell does. It's good to see you standing here, Rupert."

He snickered. "To be honest? Wasn't sure it would happen. I just knew I was spending the rest of my life in that fucking place."

I shrugged. "We're family. It's what we do."

Rupert laughed. "You're a real, tried and true badass, Bambi. We'd be fucked without you."

I paused. "Come to think of it? Yeah. You probably would be."

The guys around me laughed before Max guided me into the house. There were beers in the fridge waiting to be popped open and a bottle of wine. Just for me. I smiled and thanked John for his courteousness. Because I knew none of these assholes drank wine. Ever. And while I knew our worries weren't entirely over--what with the trials coming up now--I still felt a great relief deep in the pit of my heart.

Max lifted his beer. "To the future."

John lifted his, too. "And to the happiness it brings."

Rupert raised his glass bottle. "May families stick together for as long as they can."

They all looked at me to finish, so I raised the entire bottle of wine in the air.

"And may our asses stay out of fucking jail."

Max snorted. "Hear fucking hear."

The rest of us exclaimed together, "Hear, hear!"

I screwed the top off the wine and took a few big

gulps. I let the alcohol wash away all the what ifs and what happens nows. I let the wine fill my throat as the guys chugged back their beers. And all I let my mind think about was freedom. How we were all free from Ashton's grasp. How Max was free from his intimidation tactics. How I was free from worrying that disgusting man would come back after me. We were free from him, we were free from Benji, and--for now, at least--we were free from worry.

And we were safe.

"You guys hungry?" Rupert asked. "Or did you eat on the way back from the motel?"

Max finished off his beer. "We picked up cheeseburgers from a drive-in place on the way back. But I wouldn't mind eating again. If you're hungry."

John pulled out his phone. "Dani was right, by the way. There's a pizza place in town that's open until three. Any specific toppings?"

Rupert piped up. "You know I'm good with anything except anchovies."

I shook my head. "I still can't believe people put that nasty shit on their pizza."

"Right? It's gross. Fishy tastes don't belong on pizza."

"Though I'd eat pickled halibut like it was my day job, if I had some."

Rupert's jaw dropped open. "You like that shit, too?"

Max rolled his eyes. "Oh, here we go."

John butted in. "Three large meat supreme pizzas,

one with all the vegetables, one with nothing else, and one with hot sauce. Anything else?"

I licked my lips. "What about something sweet for dessert?"

Max chuckled. "I've already got dessert right here."

He pulled me against his side and the guys lifted their beers in the air. As if to cheer the actions they knew would take place after we were done feasting.

I sighed. "Anyway, pickled halibut is awesome. If you've got a connection, I expect you to hook me up. You know, for saving your ass and all."

Rupert chuckled. "We're family. I'd hook you up anyway. I've actually got four jars in my fridge right now. I'll give you one to hold you over. You put it on crackers?"

"I'd put that shit on anything. You should make a sandwich out of it sometime. A bit of pepperjack, some spicy mustard. Holy hell, that's eating."

Max shivered. "You guys are gross."

I laughed. "More for me, then, I guess. Don't worry, though. I'll let you know when I'm munching on it so you don't accidentally kiss me."

John chuckled. "There's no 'accidentally' doing anything around pickled halibut. You can smell that shit from a mile away."

Rupert shook his head. "And it's the best shit alive."

Max wrinkled his nose. "Nope. I'm good. Thanks."

John tucked his phone away. "Got the order placed. It should be here in about thirty-five minutes."

I leaned my head against Max. "So what do we want to do until the pizza gets here?"

We all looked around at one another before Rupert turned to face the porch.

"Want to sit outside without fear of being picked off?"

And the four of us couldn't dash outside to the porch table quickly enough.

31

MAX

I tossed the last of the beer bottles into the trash can as snores came from the living room. I brushed my hands off on my jeans and walked into the room, chuckling at the sight. Granted, it was almost four in the morning. So it didn't shock me one bit to see everyone passed out. Dani was on the sofa with her legs tucked against her and a blanket pulled up to her chin. Rupert was asleep upright in the recliner with his chin against his chest. I heard John's honking snores all the way down the damn hallway, pulling in the curtains from the other side of the house. And as I walked over to the recliner, I drew in a deep breath.

For once, I felt at ease.

I put the feet up on the chair and leaned it back, which stopped Rupert's snoring. I took the blanket off Dani and tossed it over him, knowing damn good and well the man would be passed out until noon at least.

Then I walked over and gazed down at my beautiful, wonderful woman.

I smoothed her hair away from her face, dipped down, and scooped my arms underneath her. I lifted her into the air, holding her closely against my chest. I was still wide awake. More so from excitement than anything else. For my entire life, I had walked on eggshells because of my father. I jumped at every little sound because I wondered if he was coming for me. For years, I had kept my guard up, always questioning things and always wondering if people around me were in cahoots with him. And now, for the first time in my life, I had no worries on my shoulders.

It was something I wanted to celebrate.

"Here we go," I murmured.

I kicked the bedroom door closed behind me and felt Dani stirring against my chest. I walked over to the bed and settled her down just as her eyes fluttered open. She drew in a deep breath, curling deeper into me. And as I pulled the comforter up her body, I kissed her forehead.

"Go back to sleep, gorgeous. You'll need your strength for the morning."

Her hand clapped against the back of my neck. "What if I have my strength now?"

Before I could respond, she pulled my lips down to hers. She commanded my presence, taking what she wanted as my cock lurched against my jeans. I leaned into her kiss, feeling our tongues colliding as I willingly granted her entry. Her hands threaded through my hair, clinging to me as she tugged me onto the bed. I climbed on top of her, wanting nothing more than to sink myself into her glorious curves and lose myself in her wetness.

Her nails dragged down my jacket. I sat up and slipped it off, tossing it to the side. I ripped my shirt off and dropped back down, my lips falling to her neck. Our clothes came off in a tired flurry of stunted movements and giggles. We rolled around like virgins, struggling to get the blanket away from our feet as our clothes tripped us up.

"Stupid panties," she hissed.

I chuckled. "Such a hassle. Might as well not wear them."

"You'd like that, wouldn't you?"

I let out a soft growl. "If we had our own place, you'd never have clothes on."

"Mmm, I like the sound of that."

My body blanketed hers as her legs spread wide for me. My aching cock found her pussy lips, and I felt them wrapping me up. Warming me. Slicking me with her juices as Dani kissed my jawline. I rocked against her, feeling my cock working its way to her entrance. She gasped as my tip caught against her opening. I smoothed her hair away from her forehead as her half-hooded eyes met mine.

"Please, don't ever leave me," she whispered.

I shook my head. "You'll never have to worry about that. I promise."

I captured her lips as I pushed myself in deep, swallowing back her moans. I pinned her wrists above her head, opening her body as her tits fell against my chest. Our hips bottomed out together. I felt her walls crying out for mercy. My cock thickened, spreading her more as she wiggled and groaned against my lips. I slowly drew back, feeling her arousal leaking down my balls. Oh, so wet for me. A heady sensation sent electricity sizzling up my spine.

"My God, you feel so good," she moaned.

I kissed her puckered nipple. "Not as good as you feel. Trust me."

I sucked her pert peak between my lips and licked. She jumped against me, moaning into the room as I slammed my cock back into her body. She groaned as I pulled back out, only to do it again. My tongue taunted her tits. My cock stuffed her full. My hands pinned her down while her walls clamped around my girth.

There was nothing more perfect on the planet than her.

Than the feeling of her.

The taste of her.

The sight of her.

"Dani."

"Oh, Max."

"Dani, holy fuck."

"Faster, Max. Faster. Please. Oh, shit."

Skin slapping skin filled the room as I kissed my way back up to her lips. I released her wrists, feeling her arms effortlessly fly around my neck. Her nails dug against my skin. Raking, and scratching, and tugging at the beast within. I looked down upon her--upon this woman that gave herself over to me--and my heart swelled with delight. I reached down and hooked my arms beneath her legs. I brought them up, pinning her knees against her body. Her pussy opened up for me as her jaw unhinged, and I felt my cock slip even further into her glorious body.

Then, as I stroked, her eyes bulged.

"Oh--oh my Go--what, what is that? What? What are you--?"

I chuckled as a wide smile worked its way across my face. I planted my knees into the bed and pounded into her as the frame of my bed creaked. Her back arched and her tits jumped for my viewing pleasure. I watched her entire body flush from top to bottom as her toes curled tightly. Her walls massaged my cock, pulling my balls into my body. And as I felt my ending approaching, my hips began to stutter.

"Come with me," she whimpered.

"I am. I am. Dani. Fuck. I love you. Forever. I love you so much."

"Max!"

I collapsed against her and bit into her breast, latching myself on to her any way I could. Her body quivered against me as her walls pulsed, milking me for all I had. Arousal shot from the tip of my dick, filling her and coating her walls with my mark. I sucked that patch of skin, sinking my teeth deeper. Listening to her moans and groans splashed with the occasional whimper.

Then our bodies collapsed together.

Spent, tired, and sweating.

"I love you," she panted.

I kissed the teeth marks I'd left behind.

"If there were a stronger word than 'love,' I'd use it," I murmured.

I locked myself around Dani and quickly rolled over. She giggled as I pulled her along with me, rolling us out of the mess we'd created together. With her body pressed against mine, she wiggled her way down, slithering her soft skin against my muscles until her ear settled against my heart.

I loved it when she did that.

As my fingers stroked mindlessly through her hair, I stared at the ceiling. I let my body relax against the mattress, and I didn't once peek out the window. I didn't home in on the sounds around me. I didn't keep one ear trained to the hallway. I just lay there, all of my senses tuned into Dani, as her panting turned into even breaths.

Before they quickly devolved into soft snores.

I chucked. "Sleep well, my queen."

She nuzzled against me as if she'd heard me, and it pulled a smile onto my face.

I didn't know if I'd sleep at all tonight. I didn't know if I'd wake up at a decent time, or if I'd crash in the middle of the day. And for once, none of it mattered. Such a freeing feeling, to be honest. I always had my days planned down to a T, for security purposes more than anything else. I knew the safer times to go out during the day because I was aware of my father's schedule. I knew when he'd be in town doing business, so I always made sure to stay away from the outside world until it was done.

I didn't have to do that anymore, though.

If he goes to prison, who gets his house?

Or his money?

Or his cars?

I made a mental note to call an estate lawyer in the morning to try and get some of those details. Because if all of that fell to John and me for upkeep while my father rotted in prison, I had plenty of ideas regarding what to do with all of it.

To the benefits of the Red Thorns, of course.

32
___

DANI

I smiled as I fingered the soft bruise on my breast. The warm water felt amazing against my sore muscles, especially after a long night of rest. I hadn't even felt Max get up this morning. I didn't turn over until it was almost lunch time. And the first thing I wanted was a shower.

Especially after feeling my crusty thighs brush against one another.

My fingertips slipped across the small divots that still indented themselves into my skin. Max marking me was one of the hottest things he could ever do, and I wanted him to do it more often. From the tattoo to his teeth, I didn't care what the mark was. I just wanted more of him on my body. I wanted the entire world to know that I was his, and he was mine.

"Knock knock."

I smiled at the sound of his voice. "Come in, handsome."

The bathroom door opened. "How's it going in here?"

"I mean, it's a bit lonely."

He chuckled. "While I'd love to remedy that, John's pulling me away to help him unload some furniture."

"Furniture? What did he get?"

"Apparently, a new patio set. It's pretty nice, too. It comes with one of those metal bonfire pits, too. We'll definitely have to give that a whirl tonight."

"Oh, a bonfire and drinks. That sounds like a good time."

"Maybe cook some steaks and stuff over it?"

I smiled. "Sounds like a wonderful night. I'm in. You two need any help?"

He slipped the curtain back and I giggled. "Oh, no. You stay in here and rest, gorgeous. I'll be back in about an hour."

I leaned forward and kissed his nose. "I'll be here, then."

He captured my lips softly before moving the curtain back into its original place. And I decided to go ahead and wrap things up. Because if Max was going to be indisposed for an hour, then there was something I needed to do.

A phone call I needed to place.

I washed myself down and dried myself off. I slipped into one of Max's T-shirts and slid a pair of his boot socks up my legs. With my hair damp and my breasts free from my bra, I went and stole myself a cup of coffee from the pot in the kitchen. And while I wanted to stand there and stare at a shirtless Max flexing his muscles as he hauled furniture, I knew I couldn't put this off a second longer.

So I made my way back into his bedroom and called my father.

"Danika?"

The phone didn't even ring once before he picked it up.

"Hey. It's me."

"My God. Danika. Are you all right? Is everything okay?"

I sipped my coffee. "Everything's fine. I'm calling because I want to get together with you and Mom."

"Do you want me to come pick you up?"

"No, I don't want you to do that. Listen to me, Dad. Listen to my words. I want to get together with you two. Nothing more."

He sighed. "Where at? We're still in town, so we can meet you anywhere."

"Under one condition."

"Name it."

"What I want from this meeting is to tell you guys what's been going on in my life. How I met Max. What drew me to him. How I feel about school, and my life, and my future. But I can only do that if I'm talking with people who won't pass judgment, who won't jump in during the middle of a sentence, and who understand that they can't dictate my actions by force."

"Danika, your mother and I have never once--"

"Please don't go down this rabbit hole. It's going to end well for no one. Just agree to the terms. If not for me, then for Mom. Because you know this is killing her."

He paused. "Yes. It is."

"All I want is for you to listen to my life and not judge it. That's all I'm asking you for. It's not that hard."

"It is when I want the best for my little girl."

"That's the first thing. I'm not a little girl anymore, Dad."

"No matter how old you get, you'll always be my little girl. No matter what."

I sipped my coffee. "So do we have an agreement?"

"Are you still with that man?"

"If you mean Max, yes."

"Just tell me where you are. I'll come get you. We can talk in the car, and go anywhere you want."

I rolled my eyes and threw back the rest of my coffee. I chugged it down, trying to get my mind right as my father kept rattling on in my ear. Something about just needing a drive and some fresh air to screw my head back on straight. How I was falling behind in schoolwork already. Things that only made me shake my head. Did he not listen? Would he ever learn?

Will they ever understand?

In some respects, I felt as if I were wasting my breath. And as I drew in a deep one, I thought back to that pool. The water washing around me as I sank to the bottom after Ashton pushed me in. The first thing to pop into my mind was Max. How sorry I was for putting him in that situation. The second thing that rolled through my mind were my parents, and the feeling of regret that came along with it. I regretted not letting them know about Max. I regretted not filling them in. I regretted dodging my mother's phone calls and blowing off my father to roam the streets with a man I'd fallen in love with.

I regretted not giving them the chance to see this man as I saw him. Because I assumed the worst of my parents.

But now, I wondered if I had assumed right.

"Dad. Stop."

"--I mean, your mother made me promise not to ping your phone. But if you're being held against your will, it'll be quick and--"

"We'll meet you for dinner, Dad. Okay?"

His voice stopped. "We?"

I nodded. "Me and Max. Yes."

He sighed. "Sweetheart, I don't think--"

"This is your only shot, Dad. Take it or leave it. We'll meet you at seven o'clock. At the hotel you're in. Which one are you at again?"

"I really don't--"

"Five."

"Danika, just settle down for a second."

"Four."

"Are you really counting down on me?"

"Three. 'One' ends with me hanging up the phone and never picking it up again. I'd suggest you take this moment. Two."

He grumbled. "All right, all right, all right. We're at the Hilton. On the other side of Ann Arbor. It's got a restaurant in the lobby we can sit down in."

I nodded. "Perfect. Seven o'clock. We'll see you there. And don't worry about calling the police. I've already helped Max clean things up with them and prove his innocence. So pulling that stunt again won't work."

"You've helped him with--the--cleaned--what are you talking about?"

"See you at seven, Dad."

I hung up the phone.

"You okay?" Max's voice made me jump as my phone tumbled from my hands. He strode to my side and picked it up before sitting on the bed with me. I clutched my mug of coffee and sighed. Heavily. I leaned against him as he wrapped his arm around me. And the musky smell of his sweat called to my heart.

"I love it when you wear my clothes," he murmured.

I smiled. "I'm glad. Because they're comfy."

He kissed the side of my head. "You can wear them anytime, then."

I took my phone from him. "Seven okay with you?"

"Would you give me a choice if I said 'no'?"

I snickered. "Maybe not."

"I'm proud of the way you handled that, gorgeous. You kept your poise, even though I'm sure your father didn't."

"I don't know what that bodes for us tonight. But at least he'll never be able to say I didn't try."

"And all you can ever do is try."

I looked up at him. "Are you going to see your father at all? Or call him? Or something?"

He nodded mindlessly. "I've been thinking about going and seeing him while he's in holding, yes. Because I sure as hell have no intentions to visit once he goes to prison for the rest of his life."

"Then this is your only chance to see him."

He stared off, his eyes unfocused. "Yes. It is. And I still have some things I want to say to him."

"Do you want me to go with you?"

He shook his head. "No."

"Are you sure?"

"I'm sure."

"Are you absolutely positive?"

He chuckled. "Yes, gorgeous. I am. This is something I need to do alone. I need to look him in his eyes, man to man, and tell him the things I've wanted to say for years."

My hand slid against his knee. "Well, just know the offer stands, if you change your mind."

He looked down at me. "You're miraculous, you know that?"

I smiled brightly. "I try as hard as I can."

He chuckled before he pecked my lips.

"So should we talk about this dinner you've roped me into?"

I leaned my head against his shoulder. "If you don't want to go, that's fine, too."

"I'm sure your parents would be thrilled if I didn't show up."

"I'd love to have you there, though."

"If we're being honest with one another, I'm a bit uneasy about the whole situation."

"Well, I promise you that this time, things will be okay. And if my parents kick up even the slightest bit, we're gone. You have my word."

He pulled me tightly against him. "What happens if we make it through this dinner alive?"

I sighed. "Well, whether we make it through the dinner or not, you'll have to take me back to campus. I still have some things to wrap up there. Like speaking with Hannah."

"And dropping out."

I paused. "Yes. And dropping out."

"You know how I feel about that, so I'm not going to bash you over the head with it. But a bit of advice?"

"I'm all ears."

"Get whatever records you can of yourself. I keep detailed records of my health and medical situations in case I ever need them. I'm sure there's an education equivalent or whatever. Get them so you have them, just in case you change your mind. Or want to get an associates degree. Or go to vocational school. Or something like that."

I quirked an eyebrow. "Has someone been doing research?"

He shrugged. "Possibly."

I reached up, kissing his jawline. "I might be miraculous, but you're breathtaking. Thank you for thinking of me like that."

"I know better than to try and stop you. But I always want you to have a fallback plan if you change your mind, or figure out you made a mistake."

"Thank you, handsome."

"Anytime, gorgeous."

I narrowed my eyes. "Why do I get the feeling you've got something else running through your mind?"

He sighed. "Well, John's on this buying spree thing right now. He's got more furniture he wants to get replaced. So my afternoon just got booked out."

"Sounds like fun."

He snickered. "Yeah. Right. But, that does leave our rented truck free for you to use. If, you know, you wanted to flip your schedule."

I grinned. "You mean deal with campus stuff now."

He shrugged. "Might take some weight off your shoulders, getting it done sooner rather than waiting the entire weekend."

"I think that might just be the most brilliant plan you've ever had."

"Oh. Thanks for that. Not like I didn't help you completely take down my father and his dark regime or anything."

"I mean, maybe you helped out a bit."

He winked at me. "Maybe a little more than a bit."

I nuzzled against him. "If you don't mind, just leave the keys to the truck on the kitchen counter. Once I find the strength to get into my own clothes, I'll head to campus."

He kissed the top of my head. "I'll make sure to get it done. And good luck."

"Thanks."

Because I sure as hell would need it with Hannah.

33

MAX

I clicked my tongue. "I figured he would've been discharged and in holding by this point."

Rupert folded his arms over his chest. "After a gunshot wound to the gut? Hardly. He'll be in here for probably another week or so before he's up and walking around. And you know me with my aim. Dead on, every single time."

I looked over at him. "Thank you for that."

He shrugged. "Anytime. You know that."

John interjected. "Ready when you are, Max."

I nodded. "Yep. I'm ready."

John opened his door. "Thanks for picking us up, Rupert. We'll be out in a bit. This shouldn't take long."

Rupert put the truck in drive. "I'm gonna go park in a space and keep an eye out for you two. Then we're all going to get a beer somewhere."

I unbuckled myself. "I have to be back by five, though. Don't forget that."

Rupert clapped my shoulder. "Don't worry. We'll have you back in time for you to process yourself to your own funeral."

I rolled my eyes while John laughed. "Thanks for that."

"Anytime, brother."

I shook my head as I slid out of the truck. Then John and I started into the hospital. While we knew it was going to be a headache trying to find our father's room, we certainly didn't bank in it taking almost forty minutes. One minute, a nurse was telling us one thing. And the next, a doctor pointed us in another direction. We finally got so fed up with the process that I started searching for a bodyguard instead of a doctor.

And when I found one, I pulled him into the corner.

"What can I help you with?" the kind man asked.

"I want to know where the rest of your men that are supposed to be on duty are. Because I know they're stationed outside a room. And I'm trying to find that room."

John placed his hand on mine. "You can let the man go now."

My hand fell to my side as the security guard shrugged off the phantom presence of my touch. But he also didn't hesitate to answer my question.

"Yeah. I know what you're looking for. You know only family can go up there to see anyone, right?"

John nodded. "Well, I suppose it's a good thing we're his sons, then."

I licked my lips. "Don't know if that's really a good thing. But that's enough of a family bond, right?"

The guard nodded his head. "I'd ask you for I.D.s, but I have to admit you two look like him."

My face fell flat. "I'll ignore the insult if you just tell us where to go."

The security guard pointed to the elevator. "Top floor, take a left. All the way down the hall until you come to a door with guards outside."

I nodded. "Thanks."

We followed the directions to the letter and were soon standing outside our father's hospital room. And the man downstairs wasn't joking. There were three men stationed outside the room, and none of them would let us through. Every time we tried to get past them, they simply shook their heads and shoved us back. I wasn't in the mood to be trifled with. Not only had I just spent three hours hauling furniture and picking out new shit, I had to deal with Dani's unreasonable parents tonight.

Then John talked some sense into the guys. "Here. Just take our licenses. We're his sons, and we need to see him. Now."

John held out his hand for me, waiting for my license to drop into his palm. I fished around in my pockets before I pulled out my wallet, and I slapped it into his hand. He handed both of our identifications to the men, who did everything they could to prove they were fake. They shined flashlights on them. Blacklights, too. They held them up to the ceiling and turned them around in their hands. They bent them to see if they'd snap. They looked at us over and over in order to check our pictures.

I was losing patience with these assholes.

Until they finally gave our I.D.s back.

"State your business," the lanky guard said.

I blinked. "You've got to be kidding me."

He shrugged. "Just because you're family doesn't mean you can just see him. He's a fugitive under investigation. And right now, I have strict orders to only let in investigative officers and lawyers."

I took a step toward him. "Well, you tell your boss that the captain of the S.W.A.T. team we all worked with last night has given me permission to make this visit. Got it?"

John put his hand on my back. "Max, take a breath."

I didn't back down, though. "You can even call, if you have questions about it."

The guard shook his head. "No, no. Won't be necessary. The men stationed here an hour ago relayed that information to me. Just wanted to make sure you could reiterate it back to me. The two of you are free to go in."

Fucking finally.

They stepped away from the door and the lanky guard opened it for us. I looked over at John, watching his eyes widen as the hospital room came into view. It didn't shock me one bit that he was in a massive, luxurious room all to himself. All the way at the top floor, like that somehow distinguished him from everyone else. It made me sick to look at. But I made myself step into the room anyway.

And even though Dad didn't turn his head to look at us, he knew we were there.

"Sit," he said.

I looked over at John and he shrugged.

"Or don't. The choice is yours," Dad said.

I quirked an eyebrow and turned my eyes back to the scene in front of me. Dad had his gut wrapped in a mound of gauze with a soft red dot slowly protruding through. There were beeping machines and plastic lines flowing in and out of all sorts of places on his body. They had him on oxygen. There were two I.V.s. I saw the piss bag hanging off the edge of the bed, signaling to me that he also had a catheter in. And when he finally turned his head to face us, I saw how gaunt his cheeks were.

The man looked rough.

"Are you just going to stand there? Or are you going to make yourselves comfortable?"

I shook my head. "We have no intention of staying long."

He nodded. "Well, the least you can do is come in far enough to close the door. You're letting all the damn heat out."

John and I walked farther into the room before the door closed behind us. We approached our father's bed in stride with one another. But we didn't stand too closely. Dad looked completely enthralled with the

Jeopardy episode on television. And as Alex Trebek rattled off the answers, Dad kept answering those inane questions.

"Who is Cleopatra?"

"What is mitosis?"

"What is sycophant?"

I rolled my eyes. "Dad. Can you turn that off, please?"

He held up his finger. "Just one more… oh! Who is Lot? Yeah!"

I furrowed my brow at the odd scene of my father pumping his fist into the air. He winced at the pain and quickly dropped his arm, to which John rushed to his side. I kept myself in my place, though. I didn't want to be anywhere near that man. And as John limped over to aid our father like he always had, Dad's eyes found my own.

"Come to gloat, I guess?" he asked.

I shook my head. "No. Just to look at you one last time and say goodbye. For good."

He snickered. "Just like that, huh?"

I nodded. "Just like that."

"So no empathy? Even for your own father?"

John checked our father over. "He looks fine."

Dad grumbled. "I'm certainly not fine."

John pressed a button until it turned red. "Well, I'm sure you will be with time. And this morphine."

"That stuff makes me itch."

I sighed. "John, you don't have to dote on him anymore. He holds no power over you."

John looked over at me. "You say goodbye the way

you want to and let me say goodbye the way I want to."

Dad grinned. "Yeah, Max. Let your brother have his ways."

Watching John dance around our father made me sick. But if that was what he needed for closure, then so be it. I wouldn't stop him. I sure as hell wasn't joining him, though.

"You want empathy?" I asked.

Dad shrugged. "Couldn't hurt."

"You tried to kill me three times so your drug-running business could expand. You tried to drown the woman I love. You're a greedy bastard, in general. And you want empathy?"

"I knew it was a longshot anyway."

"You're no father of mine in the first place. And even if I wanted to give you empathy, I sure as hell wouldn't disrespect Dani that way."

He scoffed. "Dani. What a weak little thing."

I opened my mouth to fire back at him, but John beat me to it.

"That weak little thing is the reason Max is still standing and you're going to prison, Dad. She has more balls on her than any of us. She was your undoing, not us. So you can think on that while you're rotting away in solitary confinement."

Dad growled as John hobbled back to my side. Then Dad looked me straight in my eyes.

"I should have eliminated you a long time ago, Max."

I shrugged. "You can rehash your regrets in prison.

John? You ready to go? Because he isn't worth our time anymore."

Dad called out. "Wait!"

The desperation in his voice filled me with a satisfaction I'd never felt before. The only thing that came close was feeling Dani wrapped around me for the first time. Listening to my father's voice crack. Seeing him handcuffed to that bed. Knowing damn good and well he was scared shitless of where he'd end up. Oh, it felt like victory. It tasted like success. And it sounded like the closing of a very, very dark chapter.

I looked at my brother. "Ready?"

He nodded. "Ready?"

Dad called out for us. "Wait, boys! Come on. I'm your fucking father, for crying out--don't you step out that door. Don't you--don't you leave me like this. Max! John! Sons!"

We turned our backs to him and not once did we look back. I was proud of John, too. Because I just knew he'd give in to Dad's pleas. We walked down the hallway as Dad's voice followed us, echoing off the corners of the deserted place. With our heads held high and our shoulders rolled back, I finally felt free from that man's shackles. I felt no remorse. No guilt. No sadness, and no grief. Our father had dug this hole for himself. He could climb out of it himself.

"I hope he likes the surprise I left behind for him," John said.

I jammed my hand into the elevator button. "What?"

Dad's voice echoed down the hallway. "Why the fuck is there piss everywhere!?"

John snickered. "Let's go. Come on, come on, come on."

My eyes widened. "You didn't."

John giggled like a little girl. "I know it's petty, but damn if it isn't hilarious."

As the two of us stumbled into the elevator, we roared with laughter at the thought of our father helplessly peeing on the floor. Getting it all over his stuff.

"Do I even want to know what else you did?" I asked.

John grinned. "Let's just say Dad has a colostomy bag, too."

My jaw dropped open. "You didn't."

"What the fuck!?"

Dad's voice filled the hallway just as the elevator doors closed, and I bent over with laughter. John slapped me on the back as I wheezed, imagining my father covered in his own piss and shit. Served him fucking right after the hell he put us through.

I finally rose up. "God, you're fucking brilliant, you know that?"

John forced his laughter to stop. "I just--I had to, you know? It might be childish, but I can literally remember pissing myself as a kid whenever that man yelled at me."

"About time he got a taste of his own medicine?"

"Fuck yeah. But did you say everything you wanted to? You didn't speak much in there."

I nodded. "When I walked in, I realized that there wasn't much I wanted to say, just things I wanted to show him."

"Like?"

The elevator doors opened on the main floor. "Like the fact that I really don't care what happens to him now."

"Well, you certainly got that point across."

"Good."

John started out of the elevator. "So how are you feeling about this dinner with Dani's parents?"

I walked alongside him. "Eh, it'll go how it'll go. But I want to be there to support her, because I know how hard it is to go against an overbearing father."

"Understatement of the year."

I opened the front door for John. "Yeah, but it doesn't diminish the pain this is putting her in."

"Let her know I'll be supporting her in spirit. And you."

"Thanks. I'll definitely let her know."

And as Rupert wrapped around to pick us up, I turned back toward the hospital. I gazed up to the top floor, where my father was surely still yelling up a storm. I gave him one last thought. One last silent prayer. Then I hopped into the truck.

"So! How did things go?" Rupert asked.

John looked at me. "Let's just say Max said what he needed to say, and I did what I needed to do."

I snorted. "You can say that again."

Rupert pulled away from the curb. "Got time for a beer and stories? Because now you've got me curious."

John shrugged. "I'm down if Max is down."

Rupert looked at me in the rearview mirror. "Max?"

I looked at the clock. "Sure, why not? I've got an hour or so before we need to really head back."

34

DANI

I knocked on my dorm room door, wary of what to expect. The last thing I wanted to do was fight with yet another person. I mean, I got it. People didn't understand the lifestyle I had chosen for myself. But I was growing very tired of people simply asserting themselves over my personal will. As if I were incapable of making decisions for myself.

But it didn't stop me from knocking on the door.

I didn't feel like I had the right to barge in. Especially since this was about to be 'just Hannah's' room. I knew Max wanted what was best for me. I knew he was simply looking out for me. But school wasn't what I wanted with my life. Not right now, anyway. Maybe in a few years, when I'd lived a little bit and really explored all of my options, I would. But I was a year and some change into college, and I still had no idea what I wanted to do with the rest of my life.

And nothing changed that fact.

I heard Hannah's groggy voice on the other side of the door. "Hello?"

I sighed. "It's me, Hannah. Can I come in?"

The door ripped open and she moved so quickly she was only a blur of blond. I felt arms gripping my neck as she slammed into me, almost knocking me off my feet. I grunted as she kissed my cheek over and over. As if I had been gone on some sort of sabbatical for years and years.

"You have no idea how glad I am to see you, Dani."

I pressed her out in front of me. "Is it okay if I come in?"

"Does this mean we finally get to talk? Will you finally tell me what in the world is going on? Because the last time I talked to your parents--"

I held up my finger. "First rule if we're going to go forward from this."

She nodded. "I'm listening."

"Lose my parents' numbers."

"When you don't pick up the phone--"

"Lose them. I'm serious."

She nodded. "Okay. I will."

I squeezed her shoulders before we walked back into the dorm room. This place felt foreign to me now. It felt like years had passed since I had been here. Or on campus. My eyes flitted around Hannah's side of the bedroom. All of her brightly-colored posters and her pristine bed. Her organized desk and her books all lined up in a row on a small shelf above her head. Even her closet was color-coordinated. Something I had envied for the longest time.

Not anymore, though.

I didn't envy a single thing Hannah had in her life now.

"Want some coffee?" she asked.

I grinned. "Got any of that hot honey left?"

"You know I do. You've hooked me on to this stuff for good."

I smiled. "Sounds like my work here is done, then."

She paused. "That doesn't sound good."

I sighed. "You might not like what I have to say. But I hope you'll let me say it, at least."

She poured me some coffee. "Of course."

We eventually sat on her bed with our hot honey coffees and sipped them quietly. It gave me time to organize my thoughts into the most succinct story possible. Because I knew she wouldn't handle the details well, nor would she let me talk for long before she started asking asinine questions. So I did the best I could and drew in a deep breath.

"I want to start off by saying that I'm sorry for the position I put you in."

Hannah looked over at me. "Hearing that means a lot to me. Thank you, Dani."

"But you also need to know that I don't regret my choices."

"I figured as much."

"I still would've made the same choices, even though I'm sorry that they hurt you as much as they did. Because lives were at stake with my actions. And I couldn't let that slide."

She turned to face me. "What happened, Dani? Tell me, please."

I nibbled on my lower lip. "I need you to know before I start that nothing has changed between Max and me. I'm still with him, and I still love him."

She took my hand. "What. Happened?"

"I need you to know that you hear me."

"I hear you, Dani. And just know that I should have listened to you. I understand that. I shouldn't have gotten your parents involved, especially since you seemed so confident in your actions. I was scared for you. I was scared for my friend. And maybe a bit jealous in the process."

I paused. "Jealous?"

"Yeah! I mean, look at you. Living this exciting life. Going with your gut. Tossing everything aside for something that feels good. I mean, look around you. Do I look like the kind of person that lives their life like that?"

I giggled. "No. Not at all."

"So, yeah. Maybe I was a bit jealous. And very worried. But I mainly didn't want you getting hurt."

I squeezed her hand. "I know, Hannah."

"Whenever you're ready with this story, I'm ready to listen."

"Well, don't be offended, but I'm just going to give you the short version. Because it's complicated. And involved."

"Whatever you're willing to tell me, I'm here for you."

I smiled. "Thank you. I appreciate that. The story kind of starts with me drowning."

She blinked. "Drowning? You're kidding, right?"

I launched into everything. How I got kidnapped. How Max's father tied me to a chair. I recounted the drowning and how Max saved my life. I told her about my parents in the hospital and that's when the tears started. She was just as angry at my parents as I had been with them, and she rooted me on as I told her about the plan we came up with to get rid of all this nonsense.

"I knew there was something weird about that Benji guy," she said with narrowed eyes.

I laughed. "Yeah. A lot was weird about him. But the plan worked."

"The police showed up at the right time?"

"Yep. S.W.A.T. and everything."

"And Randy's out of jail?"

"Rupert. But, yes."

"And his father's out of the picture?"

I nodded. "Very much so."

She sighed with relief. "Holy fuck, Dani. You really do love this man, don't you?"

I smiled. "I do. And I'll protect him at all costs. Whatever it takes. He's not bad, Hannah. None of them are. They were just being controlled by a bad man. But not any longer. They're free."

"You're all free."

I paused. "Yeah, we are. All of us are."

She licked her lips. "Can you forgive me for all this? For what I've done and how hard I fought against you?"

I sipped my coffee. "With time, I think so."

"Why do I get the feeling that's not all you want to say to me?"

"Because it's not. And I don't know how you're going to take this news."

"You're not pregnant, are you?"

My eyes bulged. "What? Hell, no! Are you kidding me? Come on, I'm not that stupid."

She threw her head back with laughter. "Well, I just thought I'd make sure!"

I snorted. "I mean, I'm dropping out of school, but I sure as hell am not pregnant."

Her laughter ceased. "What?"

I paused. "I'm dropping out of school. At least for now."

I fell silent and braced myself for Hannah's judgment. But to my surprise, she didn't say anything. So I continued.

"I'm just not happy here. And no, it has nothing to do with you. I've felt this way ever since I enrolled, you know? I didn't know what I wanted to do, so Dad had me declare his major. I was so unhappy my freshman year that I cried myself to sleep almost every night."

"I remember those nights."

I settled my hand on her knee. "I know you do. So I changed my major. It caused issues with Dad, but I figured it was worth it. But then I started classes and didn't give a shit about the subject matter and realized

I didn't want to do that either. I don't know what I want to do with the rest of my life. I don't know what kind of career I want right now. In fact, everything I do know about my life right now--everything I am confident about--has nothing to do with college for the moment."

"I can understand that."

"I want to find something that makes my soul light up. That makes me thankful to get up every morning. And HR isn't it. This school isn't it. Yes, Max makes me happy whenever I wake up, but it's more than that. If I'm going to dedicate my entire life to the practice of one thing as a career, I want to be sure about it. Like I'm sure with Max."

She nodded. "Then you have to do what you have to do."

"Which leads me to my last thing."

She sighed. "Oh, boy."

I looked her square in the eyes. "Because of everything that's happened with Max's father, the S.W.A.T. captain has suggested that we get away for a little while. At least until all of the heat dies down."

Her eyes watered. "Where will you go? Will you be safe?"

"With Max, I'm always safe, Hannah. You don't have to worry about that."

"Do you at least know where you're going?"

"Not yet. It'll be some place far enough away where Max and I can wait until his father's trial, though."

"So you're going to be gone for a *very* long time, then."

I nodded but didn't say anything. And I watched as a tear dripped down Hannah's cheek.

"When will you come back?" she asked with a sniffle.

I shook my head slowly. "I don't know. I mean, we might come back. But at this point, everything is all up in the air right now."

She paused. "Might?"

I nodded. "Yes. Might. I know it might be hard to understand right now, but I need to set out on my own. You know, really experience things. I need to be *bold*. I need to do things I've always wanted to do without worrying about what everyone else might think."

"Do your parents know?"

"Max and I have dinner plans with them tonight. If all goes well, I'll tell them then."

"What if things don't go well?"

I shrugged. "Then I won't tell them. I don't owe them this information if all my father is going to do is berate me."

She wiped at her tears. "I'm so sorry for putting you in this situation."

I set my coffee down. "Hannah, look at me."

Her eyes met mine. "Yeah?"

"Right now? At this juncture in my life? I've never felt so alive. I've never felt so happy. But these last few weeks with Max have changed *everything* for me. I'm not the same person. I don't have the same goals and passions and wants any longer. It's not possible to go back to how things used to be. To the pushover I used to be. And I need someone to understand that. Please, understand that. Understand *me*."

Her eyes danced between mine. I gripped her hand tightly as she set her coffee down. She got onto her knees and faced me as we sat on her bed, trying her best to hold back tears.

Then she threw her arms around my neck, giving me the biggest hug I'd ever received from her.

"Please don't forget about me, Dani," she whispered.

I blinked back my own tears. "How could I ever forget my best friend?"

"I want to hear you say it. Please?"

I nodded. "I promise I won't forget you. Ever."

35

MAX

My leg bounced as I sat on the couch. How much time did Dani need to get ready for this damn thing, anyway? Jeans and a T-shirt with my jacket. That's what she said would be appropriate enough for this. "Just wear whatever you want," she'd said.

But now I wondered if I was too dressed down.

"Nervous?" John asked.

I stopped bouncing my leg. "Fuck off."

He chuckled. "Hey, I'd be nervous if I were meeting the parents of the girl I corrupted, too."

I glared at him. "She's hardly a girl. You know that much."

"Out of everything I said, that's what you took away?"

I chewed on the inside of my cheek to keep from firing back. Because John's words were only confirming the one thing I feared this entire time. That, without my influence, Dani wouldn't be in this situation. No matter how much she boasted that this was for her and no matter how much she told me this is what she wanted, I still wasn't sure.

Would Dani have chosen this path had it not been for me?

"He still nervous?" Rupert asked.

I heard his lips smacking away on a sandwich as I slowly lifted my eyes.

"You'd be nervous, too, if you were in my shoes."

He barked with laughter. "Damn right I'd be. That girl was practically--"

John nudged him in his ribs and Rupert grunted. He swallowed his sandwich before casting John his own glare, and I pulled my eyes away from them. I peeked down the hallway. I really needed Dani to hurry up. We were thirty minutes away from this hotel and we needed to leave five minutes ago.

"Gorgeous! I'm sure you look fine! We have to get out of here!"

I heard a door open. "Three more minutes! Just got to get my lipstick on."

I furrowed my brow. "Lipstick?"

Rupert chuckled. "Oh, you're gonna be greatly underdressed."

I stood from the couch as my voice dropped. "Will it be ready for her when we get back tonight? Or do you need more time?"

Rupert nodded. "I've already seen it. It's perfect, Max. She's going to love it."

John came over and clapped my shoulder. "She deserves this, and so do you."

Rupert took another bite of his food. "All you have to do is be yourself."

John pointed at me. "But if you want to channel anyone in this situation, I suggest--"

Dani's voice pierced our conversation. "All right. I'm ready. I just need to find my purse. Have you seen it anywhere?"

I saw John's jaw drop open as Rupert's eyes widened. And when I turned around, my heart stopped in my chest. My God, Dani looked incredible. Like the perfect specimen of an angel that had dropped from heaven just to save me. My eyes roamed her body as I pulled away from John's grasp. The floral-printed dress she wore accented the sunkissed glow of her skin, hitting her just above her knees. The heeled boots she had on made me salivate. Her curves were accented by a bow tied behind her back. She had her hair pulled back into a half-ponytail, making her eyes sparkle as her ruby red lips curled into a grin.

She knew exactly what she was doing to me.

And it only confirmed that I was making the right decision.

"You look amazing, gorgeous."

She smiled. "You don't look half bad yourself."

Rupert snickered. "He looks like shit compared to you."

I shot him a look as Dani laughed, filling the room with her comforting, relaxing sound.

"Thanks, Rupe."

He winked. "Anytime, Bambi."

I offered my arm. "Ready to go?"

She threaded her arm with mine. "Please tell me we're taking your bike."

"In that dress you're wearing?"

She shrugged. "Why not?"

John stepped in. "For one thing, it's not safe."

Rupert added on, "And for another, the wind is going to shove that dress right up your legs the second you two hit the road."

Dani reached down, slipping her dress up. "I've got that covered."

I peeked down and saw the spandex road shorts she had on underneath. And damn it, I couldn't have loved this woman any more if she sincerely tried. I grinned as she smiled up at me, warming my frozen heart as it started fluttering against my chest. Then her wonderous voice filled my ear.

"Remember, handsome. We aren't doing this for them. We're doing this for us."

I nodded. "I know."

"I'm not expecting this to go well at all. I'm not expecting them to just automatically be okay with you and be okay with what we're about to tell them."

"I don't know if that's supposed to make me feel better or worse."

She giggled. "Just stick to the plan. Honesty above all else. No matter what they say, don't fire back."

"Unless they disrespect you."

She nodded. "Yes. If they lose all respect for the situation, have fun. But I don't expect them to do that this time. If they don't respect me, or you, we're out of there. Because if we can keep our cool, so can they. Okay?"

I winked. "You got it, gorgeous."

"Great. Now, who do I have to blow to get you to agree to take your bike?"

I growled as John and Rupert burst out laughing. Dani smiled brightly up at me before she kissed the tip of my nose, making my soul melt into a pile of goo. Damn it, she was the cutest thing I'd ever come across in my life. But fucking hell, if she didn't have a spitball fire of a strong woman deep inside that innocent soul of hers.

"Let's get out of here," I murmured.

"Ready when you are, handsome."

The bike ride over to the hotel seemed so quiet and serene compared to what we had been through. I rode without worry or pretense, without constantly checking my rearview mirrors. I couldn't remember the last time I'd taken a ride and felt as free as I did right now, with Dani tightly wrapped around me as we crossed town. I waved to a few people who waved at us. I didn't bother with speeding, or running yellow lights, or pursuing shadows I thought might be following us. I languidly drove, enjoying the view and the ride and the feeling of my entire world wrapped tightly around my waist.

But once we were seated in front of her parents, all of that faded away.

"So," her mother said as she broke the silence, "how long have the pair of you been... seeing each other?"

Dani answered. "About a month or so. Possibly six weeks."

Her mother's voice fell flat. "Got pretty serious quickly, then, didn't it?"

I looked down at Dani and watched her smile effortlessly.

"Yes, it did. And I'd like to tell you both what's been happening since Max and I started seeing each other. As soon as those scowls on your faces are gone, please."

I looked over at her father and watched him turn his head away. Ever since we walked up and joined them in their booth, he had his lips pursed. His eyes wouldn't meet mine. Her mother still hadn't looked at me, but she certainly made sure to turn herself as far away from me as possible. It was clear I wasn't welcome. But it was also clear that Dani wouldn't tolerate any of that.

"Dad?" she asked.

He licked his lips. "You can speak whenever you're ready."

Dani nodded. "Get rid of the scowl."

Her mother jumped in. "I get that you want us to respect your decisions. And we're trying. But you don't get to dictate our facial expressions after jumping down our throats about setting expectations for you that you didn't want to meet."

I nodded. "That's a good point. Dani?"

She sighed. "Fine. Okay. Yes, I--I completely get that."

Her father nodded. "Thanks."

Her mother leaned back against the booth cushion. "Whenever you're ready."

Dani nodded. "Thank you. But in the interest of time, I'd like to ask that you not interrupt and let me get through to the end before we start picking things apart. Can you do that?"

Her parents looked at one another and worry dripped over their faces. The scowls were gone, but in their places were questions and anxieties I knew we'd have to address before we left.

Everyone just keep a damn lid on it.

"All right, we can do that," her mother said.

"Dad?"

He sighed. "Just get through it as quickly as you can."

I had the great pleasure of sitting there and watching horror cross their faces as Dani recounted everything. The confrontation with my father. The chair. How she got tied to it. I watched anger rise in her father's face until Dani told him about me jumping in after her in the pool. She walked them through our plan we concocted with the police department to get rid of everyone involved. Handcuffs, the S.W.A.T. vehicle. She left no stone unturned as she filled her parents in. Their tears broke my heart. The way they sat on the edge of their seats made me wonder if they'd actually get through the story before jumping in.

But, as Dani wound things down, they stayed true to their word.

"So, yeah," she said as she leaned back, "that's what happened. From beginning, to end. Benji's in holding, for now. And once his father is discharged from the hospital, he's going straight to jail. Probably until his trial starts. But even though they're off the streets, the captain of S.W.A.T. has suggested that Max and I get out of town for a little while. Until the trial, just so things don't kick up and get messy again."

Her father blinked. "So, after all of this, the two of you are just leaving town?"

Dani looked up at me. "Yeah. We are. Just until things settle down. We're going to be keeping in contact with--"

Her mother interjected. "What about your schooling? How in the world are you going to keep up with your classes?"

I licked my lips as Dani heaved a heavy sigh.

"I actually went to the dean's office today and dropped out," she said.

Her father's voice reddened. "You *what?*"

I watched her mother put a hand in his lap to keep him from blowing his top. But I knew we were one stark revelation away from this place becoming yet another war zone. Her father drew in a deep, sobering breath. And me? Well, I wrapped my arm around Dani to keep her seated. Because I felt her growing more on edge, too.

"Danika, your education is very important," he said.

She nodded. "And so is my sanity. It's been a crazy few weeks. I need some time, and so does Max."

Her mother clicked her tongue. "When are you leaving, honey?"

Her father hissed. "You can't possibly be okay with this."

Dani leaned against me. "Tomorrow, actually."

Her mother's eyes widened. "Tomorrow? Are you kidding me!? That's not enough time. We can't possibly--you can't--but your stuff--it--"

I watched her father grind his teeth together to keep from speaking as her mother leaned forward.

"Sweetheart, that's not enough time. Please reconsider this. So much has happened, and we just--"

Dani shook her head. "I won't reconsider. I can't. But I can tell you I'll stay in touch. I'll keep you in the loop. You have my word on that. Once we get to where we're going, I'll call you. I'll tell you all sorts of stories and keep you abreast of what's happening. And I won't ever lie to you again. Not a single word. I promise you."

Her mother swallowed hard. "No lies?"

Her father turned to face her. 'You can't be seriously considering this, Rena. She's twenty years old, for crying out loud!"

She snapped at him, "And if it wasn't for your hot head and your insane actions in the first place, we wouldn't be here. Peter, where in the world do you think our daughter gets it from, huh? The not thinking. The jumping in head first. The irrational decisions based on her gut and nothing else. Who in the world does that sound like?"

Dani suppressed a giggle as I stroked my fingertips along the back of her arm. Her parents bickered with one another before her father got up and walked away.

Which didn't shock me one bit. I was proud of Dani for not trying to stop him. I was proud of her for focusing on her mother instead of indulging the walk-off and ending the dinner.

"You just have to try and see this from our point of view, sweetheart. Like we're trying to do with you," she said.

Dani nodded. "I know. I'm trying to do that. And I know this is hard for you guys. You two have dictated most of the moves I've made ever since I was born. But you also have to understand that constantly hovering and trying to control my movements is part of the reason why I never felt I could talk to you about this in the first place."

Her mother's eyes watered. "I'm sorry, sweetheart."

She took her mother's hand across the table. "I know, Mom. I know you are. And I know this is hard. Genuinely, truly hard for you guys. But from now on, no more lies. No more secrets. Complete and total transparency, from here on out."

"Can I ask just one thing of you?"

"Anything, Mom."

She sighed. "Is it possible to have this captain's number? I mean, just in case something happens while you're gone and you can't get in touch with us?"

I smiled. "I'll make sure you get it before we leave, yes."

Her mother looked over at me with eyes full of relief, and I knew we'd made a lot of progress. Maybe not with her father. But certainly with her mother.

And for that, I was happy.

"Do you have any questions for me, Mrs. Young?" I asked.

She released Dani's hand. "Plenty."

I chuckled. "I'm more than willing to answer any you have."

Dani leaned against me and I cuddled her close.

"Actually, I just have one question I need answered right now," her mother said.

I nodded. "Shoot."

"Max, do you love my daughter?"

I didn't skip a beat. "More than anything or anyone I've ever come across in my life."

She pointed at me. "Then you do everything you can to protect her while she's gone. You got it?"

"You don't have to worry about that at all. The entire reason why I've planned this getaway for us is because I know it's for her safety. She'll have a good time, we'll get our minds off things, and she'll be safe. You have my word."

Her mother dropped her voice. "And make sure she calls me. You know how she can be."

I leaned forward, winking. "I'll call you myself if I have to."

She smiled. "Good. I think we'll get along just fine, then."

Her father never did come back to the table, but that didn't seem to bother anyone. Dani, Mrs. Young, and I had a fabulous dinner together where she got to shoot questions my way and I answered them to the best of my ability. The dinner went a great deal better than either of us thought it would. And while I was sad at the fact that her father didn't feel like he could return, I knew he'd like me with time.

Once he figured out the kind of man I was, anyway.

Mrs. Young yawned. "That meal requires a nap."

Dani yawned, too. "You're not joking."

I chuckled. "I could go another round, honestly."

Her mother giggled. "With how big you are? You could go another two rounds, I'm sure."

I chuckled. "Big boys gotta eat."

Mrs. Young reached for the check. "I'll get this."

I quickly reached out my hand, wrapping it around her wrist. "Let me."

Her eyes met mine. "Let me do this for you guys. As a small gesture of peace. And don't you worry about my husband. I'll make sure he comes around."

Dani slid her hand down my arm. "Thanks, Mom. We appreciate it."

She pried my hand away from her mother's wrist and intertwined our fingers. It didn't sit well with me, her mother paying for us. But I guess it was the best decision. We'd need all of the money we could pool together for this trip we were taking. Especially after the money I'd just dropped on the gift I had for her back at the house.

"Will you call before you leave?" Mrs. Young asked.

Dani nodded. "Of course we will. We can't tell you where we're going. At least until the captain says it's okay. But I'll call you before we leave and after we land."

Mrs. Young nodded. "Okay. Good, good."

"Will you tell Dad that I love him?"

I jumped in. "That we love him?"

Her mother smiled at my words. "Of course I will, you two. Leave it to me."

Dani smiled. "Thanks, Mom."

Her mother nodded. "And thank you both for this dinner. While I'm not completely settled on anything, I feel a bit more stable. It'll take time. Lots and lots of time. But give us that time and we'll work with you."

I nodded. "Whatever you need."

36

DANI

I closed my eyes. "Well, that was… interesting."

Max chuckled, sliding on his helmet. "Interesting is one way to put it."

"At least Mom stayed for the entire dinner."

"You think you'll hear from your father tonight?"

I shrugged, putting on my own helmet. "I doubt it. But it's not my problem anymore."

"I'm really proud of you, you know."

I paused. "For what?"

"For no longer letting people in your life guilt trip you into things."

I smiled. "Thanks, handsome."

"But don't get tired on me yet. There's still a bit of business we need to see to before we head to bed for the night."

I furrowed my brow. "Business? What sort of business?"

He cracked a wry grin. "You'll see, gorgeous. You'll see."

My curiosity got the best of me on the ride back. I grew anxious in all the best ways as we crept closer to the house. I clung to Max, wondering what in the world he had in store. Had something gone wrong during dinner? Was there some sort of surprise waiting for me? Had the captain called him or something while we were eating?

I didn't know what to expect.

But as we rode down Max's street, I didn't expect to see what was there.

The street was lined with motorcycles. One behind the other, in and orderly and fused fashion. I stopped counting the bikes after twenty-two, because it was very clear to me that the entire Red Thorns crew was here. I shook my head as Max pulled into the driveway. We slid our helmets off and stowed them away. Then, without a word spoken to me, he offered me his hand.

"Care to join me, Dani?"

I slipped my hand into his. "What in the world is going on?"

He didn't answer my question. He simply led me into the house. We walked through the front door together and were immediately bombarded with cheering and whooping and hollering. I jumped at the sound. The guys clapped and pumped their fists in the air as I threw my head back in laughter. They all patted me on the back. A few gave me hugs. But not one time did Max ever let go of my hand.

It was like he didn't want to lose me in the throng of men.

For those that didn't hug me, they clapped my shoulder. They shook my hand in a brotherly fashion, and it made me feel part of something greater. Something stronger. Something more united than I'd ever experienced in my entire life. I had to keep blinking my eyes for fear that I'd cry on them. The show of strength and unity they all possessed took my breath away.

"What in the world are you guys doing here?" I asked breathlessly.

Instead of answering my question, though, the guys corralled us into the kitchen. Everyone perched where they could as Rupert and John stood at the kitchen counter, holding a wooden box in their hands. The box was massive, and my eyebrows rose in curiosity. Was this what Max had been talking about? The surprise he had for me?

"I have something for you," Max said.

I nodded. "Is that it?"

His hand fell to the small of my back. "Part of me wanted to wait until tomorrow, before we left. But this can't wait."

I looked up at him. "I don't understand. What's in that box?"

He took my hands, gazing into my eyes. "You saved my ass, Dani. I need you to know that."

"I know. I know I did."

The guys chuckled as Max snickered.

"You took charge when no one else knew what to

do. You concocted plans none of us in our wildest dreams could have ever concocted. And to do that with no one dying and barely any bullets flying around? It's not something this crew has ever seen before."

"I'm glad I could help, Max. Really."

He tucked a strand of hair behind my ear. "I've taken to heart the words that the captain said to us. About this being a fresh start for the Red Thorns. I've clawed through some serious issues in this crew to try and get us on the gray side of good. And I plan on doing that again. I plan on making this crew as legitimate as it can be. A crew that benefits this community instead of striking fear into the hearts of the shadows of this place. But that doesn't happen without you."

I paused. "You're kidding."

Max grinned as he led me over to the wooden box. He flipped the tinted glass lid open and reached into the dark cavern. I froze in my spot the second he pulled it out. My hands flew to my mouth as tears rushed my eyes. As he held up the pristine leather jacket tailored specifically to my size, he flipped it around to show me the emblem on the back.

The Red Thorns crest, emblazoned in ruby reds and stitched together in gold.

"My God," I whispered.

Max handed it to me. "Take it. Put it on."

I took it slowly from his hand and ran the leather through my fingers. How could something so durable feel so soft to the touch? I blinked back my tears and ran my fingertips along the shining silver zipper. The porch lights caught the patchwork on the front of the jacket, making the entire thing shine as bright as the sun.

"Come on. Let's get this thing on you," he said.

Max helped me slip into the jacket and I zipped it up. I held my arms out, giving the guys a little twirl as they nodded their heads and murmured among themselves. Then, after I stopped, I looked each and every one of them in the eyes.

"Thank you. Every single one of you. For making me feel like I finally have a home."

The men raised their hands over their heads and clapped. A few of them put their fingers in their mouths and whistled. I blushed as Max wrapped his arms around me, bringing me in for a solid kiss. And the second our lips connected, the thundering sound of boots stomping against the floor filled the space around us.

"Welcome to the crew," Max murmured against my lips.

And as I clung tightly to his own leather jacket, I felt the rest of my future slowly slip into place.

37
___

MAX

Rupert and John went all out for this thing. There were beers for everyone and a bottle of wine specifically for Dani. There was pizza and wings and all sorts of dipping sauces. Bones were being tossed into any cup or holding container around just to keep them off the floor. Music thumped and the guys took Dani out to their bikes to show off their own components. Their own designs. The individual ways they distinguished their bikes from everyone else's.

And through it all, my chest swelled with pride.

The guys accepted her into the fold like family. They gathered around her while she told stories. They roared with laughter whenever she poked fun at me. She made small talk with everyone and genuinely listened to them. Something I knew the crew would come to love sooner rather than later. I stood back and watched as every man fought for a chance to speak with her. To pick her mind and ask her questions and tell her stories of their own families.

It filled me with pride that she was my woman.

My future looks very bright right now.

It was the first time those words had ever crossed my mind. And it was all thanks to Dani. Had it not been for our chance encounters, I'd still be doing my father's bidding. Still running around behind him, begging for jobs. And while I knew getting our crew up and running in a different direction would take time, I also knew Dani was imperative in that switch.

She was imperative in the direction I wanted to take the Red Thorns.

Rupert nudged my ribs. "The hell are you thinking about over here, with that cheesy grin of yours?"

I snickered. "Look at how comfortable she is."

He gazed out over the crowd. "You good with that many guys around her? Because I'm not sure I would be."

"She saved them. She saved all of us. I figure one night for them to talk with their newest member before I start barging in is warranted."

"But you'll be keeping a strong eye on her, right?"

I chuckled. "That woman isn't leaving my sight."

He patted my shoulder. "There's the Max I know."

I paused. "She really fits in, doesn't she?"

"Fits in? She could damn near run this crew, if you weren't the president."

"Trust me, she's going to have her hands in this crew more than she realizes."

"I take it you've got particular plans for us?"

I sipped. "Yep. And they all require her influence."

"Why do I get the feeling that's not all on your mind, though?"

I sighed as I looked over at him. "What the fuck is a woman like her doing with a man like me, Rupert?"

He laughed. "If you're looking to me for an answer, I ain't got one for ya. Because I've been trying to figure that shit out myself since I first met her."

I shoved him. "Fuck off."

He barked with laughter. "Hey, you asked. I simply answered with the honesty you say you always respect from your crew."

"Yeah, yeah. Go take a hike."

"Love you, too, bud."

He raised his beer to me and I shook my head. But I couldn't help the grin that crossed my face. I watched Rupert go over and save Dani from the crowd of men still poking her for stories and details of the plot that unraveled. But I also watched her try to swat Rupert away. He refilled her wine glass and got her another slice of pizza. He couldn't pull her away from the guys, though.

And while I knew I'd have to do something about that later, for tonight, it was perfect.

Watching her interact as if she had always been with us was nothing short of perfect.

Rupert came back to my side. "In all seriousness, though, you two are a perfect match."

I nodded slowly. "You think?"

"I don't think, dude. I know. That girl is head over heels in love with you. I mean, a flat-out goner, know what I'm saying? She wouldn't have risked everything she did if that wasn't true."

"You have a good point."

"I have an even better one, too. Because I know you love her just as much."

I nodded. "Yeah. I really do."

"So you want my advice? Don't overthink it. Because sometimes you just have to let life take the reins for a little bit so you can hold on and enjoy the ride."

"She's the only woman we've ever inducted, you know."

"And she's the perfect model of how dedicated any woman should be to her man if she's going to be part of this family. She breaks and resets the mold, man."

"That she does."

Dani's laughter rose above even the guys before she flopped down onto the couch. They all stood around her, and I saw a few of them keeping one eye out the window. Still watching. Still waiting. Still anticipating evil and mayhem to come rolling up to the porch. I liked the fact that they'd always watch her back. That my men would always have her safety at the forefront of their minds.

But my goal for our future was to create a new life for us all.

One that didn't include constantly looking out windows.

"So you going to come join us, or what?"

John's voice piped up at my other side and I turned to look at him.

"I will in a minute," I said.

He nodded. "Good. Rupert? One of the guys is asking for you. I think our first keg has gone to shit."

Rupert held his finger in the air. "That's my cue! I got it, John. Just have the second one ready to go so I can quickly hook it up."

I furrowed my brow. "You guys need any help?"

John held up his hand. "No, no. We've got this. You just enjoy the evening."

"This is Dani's evening. Not mine."

Rupert shrugged. "She's your girl, right?"

I snickered. "Damn right."

John smiled. "Then it's your night, too. So stop being an asshole of a party pooper and get over there."

Rupert and John walked away, leaving my eyes to travel back to Dani. The guys parted, giving me a clear shot of her smiling face. Her eyes met mine and they twinkled with delight. I hadn't seen her this happy since the first time I told her I loved her. I wanted her to be this happy for the rest of her life. I made myself a solemn vow to make sure that smile never dropped from her face for too long.

Then she patted the couch cushion next to her. "You joining me, or what?" she exclaimed.

"Yeah, Max!"

"Your girl's getting lonely!"

"You gonna leave her hangin'?"

I chuckled. "I'd never leave her hanging. Ever!"

And as the guys let out a raucous cheer, I took my rightful seat next to my queen.

Ready to enjoy the party before we had to get out of here in the morning.

38

DANI

I slid out of my new jacket. "Holy shit. What a night."

Max closed the bedroom door. "I expected them to stay late, but not 'three in the morning' late."

"You let John and Rupert know that's what happens when they get three fucking kegs of beer."

He snickered. "I'm sure they already know."

"Are you sure those guys are going to be good to drive?"

"Trust me, it would take double the kegs to take them out for the night. They're good, I promise."

I nodded. "Okay. But I think you should keep your phone on for the night, just in case someone calls."

His hands landed on my hips. "Already thinking like one of the team, huh?"

I giggled as his lips found my neck. I sighed as he walked us over to the bed, making me fall onto my stomach on the mattress. His hands slid down my arms, softly pinning my wrists to the bed. And as he kissed down the back of my neck, I shivered beneath his body.

"Max, I don't think I have the energy tonight."

He gave my butt a small smack. "I know, I know."

I yawned. "I'm sorry. It's just--"

He stood up. "We've had a long day. Come here."

He helped me off the bed before promptly helping me out of my clothes. We stripped one another down as he kissed me in random places. Like my ear. And my elbow. And my hip bone. I moaned softly at the feeling of his warm lips. I tangled my hands into his hair as his fingers danced against my legs. He helped me step out of my boots and slid my dress over my head. Within seconds, I was naked. And he quickly pulled one of his shirts over my torso.

"You like me in your clothes, huh?"

He pecked me quickly. "Always."

I smiled as I watched him shed the rest of his clothes. My eyes danced over his muscles, taking stock of the thick lines that flexed for my viewing pleasure. Watching him get ready for bed seemed so mundane. So domestic. So normal. But in the best possible way alive.

I didn't want to know life ever again without Max in it.

"Staring at me, huh?" he asked.

I blushed. "Can't help it that you're good-looking."

He peered over his shoulder. "Trust me, I get the feeling."

"You stare at yourself then, too, huh?"

He tossed his sock at me and I squealed. I jumped onto the bed to dodge it, but he threw his other one and it hit me right in the face. I yelped and grabbed it with my fingertips. I tossed it to the floor as that sweaty foot smell filled my nostrils. I faked a nice gag. One that made Max roar with laughter.

John started banging on our door.

"Can you two keep it down? The whole fucking block can hear you."

I giggled. "Sorry, John!"

Max chuckled. "I'll make sure my little noise machine stays quiet tonight."

I scoffed. "Hey! That's mean."

He winked. "And it's also the truth."

I put my hands playfully on my hips as he walked toward me in nothing but boxers and that sly grin of his and wrapped his arms around my waist. He slammed me onto my back on the mattress, making my legs flail wildly. And as we wiggled our way beneath the covers, I rolled over so I could look at him.

"Ready for tomorrow?" I asked.

He scooted closer to me. "I'm as ready as I'll ever be. Are you ready?"

I nodded. "I packed up the rest of my things from my dorm and just kept them in the truck."

"So you're just going to take everything you own on this trip?"

I shrugged. "It's only four bags."

He paused. "You can fit everything you need and own into four bags?"

"I mean, yeah. Can't you?"

"No. And we're going to change that."

"Max, I don't need a lot of--oh!"

He pulled me on top of him. "I'm going to spoil you senseless on this trip."

"I don't want your money, Max. I just want--"

He cupped my cheek. "I'm going to do it because *I* want to. And if I do it right, you'll need two more bags to get your shit home. Got it?"

I paused. "Home?"

He smoothed my hair back. "Yes. Here. Home."

I smiled. "You have no idea how happy that word makes me right now."

He smiled back. "Trust me, I think I do."

My lips fell to his and I felt his hands fist the shirt I was in. I straddled his pelvis, feeling his cock rise to the occasion. But he quickly flipped me back over. I went to squeal, but he clapped his hand over my mouth. My eyes widened as his eyes darkened, and I listened as a drawer opened to my left.

My voice sounded muffled. "Max?"

His face fell. "Tonight, you listen to me. Got it?"

I nodded. "Uh huh."

He slid his hand from my mouth. "Tonight, I get to test your limits."

"My… limits?"

He dangled leather restraints in front of my face. "Yep. All of your limits."

I shook with anticipation. "What kind of limits?"

"You'll see."

He quickly wrapped the restraints around my wrists before sliding off the bed. I watched him dip down, attaching the leather thing to the bed somehow. He did it to my wrists and my ankles, spreading my legs wide. Revealing my bare pussy to the room as he stood there, reveling in his work.

"Mm-mm-mm. Dani. This position suits you."

I giggled. "What in the world are you going t-- fuck!"

His hand cracked against the inside of my thigh and I jumped. Then I watched him nod. He walked back over to that same bedside drawer and pulled out a ball attached to, well, something. And I didn't even have to ask what it was for.

Because once he pushed the ball into my mouth and wrapped it around my head, I felt him attach it to me.

"A ball gag, in case you didn't know what this is. It'll keep you quiet."

I tried moving my lips. "I'm gonna slobber on myself."

His eyes grew wild. "I sure as hell hope so."

When he blindfolded me, I felt the smallest jump of panic race through my body. And Max must've seen it. His hand cupped my cheek and his thumb stroked my skin, slowly calming me down. I felt my body settle and my heart fall back into place.

Then I felt Max's fingers traveling further down my torso.

"Max?"

My muffled sounds made him chuckle as my shirt slid up.

"Max?"

I heard something click before a buzzing sound started.

"Max!"

The vibrating toy pressed against my clit and my back shot up from the mattress. I bucked like a wild bronco against the sensations, devoid of Max's touch altogether. My cheeks flushed with need. My legs quivered with a want for release. I gasped for air as spittle dripped down the sides of my cheeks as my entire body careened out of control.

Then I felt the bed dip down by my feet.

"Max," I moaned.

I felt his cock teasing my entrance. My juices dripped onto him as he teased me with that toy. I yanked at the restraints, wanting nothing more than to touch him. Feel him. Rake my nails along his skin. But the restraints held me back. I heard him chuckling as his cock inched its way inside me. My legs locked out and my nipples puckered to painful peaks. Feeling him fill me as this toy tickled my clit was more than I could stand. And the second he bottomed out, my back arched with my first orgasm.

"Oh, we're going to have fun tonight," he growled.

I wailed through the ball gag. "Max!"

My eyes rolled back as he turned the toy up a notch. I lost all control of my body and my senses as he pounded ravenously into my body. I was at his mercy. Completely submitted to him as he played with my body however he wished. He bounced the toy against my sensitive clit. I bucked against his cock, meeting him thrust for thrust as I fell over into my second orgasm. Spit dripped down my neck. I felt my hair mangling and tangling around the blindfold as my body darted every which way, trying to figure out which way was up.

When Max turned off the toy, I breathed a huge sigh of relief.

I felt him pull out of my pussy.

I whimpered. "Max?"

I heard the heavy footfalls of his steps as he walked over to the drawer. I didn't even bother saying his name again. I knew it wouldn't help me one damn bit. My body already felt sore in the best ways possible. But the toy that quickly breached my entrance made me gasp.

Then I felt something teasing my puckered asshole.

"We'll go slowly. Relax for me, gorgeous."

I shook my head quickly, but Max's hand splayed over my stomach.

"When you're ready, nod your head."

I drew in deep breaths through my nose before I nodded my head.

The slender object breached my asshole for the first time and my world came alive. Colors burst and sizzled behind the blindfold as my eyes widened. My toes curled. My skin heated. I felt myself flush from head to toe. Between the toy filling my pussy as well as my asshole, I already felt myself dancing on the edge of no return.

Max's tongue landed on my clit.

"Fuuuuck!"

I pulled hard against the restraints. I wanted

nothing more than to lock myself around him and bury him in my thighs. He pumped the toy in and out, Slowly and deftly as his tongue made quick work of my clit. He sucked it between his lips. My toes curled as that coil in my gut wound as tightly as possible. Something clicked before the damn toy started vibrating, causing me to lose all sense of space and time.

All I knew was Max's tongue.

All I knew were the vibrations of this toy.

All I knew were my muffled grunts and groans and whimpers as his ministrations pushed me to the edge.

Before falling over for the third fucking time.

"Yes, yes, yes, yes, YES!"

I reveled in it. The power he had over my body. I lost count of the number of orgasms he gave me as he controlled every movement and sensation. He ripped the toy out and filled me with his cock again. He pounded into me relentlessly, with his sweat dripping against my neck and my face. I wanted nothing more than to touch him. To hold on to him. To cling to him while he made love to me.

And as we fell over the edge together, he released my wrists with a flick of his fingers.

Allowing me to wrap my arms around him and quake against his muscles.

39

MAX

One Week Later

Dani's soft voice came from the bed. "Everything okay?"

I peeked out the window before I let the curtain close. "Yeah, everything's okay."

"Please stop freaking out. You freaking out is freaking me out."

I looked over at her lying in bed. "Have you called your parents at all?"

She shook her head. "I told them I'd call once we actually got there."

"It makes me nervous that captain keeps pushing this travel date out on us. It's been an entire week. What the hell's going on?"

"You know she's got our best interests and our safety in mind. If she says it still isn't safe to travel, then we listen. Plus, it's not like any of this traveling expense is on us."

I sighed. "I need some of your cool right now."

She giggled. "Trust me, I'm panicking on the inside. But I've had a lifetime's worth of practice covering things up from my parents. I've gotten good at it."

My phone started buzzing against my bedside table and I practically sprinted for it. I saw the captain's number flashing on my screen and I hoped with all my might this was the phone call we needed. I placed the phone to my ear and listened to her rattle off. She spoke quickly and with urgency. Which lit a fire under my ass.

Dani whispered. "What's she saying?"

I held up my hand. "Uh huh. Yes. Thank you. We'll let you know when we're on the plane."

She squealed. "Eek! I have to get changed!"

I nodded. "Thank you, Captain. I appreciate it."

I hung up the phone and rushed to get ready. Dani and I had been packed for damn near six days now. We stayed low at my place. We followed the captain's orders to the letter. We didn't leave my house, we didn't go on bike rides, and we sure as hell didn't go anywhere near the part of town where my father's estate was.

Especially since everything regarding his estate had been handed over to me.

"You got your toiletries?" Dani asked.

I nodded. "Yep. You got your phone charger?"

She held it in the air. "Packing it now."

"You rolled your outfits like I showed you so it all fits in the saddlebag?"

"Uh huh. You remembered to pack the cash we've already drawn out, right?"

I patted my leather jacket. "Got it safe and sound against my chest."

She heaved her bag over her shoulder. "Then, tell me what the captain said and let's get the hell out of here."

"The plan is still in effect. We need to get to the airport and check in like we're taking the flight. Then, after we board the plane, we'll be privately escorted off and seen back to where we parked. From there, we stick to the map of safe roads Cap sent me three days ago. We make our way to California, and we live it up until we get the call that it's safe to return."

She sighed. "Well, I'm ready whenever you are. How do I look?"

I grinned at her leather jacket. "You look outstanding, as always."

The only thing we'd been doing in this house was eating, having sex, and sleeping. Even John was getting nervous for us, and that man never panicked until there was a reason to. Mostly. I saw the look of relief in his eyes when we came out with our bags. He gave us each a massive hug, then slipped me an envelope.

"Here. Take this with you," he said.

I shook my head. "I can't take that."

"Just take it, Max. It's not much, but it'll--"

I grabbed his wrist. "John, listen to me. We don't have a lot of time."

"Which is why you need to take the damn money."

I shook my head. "You passed the control of Dad's estate to me, remember?"

"Yeah. We went through all of that last week. So what?"

"So what? Now that Dad no longer has control of any of his things--including his bank accounts--the police don't see a reason to freeze the majority of his assets. He can't access them anyway."

His eyebrows rose. "Wait, what?"

I slipped my hand into my jeans. "Though I do want you to have this."

I handed him the new debit card as his jaw fell open.

"Are you serious right now?" he asked.

I nodded. "As a heart attack. I moved some money around and made you an account. That card is hooked to one of Dad's old investment accounts. Half of it is still invested. The other half is yours to access immediately as you need."

"How much money is in that account, Max?"

I smiled. "Why don't you just try spending some money and see if you can drain it? Because I bet you ten thousand dollars you can't."

I'd only ever seen my brother cry once. When he was in the hospital, and the morphine wasn't doing shit for his pain. But right there, in the foyer of our house, a tear rushed down his cheek. He wrapped me up in a massive hug, clapping my back hard. So hard it made me grunt. And when he released me, I nodded.

"Take care of yourself until we get back. Because we will be back, John."

He sighed. "Take care of her, Max."

Dani snickered. "More like I need to take care of him, the reckless asshole."

I chuckled. "You'll get away with calling me that once. And you just wasted your chance."

"It's funny that you think that."

John patted my shoulder. "Thank you. For everything."

I held my hand out. "Brothers 'til the very end."

He clasped my hand, our wrists bent. "'Til death take us away."

With one more round of hugs, Dani and I headed for my bike. We packed our things into my saddle bags before we slipped on as John watched us from the porch. I didn't know what kind of adventure awaited us, but I knew one thing. So long as I had Dani on the back of my bike, nothing could hold me back.

John yelled from the porch. "Be safe out there, you two!"

I lifted my hand. "And you be safe here. Keep those boys in line while we're gone. Because I sure as hell don't want to come back to any messes we gotta clean up!"

He barked with laughter. "I promise nothing, but I think Rupert's got it until you guys get back!"

I drew in a deep breath as I passed Dani's helmet back to her. We slid them over our heads, buckling them in unison before her legs locked against me. Her arms threaded around my waist, clutching me as I struck up my bike.

"You ready?" I called back to her.

I felt her nod against my back, and it settled my smile into a grin.

With the revving of my engine, Dani's laughter took over our space. The absolute best sound in the world to me, and I'd get to listen to it for the rest of my life. If she'd have me. One step at a time, though.

But eventually.

I backed out of the driveway and pushed off down the road. I waved at John one last time as he stood on the porch, watching us ride off into the distance. I peeled around the corner, revving my engine one last time. And with the honk of my horn, we left our past in the dust.

Ready to set out towards our future.

Even though my house faded into the background, it didn't feel as if I had left my home. Because my home was hitting the road with me, traveling wherever I went. Dani's thighs against my own reminded me that she was my home. Forever. And I was hers.

Forever.

And together, we were stronger than I could have ever dreamt.

With my home wrapped around me and my eyes turned toward the airport, I blazed a trail onto the highway. We still had some hoops to jump through, but I knew we'd be just fine. With Cap watching our backs and the world ridiculing my father all over the news outlets, society would bury him before the courts got a chance. Leaving all of us to lead the lives we were born to lead rather than cowering in the shadows because of a madman.

I heard Dani giggling. "What are you laughing about back there, gorgeous?"

She snorted. "Who in the world would've thought that a man like you would've ended up with a book-worm goody two shoes like me?"

My smile made my cheeks ache. "I wouldn't have it any other way, either."

"Me neither, handsome. Me, neither."

EPILOGUE

DANI

Three Months Later

I leaned against the wrought iron balcony as the sun started cresting over the ocean. We were somewhere in California. Something secluded, which I didn't think existed in this massive, overpopulated place. The sound of seagulls filled my ears as I drew in the scent of my coffee, allowing the hot mug to warm me through my palms. The sun's rays felt delicate against my skin. The smell of the ocean beckoned me to its shoreline, my toes already tingling with the need for sand between them. For three months, we'd been here. In this little beach house with a second-story balcony right on the coast.

And last night we finally got the news we were waiting for.

"Insidious Ann Arbor Gangster Found Guilty On All Counts."

Max's voice sounded behind me, and his words made me smile.

"How does that make you feel, handsome?"

He set the newspaper on the table behind me. "Relieved."

I nodded. "That's one way to put it."

"Two life sentences in prison with no possible chance of parole."

"He'll die in that place."

His arm wrapped around me. "Which is exactly what he deserves."

Max kissed my temple as I leaned against him. For three months, we'd waited for those words. We hadn't had to go back and testify, and the captain was confident that the jury would come back with a guilty verdict. And late last night, she'd called with news that would surely streak across the headlines for the next three weeks.

Ashton Ryddle would be sentenced to a lifetime of nothing.

Where he couldn't hurt anyone else.

Max shuffled behind me. "I think maximum security prison's going to be good for him."

I snickered. "If he's lucky, they'll put him in solitary until he goes crazy."

"The man's already crazy."

I shrugged. "Then crazier."

I sipped my coffee as Max's chuckle filled my ear.

"You like having your coffee out here, don't you?"

I peered over at him. "And you don't? I mean, look at this view."

He cupped my ass cheek. "I see it every morning with my coffee, too."

I rolled my eyes. "You're insatiable."

He growled. "And you wouldn't have it any other way."

I giggled as he kissed my cheek. His arms wrapped tightly around me as I stood there, looking out over the ebbing waters. He settled his chin on top of my head. I felt the ocean breeze wrapping around us. For three months, we had enjoyed this place. Cooked our own meals and woken up to one another. Made love on this private balcony while the sun set behind us. For three months, we had made this place our home. A place where no one, and nothing, could reach us.

I was almost saddened at the idea of leaving it behind.

Max's hands fell to the wrought iron railing and I wiggled my ass against his crotch, teasing him as he kissed along my exposed shoulder. He kissed back up my neck, making my skin tingle as he nibbled the lobe of my ear. And as I sighed, he ground his hardened cock against my ass.

"Care for some light morning reading? I brought the paper out with me, gorgeous."

I snickered. "Well, it is good news."

"Might be worth a read."

He nuzzled my cheek. "Think we should celebrate?"

"Didn't we technically celebrate last night after the phone call?"

His hands massaged my hips. "Can't hurt to do it again, just for good measure."

I shook my head as I turned around. The man was relentless, and I loved every second of it. My body ached from the goodness he'd poured over me last night after we got that phone call. After the captain confirmed for us that we were really free from this nightmare. Max plucked my coffee from my hand and held the mug up to my lips. I took one last big gulp before he set it on the ground, then returned to pin me against the railing.

I rested against it as I gazed into the eyes of the man I'd spent every day with for the last three months. And as his eyes danced between my own, I couldn't imagine ever loving someone more than I loved him.

"Well, I think we should definitely celebrate, then," I said.

His eyes darkened. "Wonderful."

His lips crashed against mine, like the waves crashed against the shoreline. I slid my hands up his chest, feeling his muscles pulsing for me. Part of me wished we had more time in this place. More time here to spend for ourselves now that we were free from looking over our shoulders. I knew this meant we'd be back on the road tomorrow, following wherever the pavement lead us in order to get back. After all, it's what we had been doing the last few months. Following the road in front of us to see what kind of adventures awaited at the end of our journey.

Though the itch to settle kept scratching at the back of my mind.

I mean, it's not like Ann Arbor isn't safe any longer.

Max paused. "What is it?"

My eyes fluttered open. "What?"

He snickered. "I've been kissing you for two minutes and you've practically become a dead fish. What's on your mind?"

I swatted at him. "How rude."

He chuckled. "Well, it's true. You even stopped moving your tongue."

"And here I thought you liked it when I went limp against you."

He nipped at my ear. "When I've done the hard work, yes."

I leaned against him. "I'm just thinking about some things."

"Like…?"

I shrugged. "Like, how Ann Arbor is going to feel a lot safer now that your father's off the streets."

"Uh huh."

"And how things are probably safe to return to now that the pressure of media attention is no longer relevant."

He nodded. "And the risk of fallout from the trial isn't there anymore."

I kissed his cheek softly. "Do you think about going back at all? To Ann Arbor?"

He didn't hesitate. "All the time."

I looked up into his eyes. "Do you think about going back soon?"

He shrugged. "Not particularly."

"Oh?"

He nuzzled my nose. "I have to share you when we're home. Give me a little more time to have you just to myself, okay?"

I smiled. "That depends. What do you plan on doing with that time?"

His voice dropped. "Why don't you let me show you?"

With my hands in his, he led me back into our second-story bedroom. With the doors to the ocean left wide open behind me, he led me over to the bed. As I stared up into his eyes, he slid my robe from my body. Revealing the marked nakedness he had reveled in every night since we'd been here. A grin slid across his face. He sat on the edge of the bed, pulling me between his legs. He kissed my stomach. My hips. My thighs. He kissed up my stomach until his lips wrapped around my nipples, causing my head to fall back. I gasped with pleasure as he licked them to puckered peaks. I threaded my hand through his hair as he growled against my excess. I felt my thighs warming and my pussy wetting. As his hands explored me, gripping my ass cheeks and massaging my legs, I felt more alive than ever before.

"Oh, Max," I whispered.

He kissed my pussy lips. "I love you, Dani. And that will never change."

The warm ocean breeze wafted against my back as Max slid to his knees. He spread my legs, his tongue lapping up my folds as I gripped his hair. He slid my leg over his shoulder, opening me up with his fingers.

He filled me with his digits, pumping them softly as his tongue languidly teased my swollen clit.

"Yeah. Yeah. Oooh, yeah Max. Just like--ugh--that."

My head fell back. My eyes screwed shut. His tongue stroked me in all the ways he knew how as electricity filled the marrow of my bones. As he knelt there, bringing me more pleasure than I could ever experience, I knew what I wanted. I saw my future burst into images behind my eyelids, and I smiled as shivers washed over me.

I saw Max and me in our own home.

I saw myself pregnant with his child.

I saw me learning how to ride a bike so I could ride beside him instead of just behind him.

I saw us making love in our four-poster bed.

I saw us with a bungalow by the beach, just like this one.

And as I cried out his name in ecstasy, falling over the edge, I saw a ring on my finger.

Forever his. Forever mine. And forever ours.

Thank you for reading RED QUEEN. If you loved Max & Danika, you might love Rae & Clinton as well. Don't miss their story in the Diamond In The Rough series or check out my website for a full list of my books. And if you don't want to miss the next one, be sure to join my SMS list below!

Get an SMS alert when Rebel releases a new book (US only):

Text REBEL to 77948

If you want to support me, consider leaving a review on Amazon. I'd love it!

ABOUT THE AUTHOR

Rebel Hart is an author of Dark Romance novels. Check out all the books in her #1 bestselling series Diamond In The Rough.

NEVER MISS A NEW RELEASE:
Follow Rebel on Amazon
Follow Rebel on Bookbub

Text REBEL to 77948 to don't miss any of her books (US only) or sign up at www.RebelHart.net to get an email alert when her next book is out.

authorrebelhart@gmail.com

CONNECT WITH REBEL HART:

ALSO BY REBEL HART

For a full list of my books go to:

www.RebelHart.net